'Skilfully written and p
will keep you turning t
coaster of emotions, f
The conversations in Victorian parlance and descriptions of travelling conditions are historically based and fascinating. I was gripped and unable to put this novel down.'
Maggie Colvin, author, journalist, public speaker and tv presenter

'A beautiful and encouraging story of the kind of hope and restoration only God can orchestrate.'
Tola-Doll Fisher, editor, Woman Alive *magazine*

'What an adventure Jemimah Wright has taken us on! *Isabella's Voyage* is an honest, insightful story of longing, bravery, and the choices that bring love. The heroine's determination to move forward in spite of disappointments, England's social restrictions, New Zealand's danger and Hawaii's otherworldly culture leads her to depths of love and sacrifice that could only come through the discovery of God. Jemimah has woven Providence, faith and the strength of womanhood into a tale that rings true to every heart that has dreamed of great things and faced small days. It is a novel well worth reading and hard to forget.'
Amy Peterson, author of Perpetua: A Bride, A Martyr, A Passion

'Jemimah has weaved the story beautifully; I was drawn in immediately and found myself longing for Isabella to find the freedom – and love – that she deserved. This debut novel is well worth picking up – and I am sure Jemimah is a writer to watch…'
Claire Musters, author, editor, speaker and host of the Woman Alive *Book Club*

'I fell in love with Isabella almost immediately and could not stop reading. In *Isabella's Voyage*, Jemimah Wright takes the

reader on an exotic adventure and into a love story like no other. A thoroughly satisfying read that I pray will become a film.'
Wendy Griffith, CBN News Anchor; author of You Are a Prize to be Won

'Jemimah's words flow off the page as she paints vivid pictures of landscapes and people from times gone by. Despite the characters' many challenges, this novel is a story of hope and inspirational sacrifice. I adore Jemimah's writing style and I see it as a personal gift to me that she has turned her talent to fiction writing.'
Lauren Windle, journalist and author

'Delightful, tragic, seductive, consistently absorbing. *Isabella's Voyage* is a captivating story that speaks to all of us in our vulnerability and despair, as well as lighting us up with hope and courage, in the midst of our human drama.'
Deborah Paterson, South African longboarding competitor

ISABELLA'S VOYAGE

JEMIMAH WRIGHT

instant
apostle

First published in Great Britain in 2022

Instant Apostle
104 The Drive
Rickmansworth
Herts
WD3 4DU

British Library Cataloguing-in-Publication Data

A catalogue record for this book is available from the British Library.

This book and all other Instant Apostle books are available from Instant Apostle:

Website: www.instantapostle.com

Email: info@instantapostle.com

ISBN 978-1-912726-65-3

Printed in South Africa.

Dedicated to
My parents, John and Susan,
And my husband, Alister

Contents

Chapter One

North Norfolk coast, England, September 1880

The thing about a long brisk walk, thought Isabella as she got dressed, *is that it can be a marvellous antidote to hopelessness. It is action, and that is something.*

She set out as soon as dawn's orange light brightened the sky and before anyone else was awake. Quietly descending the stairs, she buttoned up her coat and opened the heavy oak front door into the misty newborn day. It had been a cold summer, stolen by storms, and although it was early September, autumn was already showing off on the gilded leaves of the horse-chestnut tree in the rectory garden.

Despite living with her parents and sister, Isabella preferred to walk alone. This was her daily constitutional, and she used it as a weapon in her arsenal for fighting the gloom that threatened to overcome her. As she walked through the village to the sea, she kept her mind fixed on the mundane practical details of her life. She did not allow her thoughts to travel to the dreams of exploring the world; that hope had gone now. Every few steps gave her a little stab of pain in her lower back, an ailment that seemed to come and go depending on her spirits. She winced, but tried to ignore it. Her long tweed skirt and bonnet kept her warm as she walked purposefully onto the dunes.

Once at the beach she fixed her eyes on the long, flat horizon. The mud-churned waters of the North Sea absorbed her thoughts. She paused and took a deep breath, feeling her lungs expand. For a moment she was able to enjoy the view.

Isabella felt guilty for the heaviness in the pit of her stomach that did not seem to leave. It was the sense that life was passing her by, that she was playing the role of a spectator rather than a participant.

On this particular morning, walking on into the wind, Isabella tried to think of what she was thankful for. Her younger sister came to mind. Sweet, placid, good-natured Catherine. If Catherine, with her easy laugh, was able to be content, why couldn't she be? Isabella looked out to sea. She had come to the end of the beach and there was only a difficult path uphill ahead of her. She wouldn't go further today.

More than an hour since she had set off, Isabella walked back up through the gateway of the rectory.

She was still thinking of Catherine as she turned the knob of the front door, and was hit by the smell of baking bread wafting through from the kitchen. Her stomach rumbled. She walked into the wide hallway, with its polished wood floor, and after taking off her bonnet and coat, went into the dining room for breakfast.

Catherine was standing by the window, arms crossed and brow furrowed; she turned to greet her sister.

'What is it?' Isabella asked, immediately concerned.

'A telegram arrived a few minutes ago... Mama read it and left so quickly, she didn't say who it was from, but I know it's bad news.'

'Catherine!' Isabella laughed at her sister's ability to fear the worst.

'Isabella, she was shocked! I am worried it's John in London, or something has happened to one of the children.'

'She would have said if it was; it might not be bad news...' Isabella offered. 'There must be an explanation.'

Catherine sat down at the table with a sigh, and Isabella took her place opposite.

'Well, we can't do anything but wait for her to return and tell us. Let's have breakfast; no point in it getting cold.' She could see Hattie had left a covered bowl of porridge on the side counter. The new housemaid was often up before Isabella, cleaning, laying and lighting the fires before the family were awake.

Isabella poured herself a cup of China tea. The silver strainer slipped, so with her teaspoon she fished out the leaves that had escaped, and added milk. Isabella passed the teapot to Catherine, but she gave a slight shake of her head in refusal. 'Not for me.'

It was a few minutes later that Reverend Buckley and his wife joined their daughters.

'What did the telegram say?' Catherine asked instantly.

Reverend Buckley raised his eyebrows, and walked over to the chair at the head of the table.

'What a situation we find ourselves in, with so little to go on.' Isabella watched him push his reading glasses back to the bridge of his nose. He only needed them for reading, but never seemed to take them off, his kind eyes peering from above the spectacles when he talked. 'The telegram was from your Aunt Emily in New Zealand. It seems Hamish has gone missing.' He rubbed his forehead. 'She is asking for help.'

'What do you mean "missing"… is there foul play?' Isabella asked, feeling her stomach twist.

'Foul play?' Catherine gasped.

'Now, girls, let's not get hysterical,' said Mrs Buckley, but Isabella saw a redness brightening on her mother's neck, meeting her strawberry-blonde hair, not fully succumbed to the grey that was woven through it. She moved to sit down at the table.

'There isn't much information. Emily asked for you to join her, Isabella. Of course, that is out of the question. I don't know what help you could be in this situation…' Reverend Buckley said this not unkindly, but as if it was a matter of fact. 'We will write to your brother, but with his family and commitments in London, I think it is unlikely he would be able to take six months to sail to New Zealand and back.'

Isabella sat forward in her seat, eyes focused on her father, her thoughts working furiously. *Please can I go,* she silently pleaded, to God, or her father, or anyone who had the power to make it so, but she said nothing.

Reverend Buckley returned to his study, and Isabella and Catherine went to the drawing room. Their mother had an appointment to keep in Holt, the small market town five miles away from the Buckleys' home.

'Issy, if you were allowed, you would go, wouldn't you?'

'Yes,' replied Isabella, feeling a slight blush rise to her cheeks, because it was not concern for her aunt and uncle that took precedence in her mind; it was the idea she might be able to travel to New Zealand and leave, albeit temporarily, her safe, parochial life.

Catherine let out a deflated sigh. Her elbow on the side table, she rested her face in her hand.

'I wish Uncle Hamish and Emily hadn't emigrated. New Zealand is just so far away.'

At lunch the situation was discussed again.

'Hamish is such a clever, responsible sort, I can't think how he could have just *disappeared...*' Mrs Buckley said with frustration. 'There will be a cost to travel to New Zealand, and not only financial. Who could take such a length of time out of their daily responsibilities, to travel across the world?'

'Indeed,' agreed Reverend Buckley. He paused, absently putting his hand to his heart and stroking the lapel of his jacket. 'My health will not permit me to travel. So, we are in a quandary. Unfortunately, I don't know anyone in New Zealand whom we can call on.'

Isabella was waiting for the right time to speak, to declare her position. Now seemed as good a time as any. 'Father, I would be *happy* to go,' she said, feeling her heart beat faster, her corset suddenly feeling too tight. She glanced across at her mother, who shook her head with displeasure.

'Without a chaperone it would be unthinkable, my dear,' her father said.

'Surely that is not so! Times are changing, Father.'

'Isabella, *really*!' said Mrs Buckley.

Reverend Buckley searched his daughter's face and finally said, 'Let us think on it. No more on the subject now.'

For the next few days, Isabella's parents pursued every avenue to find someone to help Aunt Emily. A telegram was sent to New Zealand, asking for more information, but no reply came. Reverend and Mrs Buckley spent hours writing letters to friends and acquaintances, asking if they had connections in Auckland.

By the end of the week, it looked like an answer was found. The brother of their son John's business partner happened to be in Auckland. He would be contacted and asked to visit Emily. Isabella's parents and sister were jubilant, but Isabella was bereft. She felt as if a waiter had offered her a platter of something delicious, and then as soon as she put out her hand to take it, had whisked the platter away.

'Oh *bother*.'

'What is it?' Isabella called, hearing her father from his study as she walked past. She pushed the open door to see him drop a telegram onto his desk.

'It seems that our contact is in fact leaving Auckland this very day, sailing to Perth. He will not have time to visit Emily, and cannot help.'

'Papa...' Isabella said, stepping forward.

He looked at her and shook his head. 'I know you would like to go and be with Emily.' He paused and let out a heavy sigh. 'We need to find you a chaperone, and then I wonder if it might be a possibility.' He spoke as if talking to himself, looking out of the window. 'You would be a strength for Emily, that much is true.' Then, looking up and speaking directly to his daughter, he said, 'If Hamish is dead, Emily and the boys must come home. Are you prepared for that?'

'I think so, but really Papa, he can't be dead. I feel sure there is an explanation.'

'Until we know, we have to consider the worst. I will pray on it, and you should too.'

Isabella nodded, left her father and went to find Catherine. She tried to busy herself with the pastel of her sister that she was working on, but uncharacteristically her sitter was distracted.

'Should we invite William for supper? He might have advice,' Catherine asked as Isabella outlined her silhouette. Isabella raised her eyebrows at Catherine, who ignored the teasing in her eyes.

Dr William Fisher had moved to Norfolk a few years previously. He came to join a practice in Holt, and, as his parents were old friends of Mrs Buckley's, he was a welcome and frequent guest at their table.

'*What* a good idea!' Isabella said, knowing her sister's ulterior motive. Catherine rolled her eyes, and pretended to throw her book in her sister's direction. They both laughed and Catherine left the room to enquire of their mother.

It was agreed that William should be invited and Nathanael, the groom, despatched with a note.

William arrived at eight that evening. The atmosphere in the room changed as soon as he walked in.

'Good evening, young man,' Reverend Buckley said, getting up to shake his hand.

'Sir,' William said, with a nod, and with his left hand flattened down his thick auburn hair, before turning to Isabella and Catherine. 'You are both looking lovely,' he complimented, with a broad smile, as he flicked back the tails of his frock coat to take a seat.

As he sat down, Catherine announced, 'We have some terrible news. Our Uncle Hamish is missing in New Zealand. Isabella wants to go and help his wife, Emily, with the boys as they try to find him.' She blushed at her outburst.

'Goodness!' William said, looking at Isabella.

'I can't go without a chaperone, but I am hoping one might be found.'

'It doesn't surprise me that you would want to go, Isabella, but of course I agree, a chaperone is necessary. It's a long way.'

Isabella didn't say that the length of the journey would be a thrill to her.

'Enough about New Zealand, tell us about your day, William,' she said.

While he was entertaining them with a story of medical misadventure – always at his own expense – they were called to supper. The conversation was jovial, although William seemed contemplative. He sat between Catherine and Mrs Buckley, but Isabella felt his eyes on her.

The next morning Isabella stood in front of her easel facing Catherine; she was concentrating on getting the green of her eyes exactly right. Her sister was sitting at the window seat in the study, looking out at the late-blossoming hydrangeas and the perfectly manicured lawn.

'If you do go, what will I do without you?' Catherine asked. Isabella, aware that her sister was struggling to stay still, did not respond initially, focusing on perfecting the left eyebrow. She got it right, and looked up in satisfaction.

'I am sure one of our friends will keep you entertained! Perhaps I will come home and you and William will be engaged?'

Isabella watched her sister's face flush with pleasure, but she said with a hint of sadness, 'It is not looking promising, though, is it? He is more interested in you than me.'

'Our friendship is entirely platonic, and you know that. He is thirty-two, he's like a little brother,' Isabella said firmly, but she knew that William was drawn to her. When he had visited the night before, he and Isabella had ended up deep in conversation about his travels in India and his work with the Leprosy Mission in the Punjab. He had held a volunteer post at the mission hospital for three years. Just before his first furlough he had contracted cerebral malaria, and returned home on his doctor's insistence. After much deliberation, he didn't return to

India, but instead moved near his maternal roots in Norfolk to practise family medicine. 'A small Norfolk town is less romantic than colourful India,' he had told Isabella, 'but it has its own charms and challenges.'

Catherine had sat quietly with them, laughing at William's jokes, and busying herself with her embroidery.

Now, Isabella, focusing on her canvas, sketched Catherine's right eyebrow, and then put down the pastel to throw another log on the fire in the grate. Her mother always berated her for not calling Hattie to deal with the fire, but if it was just herself and Catherine, Isabella reverted to doing it, however unladylike it seemed. She sighed and stretched her arms up, lengthening her back, and easing the tightness she felt.

'Would you like to come for a walk?' she asked Catherine.

'It's still too cold. I think I'll stay by the fire and finish my embroidery.'

'Oh, my delicate sister!' Isabella teased.

Catherine smiled with acceptance, and stood up to look at the progress of her portrait.

'Issy, you have such talent; it's a remarkable likeness of me.'

Isabella did find satisfaction in art, but she couldn't paint all day. She gave Catherine a kiss on the cheek in thanks, ignored the briskness in the air and the dull ache in her back and went upstairs to change into her tweed dress and boots.

Once outside, Isabella tied her bonnet close. The Buckleys' gardener, Walter Olby, was edging the driveway with his spade, cutting off clods of turf to neaten the border of the lawn.

'Good morning, Walter. Wonderful work you're doing.'

He smiled, gave her a nod and doffed his cap. Isabella headed off down the lane and crossed the bracken-covered dunes to the coast. The North Sea pounded the beach.

She breathed in the salty dampness and watched the silt-filled waves. Two seals were popping their heads playfully out of the cold swell just offshore. Isabella kept walking, her back to the wind. The September sun had appeared from behind the clouds again and she already felt brighter. For some reason she thought of the cherry tree that she could see from her bedroom window. Its cycle of life seemed to taunt her; changing from naked bark to pale-green shoots, to pink flurries, and then to dark-green leaves. All the while, her life had appeared to stand still. But now, at last, she wondered if there was to be a shift in the coming season. A voyage across two oceans. Could it really happen?

'Isabella!' called a voice from the dunes behind her.

She turned into the wind to see William walking fast in her direction. He was dressed in his dark wool frock coat, one hand on his head to stop his hat from flying off. Isabella stood still, waiting for him to be close enough to hear her greeting.

'Glad I found you!' he said with a boyish smile. 'Walter said you were down here. I wanted to talk more last night, but I saw that your parents were tired – I thought it best not to stay late.'

'Hello, William!'

'Shall we walk?' he suggested, and they continued companionably along the beach.

'Aren't you working today?'

'I had a visit in the village; old Mrs Hewson's arthritis has flared up. I thought I would come and see you.' William paused and looked at her. 'Isabella, to tell you the truth, I need to talk to you.'

Something in his voice made Isabella stop. 'What is it?'

He reached out to gently touch her arm, resting his hand on her sleeve for a moment. It was a sign of affection that she was not used to from him, or any man. Glancing up, she noticed that he was sweating. She watched a trickle of moisture run down from his hairline to his neck.

'William?'

He stepped back, suddenly; something changed in his eyes.

'Oh, just that I am here to help... always here, that is...'

'Dear Will, if I don't find a chaperone, I won't be going anywhere.'

'Would it be helpful for me to tell you about my voyage to India? It was quite some time at sea…'

They walked on, but Isabella had a feeling that William was hiding something from her.

The following Sunday, Isabella sat back in the pew after singing the second hymn of the Holy Communion service. She was finding it hard to concentrate, and she guessed her sister was too. She watched Catherine absorbed in teasing a loose cotton thread out of her shawl as they listened to their father preach.

Isabella focused on the stained-glass window to her left. It was of a boat and fishermen. *Probably the disciples*, she thought. She let her mind wander, and was reminded of meeting a Chinese man who had visited their home when she was about ten. He had sailed from China to England and he spoke English fluently. He talked about brave warriors and the great mandarins, and Isabella was captivated. Long after he left, she requested books on China and wanted to read stories of the country and people so different from her own. The desire to travel was birthed in her at that point, and the feeling that she would be at home with people who were not her own.

As Isabella concentrated on the window above her, she wondered if, had she been a man, she would have joined the navy and sailed to far off ports. As it was, she had only travelled as far as Iona in the Inner Hebrides, and spent a summer as a lady's companion to a cantankerous old woman in Paris. Isabella knew her role and duty was now with her parents, but the lack of challenge or stimulation she felt was sometimes overwhelming. The sense that she was made for something more and somewhere else was always there.

The following morning Isabella was alone in the drawing room, as her mother and sister were visiting neighbours. She heard a knock at the front door, and the footsteps of Hattie running to open it. There was the sound of a man's voice she recognised.

A moment later there was a tap on the drawing room door, and William presented himself.

'Hello, Isabella, I hoped you would be in.'

Isabella rose and offered him a chair. He perched on the edge.

'I am sorry everyone is out, it's just me here,' she said, sitting back down.

'I wanted to talk to you privately, so that is helpful.'

'What is it?'

'I am supposed to be on call, so I can't stay long, but I had to say this... Isabella, would you let me be your chaperone to New Zealand?' he paused, and then added, 'As your husband?'

'My *husband*?' Isabella laughed, but her heart fluttered in panic.

William continued quickly, 'I am sure you know I enjoy your company very much, and our conversations have been the highlight of my move to Norfolk.'

'I know, William, but...'

'I am very concerned by your aunt's letter from New Zealand. I know you are adamant about going to help her and I admire you for that.' He paused. 'I think we could be very happy together.' He took a deep breath and waited for her response.

Isabella felt a flush growing on her cheeks. Could they be happy together? He was very dear to her, but what about Catherine? Of course, there had been a meeting of minds between herself and William, but he was five years her junior, only two years older than Catherine.

'Please... give me an answer,' William said with a strained cough.

Isabella saw the vulnerability in his eyes. 'William... I don't know what to say. Did you tell anyone that you were going to ask me?'

'No. I should have gone to your father for permission, but I wanted to talk to you as soon as possible. I woke up this morning with the idea and it seemed so perfect, I couldn't wait.'

For something to do, Isabella stood up and stoked the fire, her hand shaking on the poker. She thought quickly. She knew William was unaware of her sister's affection for him and she wouldn't break Catherine's confidence. The silence between them felt heavy. She sat back down, took a deep breath and then told him exactly what she was feeling.

'I cannot accept your proposal; even though it is the most wonderful thing I have ever been asked. I am sorry.'

'If you don't want to marry me now, I will wait for you.'

'I am sorry, William. I can't.'

The sound of the front door opening and female voices made them both jump.

'Say no more on this, Isabella, I have been foolish,' William muttered, walking towards the door. It was opened by Mrs Buckley.

'William, dear! I hope you are not leaving?'

'Yes, sadly it was a brief call. I have a patient to visit.'

'But where is your bag?' Catherine asked.

'Ah yes, I won't need it for this visit, I'll be back to the surgery shortly,' he sounded flustered. Catherine looked at him – and then at Isabella.

William gave a brief nod to Mrs Buckley and Catherine, and left.

Catherine sat down next to Isabella, staring at her, waiting for her to say something.

'What is wrong with William?'

'I think he was running late, that's all…' Isabella said. She stood and picked up her shawl. 'I must go and fetch my book,' she murmured.

Once upstairs in her bedroom, Isabella fell into the high-backed armchair next to the sash window. She looked out over the garden and fields beyond, the sound of William's words reverberating in her ears.

There was the cherry tree, its leaves on the cusp of russet. *Should I have said yes?*

After a while Isabella heard Catherine call from downstairs. She got up and opened her bedroom door. 'I'm up here, I'll be down in a moment.'

She checked her face in the mirror and tightened her shawl around her shoulders to protect her from the chill. Her back was aching again, and she would have to sit by the fire to avoid further discomfort.

She eventually entered the drawing room. Catherine looked up.

'You forgot your book?'

'Book?'

'You said you were going to get it?'

'Oh, yes, how silly, I got distracted.'

Catherine leaned forward. 'Issy, I know you will say I am being foolish, but I want to help William's surgery in some way; the stories of Florence Nightingale have inspired me,' she whispered. 'I know I cannot make William love me, and if he has said anything to you, you must tell me...' she paused, but Isabella said nothing. 'I want to help him, to work with him. What do you think?'

'Oh, Catherine, I...'

Isabella was saved by the announcement of lunch, relieved she did not have to answer Catherine immediately.

Chapter Two

Hawaii, January 1876

Aolani sat on the floor, leaning her pregnant body against the white clapboard wall, as the mynah bird called loudly in the trees above. Focused, she methodically threaded white and pink frangipani flowers into a *lei* while her father and older brother, Kainalu, sat in wicker chairs nearby and discussed the day. The late afternoon air was warm, freshly pungent from recent rain. Aolani stopped her threading to concentrate on the conversation.

Their father lifted himself out of his chair. He was strong and muscular, but his face was holding the pain of stiffness in his bones.

'My child, I will go and lie down now. Tell your mother when she returns.'

'Yes, *Makua*,' she said, surprised, as her father never seemed to tire.

When he was inside, she gathered her things, and ordered the servant to light the candles around the house and on the outside *lanai*. It was not yet completely dark, but Aolani felt a sense of urgency to beat back the oncoming night.

In the early hours her father woke with a high fever and sore throat. Aolani's mother said it was nothing, he would get better – he was a resiliant man, a chief, one of the *ali'i*. Aolani wondered if nobility could spare him sickness. Someone said he must have caught something from one of the *haole* merchants. Someone else suggested it was a curse, that he must have broken a *kapu*, which weakened his *mana*.

Aolani took to sitting with him; if she could be close by, it helped her not to worry. She continued to thread *leis* for something to do, stopping to help her mother cool him down with a wet cloth and try to encourage him to drink. Everyone said he would pull through, but Aolani could only see him getting weaker.

'He will not die. We will pray to *Ke Akua*. We cannot even think of his death; if we do, we will be accepting it,' her mother said firmly.

Aolani watched her brother trying to step into as many of his father's roles as he could, but some positions he could not take on. Their father was a member of the House of Nobles, appointed by the monarch on the advice of his Privy Council; he was a businessman and chief of his people. He was looked to for wisdom and direction.

Two weeks into the sickness, Aolani was sitting with her father. It was midday, his eyes were closed and his breathing laboured. She held his hand, silently praying. She heard something, and turned to see Kainalu walk into the room. As he did, their father opened his eyes and with a weak arm, beckoned for his son. Kainalu came close, and his father took his face in his hands. Their noses touched, and the chief let out a long breath.

'My blessing be upon you,' he said with a raspy, feeble voice.

He lay back on his pillow, and gave out his final breath.

'*Makua!*' Aolani cried, grasping his shoulders.

Kainalu put his ear to their father's mouth. She watched him looking for a pulse, and when none was found, he turned to her, shaking his head, with a look of desolation.

'No!' Aolani beat the mattress with her fists and then collapsed into Kainalu's embrace, as he pinned down her flailing arms. Her mother was there, and Aolani felt more than heard her cry, which rose and broke like a wave through her body, joining her own.

Word got out and soon the house was filled with the wails of grief.

The next day the chief's coffin was placed in the family's *hale pili*. Four attendants, each bearing *kahili* standards, stood like guards on either side of the catafalque, which was covered in wreaths of flowers. The *kahili* wavers stood as if carved from stone, while men and women crowded into the open doorway. Outside, a group of singers began a series of songs to his memory. Aolani watched them as if they were strangers singing for someone else, not for her father.

The vigil lasted for twenty-four hours and the next day, two of the chief's most loyal warriors tattooed the date and location of his death over their hearts. His life would not be forgotten.

When Aolani's father's body was burned there was stillness in the air. Just the crackling and spitting of the flames could be heard. No breeze playing with the palm trees. It seemed that even the birds had stopped their calling.

Early the following morning, Kainalu took his father's remains to the water. Though the family no longer held to the ancient belief that the chief's body would turn into a god, they still followed the tradition of releasing his ashes into the life-giving ocean.

From the shore, Aolani, heavy with pregnancy, watched Kainalu and ten other warriors row out in their wooden outrigger canoes. A warm wind had returned and the palm trees responded. Strands of Aolani's hair flickered and danced around her face. The canoes sliced through the waves as the sun rose over *Le'ahi*, the volcanic ridgeline jutting out into Waikiki Bay. Kainalu, and her husband, Fili, were in the same canoe. Their powerful arms plunged and pulled the paddles through the water. Aolani felt sure she heard her father's voice in the air, calling her 'his little *wahine*'. He had been an attentive father, and she had grown up in the security of his love. She remembered how, when she was a child, he would stop any meeting to pick her up and put her on his lap, or listen to what she had to say. She knew death was part of life, but this was too soon.

The men stopped just past the reef where the turquoise water became dark blue. They moved their canoes to make a circle and chanted a song of lament. The haunting sound was carried by the wind over the waters to the mourners on the beach. Aolani saw Kainalu touch the jar of ashes to his forehead for a long moment. He opened the lid and threw the contents into the ocean as the rise of the swell lifted his canoe. Each man followed by taking the white orchid *lei* from around his neck and placing it in the water. A floating remembrance to honour a life well lived.

The group of women on the beach let out a high-pitched call to the heavens.

Aolani watched as her mother swayed with emotion. She was tall, regal, with a straight back and dark, deep-set eyes. Her black hair was long and thick with silver strands running through. Aolani did not go to her mother, and she did not join the women in their calls of sorrow. She waited for her husband to come back. She needed his strength.

The canoes returned and Fili walked straight from the boat to Aolani. He was a giant of a man, like her father had been.

'*Ku'u lei,*' Fili whispered as he dropped down to where she was sitting and pulled her close. She could see there were tears in his eyes. She was not the only one to feel adrift without her father and she buried her face in the warmth of his neck.

Tucked against her husband's body, Aolani watched the waves break on the shore. They sat there until the mourners had departed, but Aolani was loath to leave the beach, the last connection with her father. This was the beach where she had grown into a woman. Her father had sat with her on the sand, helping her walk, then swim. Aolani knew when she and Fili got up to leave this spot, it would be time to look to the future. Time to focus on the child that was growing in her womb.

Kainalu walked towards them. Despite the heat of the sand, he was barefoot, wearing breeches and a loose cotton shirt.

'Sister, you need to be with our mother. I have to go to the plantation, and I don't want to leave her without any of her children close.'

Aolani looked out to the horizon and sighed. 'You are right,' she said, reaching for his hand to pull her up.

Fili rose too, and put his arm around Kainalu. 'Tell me what you need me to do.'

'*Mahalo*, brother,' Kainalu smiled, but the weight of responsibility and sadness sloped his shoulders. Aolani put her arms around him and hugged him close, wanting to imbue strength to her sibling, but her reserves were empty. She searched his eyes to see if this grief had opened up the pain of his widowerhood; although long ago now, she knew he still mourned his wife and child.

'Let us go,' Kainalu said as he pulled away.

Aolani walked slowly behind her brother and husband as they headed through the palm trees. When they got to the house, she touched the feather standards adorned with *kapa* cloth which crossed the entrance of the home. They were a sign of nobility, but what was the value of power on earth, when life was gone? Her father could have no influence from the grave. She felt a sickness in her gut, taking her appetite and stealing her joy. She stroked her belly. This baby was her first, and her father would not be there to bestow a blessing on her child.

Aolani hoped for a boy. She would give him her father's name, Kahanuola. It meant 'breath of life'. The very thing that had been taken from him.

Chapter Three

England, September 1880

Every avenue Isabella's parents pursued to find help for Aunt Emily failed. They had even thought of paying someone to make the voyage to New Zealand, but were unable to find a suitable candidate. No more telegrams had arrived; it was as if she as well as Hamish had disappeared.

While waiting, the Buckleys hosted a dinner party, as they often did, entertaining parishioners and friends.

Sir Mark Winter, a local landowner, was invited with his young fiancée, Lucy Sumner, and her parents. Isabella usually enjoyed social occasions; however, she found Sir Mark, only five years her senior, insufferable. 'Pompous, proud and patronising' had been her most recent description of him, but her parents overlooked her dislike and asked him to be their guest all the same.

At half past seven the Buckleys were all changed and dressed for dinner. Mrs West, the cook, was roasting a chicken, and the smell from the range wafted through from the kitchen into the hallway. Catherine wore a recently purchased evening gown of pale-blue silk with a low neckline off the shoulder, perhaps not in the style of London high society, but very fetching for a North Norfolk country dinner party. Her strawberry-blonde hair, like her mother's, was held back in a bun and decorated with a feathered clasp. She was not beautiful in the traditional sense, and neither was Isabella, but when she smiled her face was transformed and made her most attractive.

The guests arrived promptly and were ushered into the drawing room with its high ceiling and elegant Georgian features. Sir Mark was a tall man and always impeccably dressed. His fiancée, Lucy, was hardly more than five feet tall. They were an unusual-looking couple and, as Mrs Buckley had noted to her daughters, not an obvious match.

'Ah, Isabella, I hear you want to go to the wretched Pacific? I must say, I'm glad to be back on *terra firma* for good!' boomed Sir Mark on seeing Isabella.

She was instantly irritated, but smiled benignly. In an effort to escape being monopolised by him, she headed for the side table to pour the sherry, but she was not quick enough.

'Sit down, my dear, and I'll tell you about my experiences,' Sir Mark commanded.

Reluctantly, Isabella perched on the sofa next to Sir Mark, searching for someone to come and help dilute the conversation, but they were all busy talking with each other.

Making himself at home, Sir Mark stretched out his long limbs, so that he was taking up enough space for two people. He gave the satisfied smile of a man extremely pleased with himself.

'When I was in the navy, of course I was a natural sailor, but navigating the Cape of Good Hope, we met a storm that could have sunk us. Thankfully I kept my wits about me… would have been made admiral if I'd have stayed in…' He paused.

Isabella did not comment. Sir Mark cleared his throat, undeterred.

'The navy never took me as far as New Zealand, but I sailed the Pacific… know all about it.'

Isabella had been concentrating on a spider casting a web from the curtain rail to the gilt mirror on the wall behind Sir Mark's left ear.

'You know, I have some relatives bound for New Zealand in a few weeks. They're emigrating with their young daughter, sailing from Plymouth, I think.'

It seemed an offhand comment, but Isabella was suddenly alert. She caught her father's eye, and he gave a small nod to show he had also heard.

They were called to eat before she could ask more.

At supper, Sir Mark regaled the table with tales of one of his many adventures sailing around the world. He talked of life on board a ship, the fearful food he had had to suffer and the dangers of storms and pirates. If he had intended to trouble the reverend's daughter, it had quite the reverse effect. Her sister's eyes, however, had grown large with horror.

Just before the party left, Isabella approached Sir Mark.

'Do you think your relatives would be able to be my chaperones for New Zealand?'

'Chaperone you?' he paused. 'Well, that's a thought.'

'I would be so grateful if you could ask,' Isabella said, trying not to sound too eager.

Sir Mark shrugged in a non-committal way. 'I do not know why you want to go... but I will write and ask them. Worrying thing, this business with your uncle.'

'I am much obliged,' she said as sweetly as she could.

'Don't raise your hopes, my dear; it is unlikely your father will let you go,' Sir Mark whispered as he rose to speak to Reverend Buckley. Despite his discouragement, Isabella found herself smiling.

That night in bed, as she lay back on her feather pillow, feeling the cool crispness of the cotton sheets, she dared to hope that she would soon be on a voyage to New Zealand. It was a country she only knew about from Emily's letters and it felt as if it was the very end of the earth.

The next morning at breakfast Isabella wondered when to broach the subject, but her father came to the point after saying grace.

'Isabella, my dear. As you know, Sir Mark told us of his relatives emigrating to New Zealand. I have prayed, and I feel the good Lord has a plan in it. It may be that they can help Emily, so you will not have to go.'

This was not what she wanted to hear.

'But Father, I *want* to go.'

He winced slightly. 'Yes, so you say.'

Catherine and Mrs Buckley were both at the table, but said nothing.

'Sending a stranger to Emily would not comfort her. She needs family with her. She asked for *me* to go,' Isabella implored, trying to control her voice.

'Well, let us see what Sir Mark's relatives say,' the reverend concluded, and the subject was once again closed.

A few days later, Sir Mark's fiancée, Lucy, and her mother, Mrs Sumner, came for tea. Isabella wondered if there would be news. She did not have to wait long to find out.

The neighbours were ushered into the drawing room, and took their seats. When they were all sipping their tea, Mrs Sumner, said, 'My dear future son-in-law, Sir Mark, asked me to inform you that his relatives sent a telegram and would be happy to chaperone you on the steamer, Isabella. They will also willingly help you once you get to New Zealand.'

Isabella looked up with surprised joy and nearly spilt her tea. 'That is wonderful news!'

Catherine looked like she might cry, and Mrs Buckley let out a sigh. 'Let us talk on it later,' she said quietly.

The conversation changed direction and was mainly focused on Lucy's engagement. Both Lucy and her mother were still brimming with pride and excitement. Mrs Sumner had the habit of asking a question but never waiting for the answer, instead flitting on to the next thought. Isabella found it exhausting so she let the conversation float over her as she thought about the voyage.

After the Sumners departed, Catherine and Isabella remained in the drawing room with their mother, reading and embroidering. Isabella was waiting for her mother to broach the subject of the chaperones.

Mrs Buckley put down her book with a sigh. 'I despair of both of you – being unmarried. I have failed terribly as your mother.'

Isabella and Catherine gave each other a fleeting look. 'Not at all, Mama,' Isabella said.

'Why we have not found you both a successful match like Lucy, I cannot say.'

'At least you have us with you, Mama; surely that is some comfort?' Catherine said.

'Yes, it is. But who knows what will happen to Isabella if she sails to the ends of the earth!'

'Mama, you know I am sensible, and I would have a chaperone.'

Mrs Buckley huffed.

Isabella moved to stand up and winced as she felt her lower back spasm.

'What is it?' asked Catherine.

'Just this silly back, I do wish it would stop hurting.'

'That is another reason why you should not travel,' said Mrs Buckley.

'I am sure it will get better. I just need to keep moving.'

'Well, we can't have this turning you into an invalid.'

'I am far from an invalid, Mama!' Isabella laughed, hiding her annoyance.

But as she sat in the high-back armchair, the word eked into her soul, trying to dismantle any confidence she had in getting better. For a moment she imagined herself in future years as an invalid spinster.

Is that what I will be? she wondered.

Isabella had long since concluded she would live the life of a spinster; her previous admirers and matchmaking introductions had never resulted in the marriage that was expected of her, but she dearly hoped Catherine would find a marriage that would make her happy. If only she could help William see it was her sister, not Isabella herself, who would be a perfect wife for him.

Isabella waited for her parents' decision, afraid that any more keenness on her part would shut the door to her travels once and for all. There was not an immediate answer, but before supper, Mrs Buckley came to find her daughter, who had been in the study, trying to surreptitiously find any books on sea voyages.

'Well, there you are.'

Isabella was on the stepladder, reaching for a book on the top shelf. She stepped down and straightened down her skirts.

'Yes, Mama?'

'Your father and I have talked, and as this couple can chaperone you, then we will give our blessing.'

'Do you really mean that?' Isabella asked, amazed at her mother's turnaround.

'I *have* thought on it,' she paused. 'You *have* suffered greatly with your back and tiredness, but I now wonder if the warmer climate may be beneficial for you.'

Isabella's unspoken fear was how her weak back would manage the voyage. Despite her worry, Isabella felt elated. What she had hoped for was actually happening. *Can I do this?* She didn't know the answer, but she knew she had to keep moving forward.

Chapter Four

Hawaii, May 1876

Four months after her father's death, Aolani felt the first pangs and grips of labour. It was late at night, and she was lying in the dark, her husband snoring softly by her side. The light from the full moon illuminated the wooden furniture and Aolani felt peaceful. Until the pain came. She waited for a while, but when it was too much, she reached over to shake Fili awake. Immediately sitting to attention, hair awry from sleep, he looked at his wife. 'The baby comes?'

'Yes,' Aolani replied, rolling from the mattress to the floor where she waited on her hands and knees for the next contraction. Fili took action. He ran to call Aolani's mother from the neighbouring house, and two other aunties who would be helping to bring this new life into the world.

The labour was long, and the baby breach. As hour followed hour and no baby came, Aolani grew weak and her face dripped with sweat. With coaching from the aunties, she concentrated on her body and the child she was attempting to deliver. She tried to talk to it, to communicate spirit to spirit. *My sweet, you can come now. It is safe. Don't be afraid, I am your mother, and I will never let harm come to you.* In between the contractions she waited for a reply, for her baby to speak, but nothing came, no noise, no message.

After twenty-four hours, there was a mighty push, and the child was delivered. He was a boy, so he was named 'breath of life' like his grandfather, but despite his name, there was no breath in him. He was lifeless and blue. In horror, Aolani's mother whisked him away and tried to resuscitate him, all the time crying out to *Ke Akua* to provide healing. Aolani lay still on the bed, defeated. *There must be a miracle; my baby cannot die too.* She remembered how King Kamehameha III himself had been stillborn, but the *kaula* said he would live, and he did.

'Let him live!' she cried out.

But it was not enough and all attempts to revive the newborn failed.

'Kahanuola, my love, welcome this little Kahanuola,' Aolani's mother whispered, when it was clear the baby was gone. She placed him on her daughter's chest.

In exhaustion and devastation Aolani held her baby boy. *'E'kala mai,'* she whispered over and over to him. She was so weak from the labour, she could barely comprehend what had happened, but she felt at that moment that every good thing had been taken from her. The pain seemed unbearable. She had no energy left to fight, and she surrendered to the fact that this child would bypass the world and go straight to his heavenly home. For nine months Aolani had loved and spoken to her forming baby. The prospect of new life enabled her to arise from her father's death, but now her boy was gone too. Aolani closed her eyes. 'Fili,' she whispered.

He had been outside, but his ears were waiting for her call. Aolani collapsed in grief as he held her and together they cried, with deep, body-shaking sobs, holding their little baby and praying for a day when they would not feel as though their hearts were physically breaking in two.

Three days later, as with the ashes of his father-in-law, Fili and Kainalu paddled out past the breakers. Together they gave the child's remains to the deep. Fili asked *Ke Akua* for mercy at the same time, and for life to come to Aolani's womb again.

Aolani watched with her mother on the shore. She felt numb. She could not understand why God, *Ke Akua*, or Jesus – who the missionaries and her mother told her was good – would take life like this. She let out a deep breath and inhaled the warm, salt sea air.

Fili and her brother were nearing the shallows; she rose with her mother to meet them. Kainalu was sitting at the front of the canoe, slicing through the waves, his eyes ahead, concentrating on getting the outrigger in the right position to catch a wave. Aolani loved her brother. She knew the way he was surviving the death of his father, his stillborn nephew and the responsibility of leading the family was by throwing himself into his work.

Aolani had been in Kona, on the island of Hawaii, for the birth of her baby. Now, with empty arms, it was time to return on the ferry to Honolulu on the island of Oah'u where she, Fili and Kainalu lived. Honolulu was a small town, with no building over three storeys, but it was still the bustling cosmopolitan capital of the islands. It welcomed visitors from far-flung countries, trading with America and the Far East, very different from the gentle, slow-paced village life of Kona.

'I don't want to go back, I want to stay here with you, *Makuahine*,' Aolani said to her mother as they stood away from the crowd of relatives sitting outside singing and eating *poi* under the moon.

'My child, you must return. While there is still breath in your body there is a purpose for your life. Hold on to *Ke Akua*.'

'I don't have your faith. I want it, but I don't have it.'

Her mother sighed. 'Aolani, my daughter, you are Hawaiian. You were conceived on the breath of the wind, and delivered amid a fragrance of orchid blossom. You were born into a family of chiefs, of warriors and fighters. We are a mighty people, but only made mighty by our Creator. This is not the end. Take courage. A child will still be born from your womb.'

Aolani leaned her head on her mother's shoulder. She closed her eyes. Tears of pain squeezed between her lashes. Her mother held her, rocking her gently.

Chapter Five

Voyage to New Zealand, September 1880

Isabella's carriage arrived at the Plymouth dockside on a drizzly, grey afternoon. She peered out of the window to see the hustle and bustle of passengers being escorted on board a large steam ship. Seamen heaved huge crates of provisions and luggage for what looked like hundreds of people.

Her father had arranged the purchase of a ticket on the *Lyttleton*. She would be travelling from Plymouth down the north Atlantic, past the Canary Islands, perhaps as far west as Brazil, then south-east to Cape Town, round the Cape of Good Hope into the 'roaring forties', those westerly winds that accelerated the ship's passage. There could be storms and icebergs, as Sir Mark had illustrated in detail, both of which Catherine had been concerned about. 'And I honestly feel the monotony will be ghastly, Isabella. It will be almost *three months* at sea without stepping onto dry land.'

'Three months of watching the landscape of the water changing, of discovering new birds and sea life. I will find it thrilling!' Isabella responded; she understood that an event could be viewed in two ways, by one as a trial and by another as a possibility, an open door. She still felt this voyage, seeing the world, was the open door she had been waiting for.

However, she remembered Catherine's warnings of monotony as she got out of the carriage, staring at the *Lyttleton* – her new home. She had never seen such a large ship. Her bravery was floundering and she wished she had been able to meet her chaperones before embarking. Some moral support was all she needed. In its absence, she gave a sigh, picked up her skirts and made her way towards the vessel.

'We'll take your trunks, ma'am. May I see your ticket?' said a porter with a thick West Country accent.

Isabella reached into her bag to hand him her papers. Thanks to the generosity of her mother's inheritance, which substantially added to her father's parson's stipend, Isabella was travelling in the relative comfort of a first-class cabin in the stern of the ship. As she followed the porter up the plank, holding on to the rope at her side, she saw horses being led into the hold, joining the cows that she assumed would be used for milk while at sea. Chickens were clucking away in their coops in the open air.

At least that means fresh eggs, she thought.

Inside, the corridors were narrow, but with polished wood walls, and there was a smell of cleanliness. Isabella was taken by a porter to her cabin and had a cursory look around. It was a sliver of a room with a narrow bunk bed of what looked like teak. Before unpacking, she went up on deck to see the *Lyttelton* leave the dock. An hour after she had boarded, it pulled away with a loud toot of steam from the powerful engine, to the shouts, waves and tears from those both on the boat and on land. There was no one for Isabella to say goodbye to. That had all been done forty-eight hours earlier in Norfolk. She had taken the train to London, stayed with her brother, John, and his family in Kensington for a night, and then onwards by train to Plymouth.

Isabella turned from the crowds of strangers waving on the dock, to set her eyes on the horizon ahead, her back to all that she was leaving behind. As a woman without offspring, she felt a lack of being tethered to the earth. Her parents would likely depart this world before her. She had Catherine and her brother, but the gossamer thread of belonging seemed to be vulnerable, leaving her fearful of feeling emotionally adrift on the large ocean they would be traversing.

It took almost two hours before they lost sight of land and were in open sea. Isabella was intrigued by the slow, undulating movement of the ship and the creaks of the wooden boards and fixtures. The second name on the cabin door indicated that she was supposed to be sharing with a Miss Hartley, but Miss Hartley never appeared. Isabella was relieved, as two crammed into the room would not have been comfortable.

She was looking for something in her large carpetbag when she came across the present from old Walter, the gardener. He had given it with deference and a little bow after church the Sunday before she left. Isabella smiled at the memory. She unwrapped it and found a well-worn copy of *The Pilgrim's Progress*.

Isabella flicked through the pages, having read John Bunyan's book many years before. She would start it again straight away. As she was holding the book her eyes fell on the pile of letters from William and her family. She had been told she could not open them until on board. She sat on the bed and read William's first:

My dear Isabella,

I am writing this letter at five in the morning as I want to give it to you before you depart. I can't quite fathom that you are leaving us today, and for such a long time. I want you to know how much I will miss you. I respect your decision. If you change your mind, I will be waiting for you on your return. I will pray daily for your safe travels and a happy conclusion for your aunt and uncle.

Affectionately yours,
William

William. She tried to ignore the attractive picture of being his wife that had formed in her imagination. He was a good friend; would it have mattered if she did not love him? If it had not been for Catherine, she wondered if her answer might have been different. The thought made her feel anxious, as if the course of her life might have taken the wrong route and it was now out of her hands.

While Isabella was reading the letter for a second time, there was a knock at the door. She opened it to a smiling woman with thick, wavy, dark hair. It was piled into a fashionable bun at the back of her head, with ringlets falling around her face.

'Hello, are you Miss Buckley?'

'Yes, Isabella.'

'I hope I am not disturbing you, I wanted to introduce myself. I am Elizabeth Cornish. My husband is a cousin of Sir Mark Winter?' she asked almost in a question, as if waiting to see recognition on Isabella's face. 'He told us that you would be on the steamer. We are with our daughter, Eleanor, three cabins down from you.'

'Yes, I was going to come and find you. How do you do?' Isabella smiled, shaking her hand.

'We will have plenty of time to get to know each other, but I wondered if you would join our table for supper this evening?'

'Thank you, I would love to.'

'Wonderful, I will leave you to your unpacking, then. See you at seven?' Elizabeth said.

Isabella smiled and nodded, relieved that she felt they were going to be friends.

A few hours later, a gong signified that dinner was served for first-class passengers. Isabella, now changed from travelling tweed into her blue silk, made her way to the saloon. Stewards were running to and fro in their smart uniforms and white gloves. Isabella scanned the passengers for Elizabeth's face, holding on to a rope railing to keep herself steady.

'Over here!' came a call from behind her.

She turned to see Elizabeth seated at a table with four others.

'Do join us,' she said, rising with the others to welcome Isabella. 'Sadly my husband isn't with us; he is already suffering from seasickness and confined to our cabin.'

'Oh, I am sorry.'

'All the more for us!' replied one of the other diners.

Shaking their hands, Isabella smiled and took her seat.

'What leads you to be travelling to New Zealand?' asked the middle-aged man opposite her, once the starter of tomato soup had been served.

'My uncle emigrated to New Zealand three years ago, but recently we got news that he has disappeared. I am going out to help my aunt and nephews,' Isabella said before taking a sip of the tomato soup.

'Disappeared?' gasped the woman next to him, with eyes wide, her hand instinctively going to her throat. 'That sounds positively terrifying. Do you think he is dead?'

Before Isabella could answer, Elizabeth broke in, 'I am sure there will be a happy end to this mystery,' she said with an encouraging smile to Isabella. 'Who would like water?' she asked, offering the glass jug that had been in front of her. The subject of the conversation changed, but Isabella was stuck with the woman's question.

It was strange they had heard no more from Aunt Emily. Isabella knew her farm was two days' ride from Auckland, and their three sons were young still. It could be the news was bad, but Isabella had felt optimism from the start that all would be well. She had no proof, of course, but just a confidence that she hoped would not leave her now.

Chapter Six

Hawaii, June 1877

When Aolani realised she was pregnant again, her immediate reaction was fear. 'What if I lose this child too?' she whispered to Fili as they lay on the straw mattress in the dawn light, listening to the melodic rush of waves breaking in the distance.

'He will live,' Fili said firmly. In reality, Aolani understood he could not know, but his words gave her comfort. She chose to believe him, but she did not talk to this baby as she had her firstborn, in case the chance to be a mother was taken from her again. 'If I love this baby less, it will hurt less if it dies,' she told herself.

Aolani spent her days with her mother, who had travelled with them to Honolulu, while Fili was working. She was weary of company, only allowing her family close. Fili tried to encourage her to meet people and celebrate her pregnancy, but his efforts were usually fruitless – until one morning he reminded her of the upcoming Kamehameha Day celebrations.

'We are invited to the Hawaiian Hotel. Kainalu will be with us…'

'Fili, I don't want to go. I don't want to talk to people I don't know.'

Fili sat next to his wife and put his arm around her. '*Ku'u lei*, all the islands are celebrating; it is right for us to, as well.'

Aolani's mother entered the room. 'Lani, it is important. This is not just about you.'

Aolani rolled her eyes. Her mother saw, and said more softly, 'This is about the unification of our islands. It is your duty to be there.'

Aolani did not reply, but she knew she would have to give in. She also knew she might enjoy herself. 'I'll think about it,' she said, standing to leave the room.

Aolani eventually acceded to Fili's encouragements, only because she loved her husband, and she knew it was time to rise out of her mourning. She wore a fashionable bustle with her skirts, and placed a flower crown on her head, arranging her thick brown hair in a braided bun instead of keeping it down. Although she was six months into her pregnancy, her bump was small, which concerned her, but it was not too small that she did not have to loosen the laceable slits down the side of her corset.

Looking in the long mirror now, she hardly recognised herself. No more loose dresses, she was now attired in the formal, restrictive clothing of the Europeans. Her silk dress had both a high neck and long sleeves. She smiled at her reflection, pretending for a moment she was an English lady, with dainty pale hands and impeccable manners. She gave a little curtsy and then burst into laughter. Picking up her skirts, she walked out to the waiting carriage.

The hotel, near Waikiki, had two storeys and was made of stone, with two deep verandas festooned with clematis and passion flowers. There was a shady lawn at the front. The large, open reception rooms of the hotel were bright and airy, filled with the fragrance of the frangipani trees outside. The flowers' sweet, pungent smell was wafted around the room by the warm breeze coming in from the ocean.

Chinese waiters stood at the entrance with trays of drinks welcoming the great and the good of Hawaiian society into the hotel. Despite the luxury of the party, as Aolani feared, the evening was all small talk. She was stuck with a group of women discussing their horror at the increase in the cost of imported fabric. Aolani was tired, and wished she had not come. She was about to ask Fili to take her home, when Kainalu called her over to meet another *haole* couple.

'May I introduce you to my sister, Aolani. She is married to Fili, whom you know. Aolani, this is Mr and Mrs Fortnum from England.'

'Ah, England!' Aolani said, feeling her face brighten.

'Mr Fortnum has been helping us with our export contracts at the farm.'

'Pleased to meet you,' Aolani said, shaking their hands. Mr Fortnum wasn't quite as tall as Aolani, and round in shape with a mop of unruly curly hair. Mrs Fortnum was all smiles, and because of the heat her cheeks had begun to have a rosy glow. They talked together for a while, until Mr Fortnum and Kainalu went to find Fili to get his insight on a matter of business.

'Are you enjoying your time in Honolulu, Mrs Fortnum?' Aolani asked when they were left alone.

'Oh, I am, but do call me Emma,' she said, adding, 'Would you join me outside? We can watch all the chitchat from the comfort of those chairs. I am longing to rest my legs and enjoy the evening breeze.'

Aolani laughed, briefly placing a hand on her stomach. 'I would love to.'

They sat down, and Aolani felt the relief. 'I am very glad to meet someone from England; I find it such a romantic place.'

'Oh yes, I miss it terribly, even though we are in paradise! We have been here three years now; I can't think why I haven't met you before. Likely because I spend too much time at home raising my boys! We decided not to send them home to boarding school, but have tutors to teach them.'

'Has that worked for them?'

'It has been *somewhat* successful. We had to let one tutor go when we realised he knew less than our oldest. Then another ran off with a Chinese girl. Our present tutor is professional and thankfully very strict – long may it last!'

Aolani laughed again. She hadn't laughed in a while and it felt good. 'What about your husband, what does he do?'

'Oh, he has all the fun! He works as an adviser for King Kalākaua.'

Aolani listened to the way she talked, and repeated the vowels in her head. When a waiter came over and Mrs Fortnum asked for 'water', Aolani tried to mimic.

'Worrter?' she said.

'Oh goodness, is that what I sound like?' Emma smiled, and then her face became serious and she leaned forward. 'I noticed you put your hand on your stomach when we moved to the chairs. I hope I am not being rude, but are you expecting your first child?'

'I am,' Aolani replied. 'But it is not my first... I lost a baby.'

'Oh, my dear,' Emma said. 'I understand something of your pain; we lost our fifth child seven months into my pregnancy. It was when we had first moved here, and I knew no one. I just wanted to go home.'

'Tell me, how did you survive it?' Aolani asked, blinking back tears that seemed to arrive too swiftly nowadays.

'I don't know; sometimes it is still painful. But I believe I will see my baby again in heaven, and you will too.'

'I hope so,' Aolani said, with lingering doubt.

They left the party, both later than expected, agreeing to meet again soon. Aolani felt she had finally found someone who understood what she was feeling.

'I admire the British,' Aolani said to Fili in their carriage home.

'I don't think it is an inherited admiration,' he laughed.

Aolani knew he was referring to her mother.

Kainalu, now in Kalākaua's cabinet, had been commissioned to work with the health minister to help combat the growing problem of leprosy in the indigenous population on the islands. The House of Nobles had debated the subject, and there was real fear among the people. After the smallpox epidemic of 1853, the politicians did not want to take any chances. Kainalu had a meeting with the royal physician, a Frenchman named George P Trousseau, the day after the party.

'*Mon ami*, separation is the only answer, this blight and curse from the Chinese is so contagious.'

'So we must find the lepers and send them to the colony at Kalaupapa?' Kainalu questioned.

Dr Trousseau took his glasses off and rubbed his eyes.

'Yes, it is the only way to protect these islands from an explosion of the sickness. But I cannot go to your people to find the lepers – they hide them.' Dr Trousseau tapped his hand on the side of his chair in frustration. 'We need to employ a Hawaiian to travel to the islands to educate the people.'

'I could do that job,' Kainalu said; it seemed obvious to him, but the doctor was visibly taken aback.

'*Non, mon ami*, I was not implying you should go.' He paused. 'Why would you want to surrender your comfort to travel the length and breadth of Oah'u, Hawaii, Maui, Lanai, Kauai and probably Moloka'i? No, we'll employ someone, it will take months and be lonely work.'

Kainalu looked out to the garden surrounding the building, contemplating what he had suggested. He was ready to do something; he had felt impotent stuck in political discussion knowing that it was action that was required.

'If I can help stop the spread of leprosy, then I will do it,' he said.

Leaving the comforts of home would not bother Kainalu. He was happy to sleep under the stars, and from a young age the beach had been his playground. He could easily buy *poi*, catch fish and harvest coconuts to sustain himself, but he knew that it was unlikely that he would have to supply his own food. The Hawaiian people were a generous race, and in all likelihood Kainalu would be looked after and fed royally in every village he visited.

'Well, *mon ami*, if you insist,' Dr Trousseau said with a shrug of his shoulders. 'Of course, you will be supported by the Board of Health, and we can give you details of every community you need to contact. As for rounding up the lepers, I wonder if it would be best to leave that to others. If you can tell us where they are, we will send for those who won't come voluntarily. It sounds *un petit peu* barbaric, but what else can we do?' He sighed, collecting his papers from the table and looking at Kainalu with a smile of resignation. 'For the greater good,' he said, and then, rising from his chair, asked, 'So, when can you start? The sooner the better.'

'My sister is going to give birth in a few months' time, perhaps I will begin here, in Oah'u, and stay on the island until the new life has arrived, and from there travel to the outer islands.'

'*Bien*, I will make the necessary arrangements. Could we meet again in a week, so I can give you the supplies and information you will need?'

'Very good, *mahalo*,' Kainalu said, and then turned to leave the doctor's office.

'*Non*, thank *you*, you are doing a great service.'

Kainalu rode over to Fili and Aolani's home. Aolani was lying down on a straw mattress on the *lanai* when he arrived. She was fanning herself with a banana leaf; her legs had swollen so much that it was uncomfortable to walk.

'Sister, you look busy,' Kainalu joked. She attempted to hit him with the banana leaf but missed.

'I am so bored; give me news, what is happening in town?'

'Same same, the sky is blue, and the ocean is turquoise, the palms wave in the breeze and Honolulu is full of visitors from the steamers coming in.'

'I know that, but tell me something more interesting,' Aolani implored.

He paused. 'I have a new mission. I found out today.'

'What is it?' She asked, sitting up on her elbows.

'I will be travelling to tell our people that leprosy is contagious, and we must separate all lepers if we don't want these islands to become full of them.'

Aolani looked at her brother in shock. 'Why do you want to get involved with leprosy? Keep away from the lepers, brother.'

'Have no fear, *wahine*, I will be safe. I will stay on Oah'u until your child comes, and after I have met the babe and given my blessing, I will leave for Hawaii and the other islands. I estimate I will be gone for five months if I do this job with diligence.'

'Kai, that is a long time.'

'Cheer up! You will be preoccupied with the newborn. You won't even realise I am gone,' he said, giving her a wink as he walked into the house, not waiting to hear her answer.

Chapter Seven

Voyage to New Zealand, October 1880

The steamer chugged through the night, driving its way slowly across the seascape. Isabella slept deeply, perhaps from the sea air or perhaps making up for the fact she had not slept much in the days preceding her departure.

The early morning light woke her as it streamed through her cabin's polished bronze porthole. For a moment she forgot where she was, until she heard the gulls overhead.

She lay content in her bunk, listening to the constant groan and hum of the steam engine, and the sound and movement of the sea.

Sleepily, she lifted her head, with her thick brown hair escaping its long plait, she looked around her little cabin. There was nothing to do but get up. After she had dressed, she opened her door and saw Elizabeth walking down the corridor towards her, hand in hand with a small girl.

'We were just coming to see if you would join us for breakfast,' Elizabeth said.

'Thank you, I will,' Isabella replied, and then, bending down to shake the little girl's hand, asked, 'You must be Eleanor?'

'Yes,' the girl replied shyly, hiding part of her face with her mother's hand.

'How old are you?'

'Four!'

'Just turned four!' her mother added.

'My, what a big girl!'

Eleanor's smile broadened.

They walked into the saloon, Eleanor still holding her mother's hand. Then she reached out to hold Isabella's too. Isabella happily took it. They took their seats at a table laid for four next to a porthole.

Elizabeth's husband, Hubert Cornish, joined them after a few minutes and bowed politely to Isabella. He looked very pale.

'Miss Buckley, I am very glad to meet you.' He was a patrician-looking man, thin, with greased-back brown hair and a clipped moustache. His voice was deep and commanding.

'I heard you were unwell; I do hope you are feeling better?' Isabella enquired.

'Yes, thank you. I am not quite right,' he said, sitting down and inspecting his place setting. 'But I am sure by the end of the day I will have found my sea legs.' He pursed his lips. 'Now, you are acquainted with my cousin Sir Mark Winter? As you know, he wrote to us about your circumstances. If there is anything we can do to help once we all arrive in New Zealand, please let us know.'

As Elizabeth poured tea into porcelain teacups, Hubert picked up a knife and turned it over, tutting. Loudly he called to one of the stewards and, unaware, or perhaps, thought Isabella, aware, of passengers watching him, handed the man his knife, fork and spoon.

'These are dirty; polish them up, my man. You would never see something like this at my club in London so I don't see why we should have dirty knives and forks in a first-class dining room.'

The steward apologised with deference and took the offending cutlery away. After a few minutes he returned, placing the now shining knife and fork at Mr Cornish's place.

'Yes, much better. Let's keep standards high,' he said, without looking at the steward.

Isabella watched the steward's impassive face. She wondered if he had polished the knife, fork and spoon with a surreptitious spit and rub. She took a sip of her tea and glanced at Elizabeth, who had a polite smile fixed on her face.

Eleanor was staring out of the small porthole into the huge grey sea that surrounded the steamer. She was a delicate girl, very small and slight. Isabella felt sorry for her having so few other children in first class to play with.

After breakfast, Elizabeth, Eleanor and Isabella went for a walk on deck. They had to wrap up warmly and the cold wind startled Isabella with its strength. Mr Cornish, although invited by his wife, was otherwise engaged with some paperwork in their cabin and wanted peace and quiet.

As they perambulated up and down the portside, Isabella found her balance in the constant movement of the ship. There was a section for first class passengers only, and a line was painted on the wood so that no one from steerage would cross over.

'What a relief we don't have to be in steerage. Imagine how sick we would feel,' Elizabeth commented as the ship rose and fell with the swell. 'I am told they sleep in tiers of bunks in different compartments for men, women and families. Our cabin is small, but I am grateful for the privacy.'

As they walked, Isabella watched fellow first-class passengers making themselves at home, everything still new and intriguing. They were establishing routines that would be adhered to throughout the journey: finding favourite spots to read their books and take exercise. Friends were being made that perhaps would be regretted later, having no easy means of escape from unsolicited conversation. Isabella's habit was to deflect conversation back to Elizabeth; she knew nothing was worse than being talked at, and she wanted Elizabeth to choose her company, not try to avoid it.

But Elizabeth and Isabella were easy companions, and spent most afternoons together, either walking along the deck talking, or entertaining Eleanor. The two women, with Eleanor often on Elizabeth's lap, would sit on deckchairs away from the wind, the sun kissing their faces intermittently, whenever it poked through the clouds. From time to time they saw other ships, and they played the guessing game, laughing as they narrowed their eyes to wonder at the vessel and where it was sailing to.

When Eleanor was tired, they sat in companionable silence, reading. A makeshift library was formed in first class where people could share and borrow what they wanted. Isabella had finished *The Pilgrim's Progress* and was currently engrossed in Dickens' *Pickwick Papers*. When she wasn't reading or playing cards, she painted, setting up her miniature easel on deck and trying to sketch the movement of the sea and the passengers in groups, but she found it difficult. Portraits were her strength. She needed a subject that stayed still.

One afternoon, Isabella, Elizabeth and Eleanor were on deck watching some of the passengers from steerage put out lines to fish off the side of the steamer. An old man with ruddy cheeks and wild, white hair saw Isabella watching.

'Tryin to catch summat to add to the pease soup an' dried potatoes!' he said jovially.

Every time a fish pulled at the old man's line there was a flurry of excitement from the crowd that had formed.

'I think I've got a big un, might be a barracuda!' he called.

The crowd all stood to have a closer view as he pulled and reeled in his catch, his rod looking like it might snap at any minute. One of the other steerage fishermen came to help, looking across at Elizabeth, who was standing next to Isabella. He smiled and winked at her. Isabella saw Elizabeth blush and look away, but also watched as her gaze returned to the man. He was handsome, thought Isabella, with very dark hair and a thick moustache. He was wearing a white shirt and waistcoat without a jacket, despite the breezy temperature on deck.

Isabella was not surprised that the man had chosen to look at Elizabeth and not her. Her chaperone was striking, with her peaches-and-cream skin and large brown eyes. The same face that had attracted Hubert was attracting other men on the ship. Isabella wondered why she didn't feel jealous; was it because she did not expect such attention, or simply because Elizabeth was unaware of the effect of her looks, and this natural humility made her so easy to like?

When Isabella considered herself, she knew she was not what fashion would call a beauty. She wasn't the pale English rose that was deemed by many as the height of attractiveness. As a younger woman she had compared her looks with others, and felt downhearted when she came up short. It was a passing comment from Walter that had changed her thinking: 'A flower does not think of competing with the flower next to it; it just blooms.' He had been talking of the roses showing off their vibrant yellows and pinks in the front border, but Isabella was struck by the truth of his words. She had decided to 'just bloom', although as the years went by this had not been so easy. 'Wilting' was a more accurate way to describe the dimming light of hope that affected her external features so significantly. Isabella had decided to focus on what she liked about herself: her hair, for instance, the same dark brown of her father in his younger days, was thick and long. She liked her blue eyes, and she had good straight teeth, for which she was grateful. Her mother suffered with false teeth after her own had decayed, and Isabella now religiously cleaned her own after meals with her tooth powder and horse-hair toothbrush.

The men were still trying to haul in their catch, but it was causing some difficulty.

'Let's go inside, I am getting cold,' Elizabeth said, taking Eleanor's hand and walking away from the fishermen. Isabella followed but looked back as they opened the door to the deck below. The fisherman was watching Elizabeth with a faint smile on his lips.

That evening, Isabella and Elizabeth were sitting in the long promenade saloon at the stern, called the 'cuddy'. The room was filled with a mist of cigar smoke, as the men were smoking and drinking at one end and the women playing cards and talking at the other. Eleanor was safely tucked up in her bunk, and Elizabeth indicated an empty sofa, away from the group of ladies. Another passenger came to sit with them, but then changed her mind and joined the card game.

'It's so nice to have you to talk to,' Elizabeth said.

A steward came to ask if they needed anything.

'No, thank you,' Isabella smiled.

'Mr Cornish has many talents, but communication isn't his strongest. He can go for hours without saying a word to me,' Elizabeth said, giving a hollow laugh.

'How did you meet Mr Cornish?' Isabella asked.

'My father owned a farm in Dorset and he was losing money. Hubert helped him and gave a very generous interest-free loan, and in fact my father then sold the farm after my mother died. Hubert is fifteen years older than I, but he asked my father for my hand in marriage. I was young and flattered. We married seven years ago.' Elizabeth paused, and then said in a quieter tone, 'Marriage has not been what I expected, but Eleanor makes everything worth it.'

'Would you have more children?' Isabella asked, hoping her questions did not appear too direct or inquisitive.

'I would love to, but none have come yet. I am praying that once we reach our new home that will change.'

'I am sure it will!' Isabella smiled and noticed Elizabeth's eyes glisten.

Elizabeth composed herself quickly. 'The party line of why we are emigrating is that my husband has always wanted to travel to the colonies. When a business opportunity came up, he said it was right for us as a family. What he doesn't say, and please don't mention it, is that he made some bad business decisions and lost a lot of money. Both ours and that of two friends. He was even accused of being fraudulent, although thankfully it never went to court. I suspect he is making us leave out of shame, but I understand it is difficult for him to do business at home now. I do feel sorry for Hubert; his reputation is very important to him, and it has taken a battering.'

'It must have been hard for you too.'

'It was difficult watching him struggle through, knowing I couldn't do anything. He didn't talk to me about it much. He said he didn't want to worry me, but I worried more not knowing.'

'I hope the opportunity in New Zealand redeems this for you all.'

'Thank you. I know I can trust you with what I have told you.'

'Of course.'

As it was late, Isabella said goodnight, and they both retired to their cabins.

Isabella changed into her cotton nightdress and blew out the oil lamp. In the darkness the cabin became alive with shadows and the now familiar noise of creaking wood and the rise and fall of the steamer pushing through the water. It felt good to be brought into Elizabeth's confidence. Isabella felt happy as she lay in her tight little bunk with her eyes open, becoming accustomed to the darkness.

The fresh air had made her tired, but it was different from the thick, dark tiredness she usually felt at home, when her backache exhausted her and she had to fight a sort of melancholy. Isabella suddenly realised that apart from an occasional queasy feeling from the movement of the ship, she hadn't felt ill at all since she had got on the steamer. Her back pains had almost disappeared. She did not dare believe they were gone for good, but committed to rejoicing each day that she was free from pain.

Isabella woke early the next morning with the remains of a dream so vivid in her mind that it seemed real. In the dream she was lying on the wooden deck of a sea vessel, her body moving with the gentle rise and fall of the waves. She could see a tropical island with high mountain peaks shimmering like a mirage in the distance. It seemed to be pulling her closer.

Without warning, time jumped and Isabella found herself on land. She looked around her. There was a rock jutting out from the beach so she picked up her skirts to climb up and sit on it, facing the deep cerulean ocean. Tall palm trees surrounded her, waving in jubilation to the clear blue sky. Peace flooded her being and she embraced the warmth of the sun on her face. Isabella didn't question the fact that she was apparently so far from home. She felt a sense of urgency. She seemed to know that someone was waiting for her. The air was warm and alive with the calls of birds in the trees above her.

Isabella opened her eyes with a feeling of wonderful anticipation. Leaving the cabin, she realised she was too early for breakfast, so she walked upstairs and opened the heavy portside door to watch the sun rising in the east. She stood on deck as the sky turned pink and then orange with the rising sun. *Could there be something more for her?* The dream still lingered, and she wondered what new horizons would open for her, travelling to New Zealand.

She could have stayed on deck for longer, if it wasn't for her stomach reminding her that she needed breakfast.

The next day was Sunday and the passengers had their church service in the cuddy. When it finished, a steward informed the congregation that they were nearing Cape Town where they would have a coaling stop and correspondence could be sent. The steamer would get there the next day, so Isabella went to her cabin to finish her letters home.

While she was writing, she heard a faint knock at the door.

'Hello?' she called.

Slowly the door opened, and Eleanor's ribboned head popped round; she had a ragdoll under her arm and her eyes glinted mischievously.

'Eleanor, come in,' Isabella said, patting the side of the bottom bunk. With a grin the girl opened the door wider and jumped up on the mattress.

'Are you hungry?' Isabella asked, reaching up for a box of peppermints in the cabinet beside her bunk. 'Would you like one?'

'Yes, please,' Eleanor said, holding her hand out to receive it.

'And who is this?' Isabella asked, pointing to Eleanor's doll.

'Molly,' Eleanor answered, as she sucked the sweet. She looked at Isabella solemnly and then asked, 'Why are you alone?'

'Oh,' Isabella answered, surprised and not sure how to answer; the very question made her feel suddenly sad. With a brightness that she hoped disguised her deflated feelings, she said, 'I am going to visit my family in New Zealand, then I won't be alone!'

Eleanor nodded, as if she was satisfied with the answer.

She picked up Isabella's silver hairbrush, playing with it, before attempting with a giggle to brush her own hair. She asked about Isabella's wristwatch, wanting to put it on her own arm. Isabella let her, and enjoyed answering her less direct inquiries.

Eventually Isabella heard Elizabeth's call and Eleanor jumped off the bed, but not before giving Isabella a peck on the cheek and a polite 'thank you for the peppermint'. Isabella smiled as she watched her go. She had always loved children. Her maternal inclinations had begun to flourish when Catherine was born. Isabella, then seven years old, took her position of older sister very seriously.

Chapter Eight

Hawaii, autumn 1877

On the very day that Aolani's mother said the baby would be born, Leilani came into the world. She was a girl, which was the first surprise – the second being that she had the exact same heart-shaped birthmark as her grandfather on the small of her back. This was taken as a good sign. Her grandmother in particular felt it was *Ke Akua* speaking. Leilani was His blessing to the family.

Once Aolani came to terms with the fact she had not delivered a boy as they had expected, she fell in love with her daughter. Leilani was a docile baby with soft brown hair and almond eyes shaped just like her Uncle Kainalu's.

Kainalu left for the outer islands in October, a month after Leilani was born, having ridden the circumference of Oah'u, visiting the sugar cane farms and villages. He would spend a few nights with each community, speaking to the chief or plantation owner and then gathering the people together to educate them about leprosy.

One afternoon he stopped at a plantation in the town of Waialua looking over the north shore of Oah'u, thirty miles from Honolulu. He introduced himself to Mr Price, the American plantation owner, who instructed his foreman to gather the workers.

The men and women congregated straight from the fields. They were hot, tired and hungry. *Not the best timing*, Kainalu sighed. He introduced himself by saying he was the son of Kahanuola, whom everyone had heard of and respected.

Kainalu hoped it would make ears open to what he was about to say.

'*Ma'i pake* will destroy our people and ruin our islands if we do not act now. Don't be afraid to come forward for testing if you think you have the disease. If you don't come forward, it will spread, and our islands will never be the same.' Kainalu paused, looking at the faces of the workers. They were made up of Hawaiian men and women, as well as Chinese, Japanese and Portugese immigrants.

'You call it *Ma'i pake*, and blame my people. But it is also named *Ma'i ali'i* – chief's sickness,' said a Chinese worker, in a mixture of broken English and pidgin. 'You come here, tell us surrender friends, banish them, when *your* family cuda brought disease to *us.*'

There was an intake of breath among the Hawaiians. No one should speak to a son of a chief in that way. The Chinese labourer threw down his hat and left the assembly.

Kainalu waited. Eventually he said calmly, 'We do not know exactly how leprosy came to be on our islands, but what we do know is that it is spreading rapidly. I am not ascribing blame, but I urge you to act now. If you know someone with symptoms, we need to apply a quarantine.'

There was low-level mumbling. Kainalu wondered if there was someone among the crowd who had the disease, because of the lack of eyes meeting his own.

When he had said his piece, the foreman dismissed the workers. Kainalu didn't stay in the plantation that night, although warmly welcomed by Mr Price. He had been frustrated by the outcome of the meeting and decided to camp on the beach nearby.

He tethered his horse and then built a small fire to roast the fish he had been given. The beach was empty. No fishermen, no children having a final play in the ocean waves before bed. Kainalu relished the peace. He watched the sun set behind the ocean and the sky become a pattern of vibrant red, orange and pink. The show of extravagant colour in the sky could not be for him alone, but he felt it had been sent to soothe him.

Since his time in Maui ten years previously, he had sensed the presence of *Ke Akua* with him. But this magnificence in the sky needed to be witnessed by more than one pair of eyes. Kainalu suddenly had a deep desire to share what he was seeing with someone else.

Since the death of his wife, Kainalu had shut off any prospect of another woman coming into his heart. He did not want to marry again; he could not bear risking the pain of loss. But now, perhaps, he was changing his view. It would be nice to have a woman to come home to, someone he could talk to about his work, who would share his interests and passions, a woman who put others before herself. He knew character was more important than the externals that had turned his eye in his youth. Now he was thirty-eight, he was looking for a partner, an equal. As he watched the movement of the ocean, Kainalu prayed to *Ke Akua* for this woman to come to him.

The next morning Kainalu headed straight back to the plantation. He didn't announce his arrival, but tied his horse to a tree at the entrance of the farm and walked down the track to the workers' houses. He walked slowly, not knowing exactly what he intended to do. The cloudless sky promised a hot day ahead. A bell chimed, and children of the plantation workers ran to a wood-and-thatch cabin for school. Kainalu had been educated at the Royal School in Honolulu, a school started by missionaries solely for the sons of chiefs. The lessons were in English and Kainalu had been raised to become a leader of the people. This little plantation school would teach the rudiments of reading and writing, but Kainalu knew it was likely the pupils would not stay for long, having to work the fields from a young age, or preferring the lure of the ocean over the discipline of class.

He waited under the shade of a palm and watched as about fifteen children entered the building. Most had bare feet, not from poverty, for they would be well provided for on the plantation, but for an island child, shoes were deemed unnecessary.

A little girl was the last to enter the school. She looked like she had both Hawaiian and Chinese blood in her veins. She was a pretty little thing, about six years old, but clothed in the most ridiculous outfit. A dress that would have been understandable in a colder climate covered her body from head to foot, and was a size or two too big. It had long sleeves and a buttoned back reaching to a high neck. The material may have been silk, but it was ragged now, and had lost its sheen. The girl did not seem bothered by her restrictive clothing, but sang a little song to herself as she entered the school.

'Kainalu, I didn't expect you so early,' came a voice from behind him.

Kainalu turned to be greeted by Mr Price. 'I am sorry, I was about to come and find you.'

'Not to worry, now; do you want to examine each worker? I haven't noticed any sign of the sickness, but I don't want it here and am happy to take any precaution. Perhaps you would be better qualified to recognise the symptoms?'

'Yes, my thoughts exactly. Would you have someone to assist me with the women?'

'Our nurse can help. I will arrange for my labourers to present themselves. If you would like to wait in the meeting room, they will come to you.'

Kainalu spent the morning inspecting the workers. None of them had known he was returning. Many looked surprised to see him again. Kainalu checked the men for lesions on their skin or loss of sensation in their extremities. Everyone seemed to be clear. The Chinese man who had exploded in anger the night before came in for his turn. He was now subdued and obligingly took off his shirt to reveal his chest and back. Both were free from any signs of leprosy.

By two o'clock, Kainalu had finished his work and was ready to leave. He had found no lepers among the plantation workers.

'Glad to hear it, that has put my mind at rest,' said Mr Price as Kainalu began to walk back to his horse.

'It is good news indeed. Good day, sir,' Kainalu replied, but he was confused. He had relied on his intuition in the past, and this time he had been sure the disease was on the plantation. The fact that he appeared to be wrong rankled him.

Kainalu walked past the school, which was empty now, the children playing outside. He noticed the girl with the cumbersome clothing playing by herself. She appeared quite happy, but it seemed the other children were avoiding her, or she was avoiding them. She was lifting a piece of coloured glass to the light, and smiling at the patterns the sun was making through it. It was then that Kainalu saw her left hand. It had been hidden under the long sleeves of her dress, but was now revealed.

The top of her second finger was missing, and there was a bandage around the hand.

Of course, it could have been from an accident, which was probable living on a plantation. But it also could have been from loss of feeling in her fingers because of leprosy. His heart sank; was this innocent child a leper? He stood, watching her, wondering what to do, when all of a sudden a Hawaiian woman came round a corner and looked at him sharply. She called the girl, who stood up and quickly ran from sight into one of the workers' homes.

Kainalu followed the child, but when he went into the house there was no sign of her; just the woman who had called the girl, sitting calmly on the ground stirring a calabash gourd bowl of *poi*, as if nothing had happened.

'Where is the girl?' Kainalu asked.

'There is no girl,' the woman replied, not looking up. Kainalu saw her fingers tense around the calabash.

Kainalu got down on his knees. 'Is she sick?' he asked. The woman did not reply. 'I know this is hard,' he said, putting his hand on the woman's shoulder, forcing her to look at him. 'But she needs medication.'

'No!' the woman cried, pushing his hand away. 'I won't let it happen!' – her attempt at concealing her daughter gone.

Kainalu sighed. 'I just need to see her; will you bring her to me?'

The woman stayed where she was, staring at the ground. Kainalu looked up and saw a foot peaking around the back door. He slowly walked over, and smiled as he saw the little girl hiding.

'Don't worry, *wahine*, I am not going to hurt you,' he said, crouching down to her level. 'Can I see your hand?'

Shyly she pulled up her sleeves and revealed the hand with the missing finger. Kainalu found a sharp stone, and pushed it into the brown dusty skin of the girl's foot, not so much that it would break the skin, but enough to hurt. She did not flinch.

He sighed again. Her mother had come to see what was happening. She had silent tears falling down her face. Kainalu felt wretched.

'We will send someone in a week to collect her.' He paused before adding the words of Dr Trousseau: 'It is for the greater good.'

'Her name is Maima,' the woman said, looking up at Kainalu. Taking a deep breath, she brushed her tears away. 'Please look after her.'

'I will. She will be taken to the Kalihi Kai receiving station; you'll be able to visit her. There are other children, so she won't be alone. We will give Maima the best hope for living. Do not worry, *Makuahine*, trust *Ke Akua* with your girl.'

As a token of comfort, Kainalu held on to the woman's shoulder and squeezed. He knew only too well the feeling of having the one you love taken from you.

Mr Price showed sadness in the revelation; Maima was obviously loved by all. Her mother and father and her two siblings would now have to be watched carefully in case they had leprosy lying dormant in their bodies.

Kainalu was not surprised when he met the girl's father. It was the Chinese man who had shouted in anger at the first meeting.

'I only recently seen the ulcers on Maima. We tried to hide them by dressing her in long dresses and telling her she must not play with other children. She burned her finger a few months ago. Her grandfather, he died of leprosy. Maima lived with him and her grandmother as a little girl. She only come to the plantation not long ago.'

'I am sorry,' Kainalu said to him. 'If she has to go to Kalaupapa one of you could join as her *kōkua*, but that is a big sacrifice. I know you have other children.'

The man looked down at the ground, trying to control his emotion. He knew his family were now seen as unclean. Kainalu presumed they would not be able to stay at the plantation, even if Mr Price let them; there was too much fear and stigma attached to the disease. They would have to find a new community and start afresh, learning to live without the joy of their daughter with them.

Kainalu left with a heavy heart.

He returned a week later with the health officers to collect Maima. He didn't usually partake in this side of the work, but as she was so young, he wanted to see her get safely to Kalihi and make sure the staff there treated her well. Perhaps it was because of the birth of Leilani that he was so saddened by Maima's bleak future. His little niece was so beautiful, so perfect. He could not imagine her being taken from the family. Maima was beautiful too, and to her parents she would always be perfect, despite leprosy's dreaded rampage of her body.

Maima went quietly with Kainalu. He knew that she didn't fully understand what was happening, and thought she was going somewhere to get better. What she didn't know was that she would eventually be separated from her parents forever.

Chapter Nine

Arrival in Auckland, December 1880

The trade winds were now encouraging the steamer along, and there seemed an air of excitement among the passengers, many of whom were about to start new lives and establish themselves in New Zealand.

Isabella was to have dinner at the captain's table and, while she was dressing, she thought of wearing her pearls. Her small trunk contained her few precious things and she searched it thoroughly. The light of the cabin was dim, but her fingers eventually found the black velvet pocket that contained the necklace.

As she placed the cream pearls around her neck, William's face popped into her mind. He had once told her she looked very pretty in her pearls and said that she should wear them more often. Isabella wondered what he was doing, wondered if he was spending time with Catherine. *Why am I thinking of William today?*

Recently she had fallen asleep imagining the prospect of being married to him. It never felt right, but at this moment she wished he was with her. Above everything, she missed his friendship. Elizabeth was a wonderful substitute for Catherine, but Hubert would never be an easy friend. However, Isabella was beginning to notice a softening in him. The sense of humour that once was so lacking now seemed to appear, and with it, a little kindness. Isabella realised she even liked being around him now.

'Can I trouble you to join us to make up a four?' he had asked Isabella the previous day, pointing towards the bridge table in a corner of the cuddy with fellow guests Reverend and Mrs Peabody ready and waiting. 'Elizabeth is tired and would rather not play.'

Isabella had been reading her book, but had read the same page twice and yet still could not say what was written.

'With pleasure,' she replied, putting down the novel. Even though she had played more games of patience than she thought possible, cards were still one of the best ways to pass the time on the steamer.

'Wonderful. Now remember, concentrate, and follow my lead,' he said under his breath as they walked over to the table.

'Of course,' she sighed, already wishing she was back with her book.

He seemed to realise his error. 'What am I saying? You are a marvellous player,' he laughed, pulling out the chair for her to sit down.

'You are too kind,' Isabella replied as he pushed her in. Reverend and Mrs Peabody both smiled at the hint of sarcasm in her voice that she didn't really mean. She appreciated his new humility.

During the game Isabella watched Hubert. He sometimes laughed at his mistakes and was generally good-humoured. Perhaps the stresses of leaving England and the burden of failure were coming off his shoulders? He even remained calm when he and Isabella eventually lost. Earlier on in the journey Isabella knew that a game of bridge with him would have been excruciating. Hubert Cornish was not a good loser, and being his partner, it would have taken the joy out of the game for Isabella.

A few hours later, when Isabella, Elizabeth and Eleanor were sitting on deckchairs at the stern of the ship, Hubert came to make certain they were happy and had everything they needed. It seemed an entirely unselfish act, and one that had previously been rare from him. Seeing they were cared for, he then returned inside to read.

Isabella had started an oil portrait of Elizabeth and had observed a change in Elizabeth's countenance over the past weeks. Her eyes had been weary when they began the voyage, but now, Isabella noticed a new light in her friend's eyes. Hope had come back.

Isabella looked at her reflection in the mirror. She touched the pearls around her neck. It was time to go to dinner, no more thinking of William. As she shut her cabin door, she realised that she would not mind if she was seated next to Hubert.

The next day, there was an announcement that before the *Lyttleton* arrived in New Zealand they would be passing a steamer returning to England. A small boat would be despatched with any letters the passengers wanted to send home. All on board had approximately an hour to get their letters to a member of the crew who would ferry them across.

Isabella quickly went to her cabin and finished a six-page letter to Catherine, as well as a long one to her parents. She didn't write to William, but she knew Catherine and her parents would share all the news she had given them.

Right on time, the steamer appeared on the horizon, and a small boat was duly despatched off the side of the *Lyttelton* with the precious correspondence. Isabella had mixed emotions as she saw the ship going off in the direction from which they had come.

At breakfast the following day, Isabella talked to Hubert about her next steps once had arrived in Auckland. 'Why don't you stay with us at our guesthouse for the first few days, and then find the next course of action, once you have assessed your surroundings?' he suggested.

'Can't you stay with us always?' asked Eleanor, who had quietly been eating porridge next to Isabella.

Isabella put her arm around her and gave her a kiss on the top of her head. 'Wouldn't that be lovely?'

Seeing New Zealand come into sight was hugely thrilling for Isabella and the other passengers. At last, their voyage was ending, and a new one beginning. As the *Lyttleton* travelled through the narrow Auckland isthmus, Isabella felt growing excitement at the thought of seeing Aunt Emily. *Surely Hamish will be with her now.*

Within four hours the steamer ended its passage in the hot and humid Commercial Bay. Their journey was over. It was now December 1880 and Isabella had been at sea for almost three months. She stood on deck to look at this new land; the impression was that it had seen better days. Flags drooped in the stifling air; she watched men on the dock who seemed to be plying their tasks mechanically, on the verge of sunstroke. A panting dog with a flabby and protruding tongue hid himself in the shadow of a building. It did not feel like England; the design of the buildings were more like those of American cities she had seen in pictures.

After the palaver of arranging trunks and registering each person at customs, Isabella and the Cornishes climbed into a waiting buggy.

'The ground feels as if is moving,' Eleanor said, holding on to the side of the carriage and looking out with uncertainty. They were silent as they took in the buildings and industry around them.

'Oh, for a sea breeze!' laughed Elizabeth.

'I am too hot,' moaned Eleanor, her hair plastered to her forehead under her sun bonnet.

'We all are, my darling. Chin up, we'll be at the guesthouse soon enough,' replied Elizabeth.

The travellers eventually arrived, red-faced and perspiring, at the large one-storey house. It was on a coastal hill, with a winding road down to the water.

'Welcome, welcome!' called an elderly woman as their buggy parked up at the house.

Hubert stepped down. 'Mrs Hunt, I presume?' he said formally.

'Yes, and you must be Mr and Mrs Cornish. We are delighted to have you stay.'

'I wonder if we could take advantage of your hospitality further. Can I introduce you to our friend, Isabella Buckley? She has been travelling with us.'

Isabella stepped down from the buggy, smiling warmly at the woman.

The old lady's face fell. 'We have no rooms available, I am afraid. We are full now with your family in the two last rooms.'

'Are you sure there isn't somewhere Isabella could stay?' implored Elizabeth.

Isabella felt her friend's concern for her, but ever pragmatic, she began thinking of what other options she might have. There would surely be another guesthouse or hotel nearby.

'Well, there are two beds in the little girl's room,' the lady suggested.

Elizabeth looked at Isabella. 'Would that suit you?'

Isabella valued her privacy and had appreciated her own space to retreat to on the boat, but this wouldn't be for long. It would be fun to share with Eleanor, and it would mean she could stay with her friends.

'I would be delighted.'

The proprietor, who did not seem to take changed plans in her stride, said she had to get the room ready and would be another fifteen minutes. 'My help has gone for the day, so it is just me and the cook... Please, follow me inside,' she said as she walked back into the guesthouse.

'Come on, down you get,' ordered Hubert to Eleanor, who was still sitting in the buggy.

With a look of reluctance, she stepped down, and her father lifted her onto the ground. Elizabeth took her hand and they all followed into the house, where they were directed to wait in the relative cool of the sitting room. After a while, an elderly man joined them.

'Welcome to our humble guesthouse. I am Mr Hunt.' He was a slim gentleman, with grey, pomade-smoothed hair and a white beard.

Hubert stood up and reached out his hand to shake Mr Hunt's offered hand. 'How do you do? We met your wife a little earlier. We are exceptionally pleased to be staying at your establishment,' Hubert said, and introduced Elizabeth, Eleanor and Isabella.

'We like it, although we're probably getting a little old to keep the business up. Mrs Hunt likes meeting all the guests,' Mr Hunt said, with a wink at the group.

Mrs Hunt returned, and offered glasses of cooled lemon juice. Conversation seemed to be sapped out of the voyagers, but Mrs Hunt prevailed, seemingly delighted to have people to talk to.

'There are some lovely places for you to see in Auckland. The heat will prevent you from walking, so we can hire you a buggy. If you go west, you meet the Tasman Sea and black volcanic rock. I do love it there, it's so wild. But if you want something more refined, there is the waterfront, or indeed you can visit Mount Eden for a panoramic view of the city.'

'That would be delightful,' Elizabeth said politely, beads of sweat buckling on her upper lip. Eleanor was limp at her side, staring out of the window.

Isabella could not stop thinking about Hamish and Emily.

'What about the natives, the Maoris? Do you know any of their history?' Hubert asked, valiantly keeping the conversation going.

'I'm sure you know about the Muscat Wars and the Treaty of Waitangi back in 1840. The Maoris are an interesting race; they are warriors really. Their tattoos can make them look somewhat frightening, but in general we seem to be living in harmony with each other. They call this place *Aotearoa*, the Land of the Long White Cloud,' said Mr Hunt, then, turning his attention to Isabella, 'What brings you here?'

Isabella, as clearly as she could, explained about her aunt and uncle, and the disappearance.

'We sent a telegram that I was coming, but as far as I know there has been no response. I would like to ride out to their farm as soon as possible.'

'What are their names? I am surprised I have not heard of this.'

'Hamish and Emily McGuffy. They have three young sons with them as well.'

'McGuffy? I recognise the name, but can't say I have met them. To put your mind at ease, there has been no news of murder or death in the farming community recently. If there was, I would have read about it.'

The news did relieve Isabella somewhat.

'I need to find them as soon as possible.'

'Well, we could help with a guide and horse tomorrow morning – if that's not too soon?'

'Tomorrow would be wonderful.'

'Excuse me,' Hubert butted in. 'Is it safe for Isabella to ride all the way out there? A woman travelling alone is a very bad idea. And we don't know what has happened to her uncle.' Turning to Isabella, he said more gently, 'Why don't you wait a week or so, and then we can accompany you once we are all set up?'

'Thank you, Hubert, I understand your concern but, as I said, I really must get to my family as soon as possible,' she said firmly, and then said to Mr Hunt, 'I will accept your offer for tomorrow.'

'Very well, we can supply both the horse and guide at a very agreeable price, and Mr Cornish, New Zealand is a safe country, so she has no fear of brigands and bandits here.'

'Glad to hear it,' he said briskly. 'Isabella, I can't stop you, but I urge you to be cautious.'

'Thank you, Hubert, I will be.'

'Sharkey gets fidgety if he's stuck in Auckland for too long. He'll be glad of the trip,' said Mr Hunt.

'I cannot thank you enough,' said Isabella, wondering whether he was talking of the horse or the guide.

Elizabeth moved to sit next to Isabella and put her arm around her in comfort. As she did, she stifled a yawn.

'Oh, my dear, you are tired; how about a rest before dinner for everyone?' suggested Mrs Hunt, as if suddenly aware of the lethargy of her guests. There was an almost imperceptible sigh of relief from Elizabeth.

Early the next morning, Mr Hunt waited for Isabella by the stables, with both horse and guide.

'Let me introduce you to Sharkey – he has worked for us for years, and I would trust him with my life.'

'Good morning,' Isabella said, summing up the short but upright man. He reminded her of a jockey with his slim physique and slightly bowed legs.

'Pleased to make your acquaintance, ma'am,' Sharkey replied in a strong Irish brogue.

'I've given Sharkey the address you gave me last night. We estimate it's about sixty miles from Auckland. It should be at least two days' ride. Camping will be more convenient, if you want to get there sooner, as you won't have to make a detour to a guesthouse, but are you happy with that?'

Isabella balked slightly at the thought of camping alone with a man she did not know, but decided there was no other option.

'Yes, that will be fine,' she said, in what she hoped was a confident, businesslike tone.

Full of nervous anticipation, Isabella followed her guide along the Great South Road. After so many days at sea she was glad for some exercise, but her body took a while to ease into the saddle again, her muscles slowly waking up from three months of inactivity, except for her gentle deck circuits.

The lack of December rain had left the landscape a dry yellow brush. Tall, thirsty trees and calla lilies drooped with the high temperatures, and dusty thickets sheltered the cicada, their call filling the hot air.

Riding side saddle, as was expected from a lady, was not at all comfortable in this weather. Isabella realised she would have to purchase lighter clothing if she was not going to faint from heatstroke, but she was grateful for her wide-brimmed bonnet keeping the sun out of her eyes.

She glanced over at Sharkey as they rode. He had made no effort at conversation with her.

'Tell me, Sharkey, how long have you been in New Zealand?'

'Over ten year, ma'am.'

'And what about your name – you can't have been christened Sharkey?'

He looked back at Isabella without reaction. 'I was christened Augustus O'Shay in County Derry, many a year ago now.'

'That's quite a name. I can see why Sharkey might be easier to go by.'

He gave a polite nod in agreement.

She was about to ask how he got the nickname, but he seemed disinclined to talk and she didn't have the energy to persist. She was feeling as dusty and drooping as the lilies they had passed.

Sharkey wore a sort of cowboy hat, which protected him from the sun. When he had removed his hat on greeting her earlier that morning, Isabella had seen he didn't have much hair at the top of his head, but kept whatever he had held together in a scruffy ponytail.

After five hours of riding, they made a stop for water and lunch and then mounted up again. Isabella would have liked to have rested longer, but desire to find Emily spurred her on. As the hot sun began its descent to hide behind the horizon, she was relieved when Sharkey motioned to the spot where they would camp for the night. They led the horses off the main road and into an opening surrounded by small brush-like trees. There was a brook with water bubbling up from the ground. Isabella went to wash her hands and the dust and sweat from her face in the cool, refreshing water. She wanted to lie her whole body in it, but felt restrained by decorum, so instead took off her boots and plunged her feet into the brackenish water. The cool tingling she felt travelled up from her red, swollen feet and revitalised her.

Sharkey quickly set up a canvas tent for Isabella. Once the tent was up, he got to work collecting wood, whistling a melancholic tune as he worked. He then started the fire, boiling water in a tin saucepan so that they could have tea. He was about to cook eggs in an old frying pan that he had tied to his saddle, when Isabella offered to help. Silently he handed her the pan and she cracked the eggs over the heat to fry.

When they were ready, she passed the pan to Sharkey, and he served them on two slices of bread. Isabella ate hungrily. She felt a sort of giddiness in her body, and did not know whether it was physical, from the long ride, or anticipation of what she was about to find.

The meal passed in silence. As the sun set and darkness fell, they turned in for the night, Sharkey sleeping by the fire.

Isabella, although not comfortable, managed to sleep. She was awoken by the dawn chorus and, opening her eyes, peered through the canvas flap of her tent to see Sharkey, already packing up the camp. Water was again boiling on the fire.

'Mornin', ma'am,' he said, looking up, and then turning away respectfully.

It wasn't long before they were back on the road. After breaks mid-morning, for lunch and then another after a few hours' riding, Sharkey indicated a sign next to a track off the main road: 'McGuffy's Lodge'. Isabella swallowed but her mouth was dry. They turned down into the track and rode a while until they came into an opening leading down to a valley.

'This is it,' Sharkey stated, indicating a house with his eyebrows and a nod of the head in its direction.

Standing solitary in the middle of a field below was a property surrounded by tall gum trees; a riverbed snaked behind it. It was beautiful even in the heat and dust, but Isabella soon realised there was no sign of life, no noise of children, no windows or doors open to bring air into the house.

'Let me ride down. You stay here,' Sharkey said.

'No, I will go with you,' she said, giving her horse a kick and trotting down into the valley. Sharkey followed behind, and rode in front of Isabella as they got to the house.

'Aunt Emily! Uncle Hamish!' Isabella called out, but there was no reply.

Sharkey jumped off his horse, tied it to a post and walked up to the house. Isabella watched, holding her breath as he knocked on the door. Silence. He tried the handle. It was locked. He walked around the covered veranda, peering into the windows. The interior was hidden by closed curtains, save for one window.

'There is nothing here. They must have left,' he shouted to Isabella.

Sharkey walked over to her, his hat in his hands, and used a large red handkerchief to wipe the sweat from the back of his neck. Isabella indicated that she wanted to dismount, and he helped her off her horse. She walked towards the house and he followed. Sharkey was right; it was empty – no furniture or belongings. Emily and Hamish were definitely no longer there. Isabella's mind raced with terrible scenarios.

'We'd better get back. I don't think we can stay here,' said Sharkey, nervously scanning the perimeters of the valley.

Isabella wondered what he was expecting to see, but didn't want to ask. She had been planning to find Emily and stay with her, and then get her trunk sent along later from Auckland. Now, in the absence of her aunt, uncle and nephews, she had no choice but to make the two-day journey back to the city and try to find out any information she could about their whereabouts.

As Sharkey didn't want to stay at the homestead, they decided to ride a bit before setting up camp.

'If we go fast we might be able to get back in a day tomorrow, but we'll have to make up a bit of distance now. Are you happy with that?'

'Yes, I quite agree,' said Isabella.

They rode for three hours, Isabella getting more concerned with every mile. Sharkey set up camp just before nightfall. A full moon illuminated their surroundings, and they silently got on with the duties of feeding the horses and lighting a fire. Sharkey was about to unpack the canvas tent but Isabella stopped him.

'Don't worry about the tent, I'll sleep on my pack out here; it'll be quicker in the morning, and we can leave promptly.'

'If you're sure?'

Isabella didn't reply, but put her saddlebag down. She would take off her boots, but that was all.

After the fire was lit, Sharkey boiled water and gave Isabella bread and some cheese that had become slimy from the heat. She then lay down and shut her eyes. Sharkey did the same thing and a few minutes later Isabella could hear his faint snoring. When she realised sleep was not coming, she opened her eyes again and looked up at the huge velvet sky above, with stars so bright and big, they seemed closer than normal.

As the fire embers slowly went out, Isabella watched the stars, praying for her aunt and uncle, until at last sleep took her.

When she awoke, Sharkey was sitting by the fire, drinking slowly from a mug.

'Shall we depart?' Isabella suggested.

'I can if you feel up to it, but it's only five in the mornin'.'

'Let's go.'

It took them fifteen minutes to pack up, and ten hours later they arrived, hot and tired, back at the Hunts' guesthouse.

Hubert looked up from the veranda in surprise to see Isabella following Sharkey back into their courtyard. He walked down to meet them.

'I didn't expect you back – what's the news?'

'They are gone; the place is empty. I don't know where they are.' Isabella's voice quivered. Fear for Hamish and Emily's safety had only increased, and exhaustion from the long ride exacerbated her feelings of concern.

'What do you mean? Your family were not there?' Hubert paused, and then called into the house, 'Elizabeth!'

'Yes, darling?' came the faint reply.

'Come outside, Isabella is back.'

Elizabeth came running out with an excited smile, but stopped when she saw Isabella's hot and dusty face.

'Isabella! What happened?'

Before Isabella could speak, Hubert spoke for her. 'Her family were not there.'

'Well, someone must know what happened. Let's talk to the Hunts,' Elizabeth said matter-of-factly, motioning to Hubert to help Isabella off her horse.

'Mr and Mrs Hunt have both just left for an appointment in town,' Hubert said.

'Oh dear… would you like some tea, then? Or water? Or… whisky, while we wait?' Elizabeth asked.

Isabella was touched at her friend's concern. 'I think a glass of water, for now.'

She thanked Sharkey, and he made a neat bow, took the horse's reins and led them to the stables behind the house.

Once inside, Eleanor sat sweetly next to Isabella, and Hubert asked questions about what she had seen, trying to deduce an answer to the puzzle that now presented itself.

When Mr Hunt returned, he sent a message to a friend who farmed near Isabella's aunt and uncle and asked him to come to see them.

Isabella went to bed early that night, but she slept fitfully and was woken by a nightmare. Emily and Hamish had been carried away, and the children were lost in the woods. Isabella could see them, but as loud as she called, they didn't hear her. She woke suddenly in the pitch black of night, her sheet no longer covering her and her nightdress wet with perspiration. She told herself it was just a dream. There would be an explanation.

Mr Jones, the friend of Mr Hunt, arrived two days later, a sturdy man with a long nose and weatherbeaten face. He was a Welshman, and he was immediately helpful.

'I know the McGuffys well, but they have left to go back to England,' he answered, as soon as he knew Isabella's question.

'When?' Isabella asked, shocked.

'Just two weeks ago. Your uncle had been attacked and robbed – he could have been killed. From what I understand, he was found by an old Maori woman who looked after him until he recovered, but it was weeks before he was reunited with his family. They tried to continue on the farm, but your aunt couldn't do it. She insisted they return to England…'

Isabella listened in disbelief. She had come all this way and had missed them by two weeks! Perhaps the letters home she had sent from the *Lyttelton* had been rowed to the very steamer they were on!

'Surely Emily got the telegram and letter from my mother saying I was coming. I don't understand why they didn't wait for me,' Isabella said.

'Post has been a real problem of late; we've had big delays in telegrams and letters getting through to the farms – this heat has had everything off kilter. It could be that your communication never got to them,' said Mr Jones.

'What do I do now?' Isabella said, more to herself than to anyone else.

'Why don't you stay with us for a few days? Take some time to think about what to do. You don't have to make a decision now,' said Elizabeth

'Take a few days, and then the answer will be clear,' said Hubert. 'It is, of course, good news that they are all alive and well.'

Isabella realised he was right, she should be rejoicing. Her worst fears had not been realised. Her aunt and uncle and their boys were safely on their way home. What did it matter if her plans were changed? This voyage was about more than coming to help Aunt Emily; it was an adventure, a chance to break free, and it didn't have to end now.

Later that night, after writing a letter home to her parents, Isabella lay in bed contemplating her options. She could get a passage on the next steamer and return home straight away. Or she could stay in New Zealand for a time and visit more of the country, or... was there another option? Something was nagging at her, but it wasn't until the next morning that she remembered what it was.

Isabella woke from the same dream that she had had while on the *Lyttleton*. The picture seemed more vivid now, of arriving on a tropical island, a new Eden. She had the sense that the island was calling her. But she had no idea where it was, or even if it existed.

Chapter Ten

Hawaii, July 1878

By the summer of 1878 Kainalu had returned to Oah'u. His mother, now called *Kapuna Wahine* in respect for her position as grandmother, wanted him to live with her in Kona. Kainalu, however, was still tied to Honolulu with the Board of Health and its work and also needed to support Fili, who was running the family plantation on Oah'u. A reciprocity treaty with the United States, endorsed by the senate, had guaranteed American markets for Hawaiian sugar. 'A golden opportunity to expand the business and sell our sugar for an exceptional gain,' Fili had said with a grin when they heard the news, slapping Kainalu on the back. Fili was not a greedy man, but he liked to make a profit. He was focused on running the business to embrace expansion, and Kainalu trusted his judgement.

Leilani was a happy baby. Her life appeared to mark the end of a pattern of death, an olive branch of hope that signified a new season for the family. Kainalu watched how Leilani gave his sister such joy. Aolani would sit for hours holding her baby girl in her arms, content to smile and play, their eyes locked on to each other's, Leilani taking in every fold and crevice of her mother's face, her eyes fringed with long, dark lashes.

'She's growing well,' Kainalu said, crouching down to have a closer look at his little niece.

'She has decided not to sleep at night, only in the day,' Aolani replied, her eyes heavy with tiredness.

'Get someone else to wake up with her to give you a rest, sister.'

'I don't mind, Kai,' she said. 'I have dreamt of and prayed for this baby. I can embrace the sleepless nights… for a little while longer!'

Kainalu stroked Leilani's downy hair. His daughter would have been a teenager by now. He felt a pang in his chest, but stood up to distract himself, not wanting to linger on the memories.

As in most Pacific islands, it could be said that it was not one person that raised a child, but a whole village. That was true for Leilani. Aolani had many helpers and her family were constantly near. *Kapuna Wahine* visited often to see her granddaughter and Leilani was her joy.

Kapuna Wahine was eager for Kainalu to marry again. She wanted a Hawaiian *wahine*, a chief's daughter, for her son, who would provide her with more grandchildren to cherish and love.

'What are you waiting for, Kai? I will find you a wife,' she insisted.

But for the moment Kainalu was able to sidestep the conversations. Again he had to remind his mother that the wife he had adored was dead. He didn't tell her that he was beginning to feel open to finding love once more.

While working to improve Kalihi receiving station and the Kalaupapa leper colony, Kainalu visited Maima every week. Her parents' visits had become fewer and fewer; the effort to get to Kalihi made the trips physically and emotionally difficult and they had made the choice not to be her *kōkua* for the sake of their other children. Her mother was heartbroken after each visit; she knew Maima would be transferred to Kalaupapa soon. When Maima moved to the island colony it would probably be the last time her parents would see her on this earth.

'Uncle Kai!' Maima shouted when she saw his horse arrive at the high gates of the compound. Kainalu was warned that he shouldn't have close contact with the lepers, but something in him could not hold back from embracing the little girl. She had so little physical contact that he wanted to lift her up in his arms just as her father would have done. At least she had other children to play with, he told himself. A child alone surrounded by leprous adults would be a lonely scenario indeed.

Kainalu would often leave Kalihi heavy-hearted, as the treatments for the lepers were not able to give a cure, only stave off the encroaching illness. Seeing bodies becoming more and more disfigured over time caused him distress that he could not bury, and made him more determined to see the islands free from disease. He knew there was an incubation period of three to seven years, and then the diseased person would lose feeling in their hands and feet. Blindness could occur, and because of the compromised immune system, many would die of tuberculosis or influenza. It was a heavy burden for him to watch.

Kainalu found release in wave-sliding or *he'e nalu*, as his people called it. He was one of the most skilled surf-riders on Oah'u, and had inherited his *wili-wili* wood board from his father. The *wili-wili* was reserved only for royalty, and was *kapu* for commoners to use.

'What is it about this sport that you love so much?' Mr Fortnum asked one day, after Kainalu returned from an early morning excursion. 'Isn't it all about the gods and worshipping the ocean? Surely you don't do that?'

Kainalu laughed. His friend knew about his allegiance to *Ke Akua* and rejection of the gods of his ancestors.

'Wave-sliding has a deep connection with the spirituality of our Polynesian culture. Surf-riders pray to the gods for protection and strength in the powerful ocean, but I now pray to *Ke Akua*. He is the unknown god to many of my people, but not for much longer. We are made to praise, to look to something to worship. If I did not know *Ke Akua*, of course I would still worship the power of the mighty ocean. But now I know its Creator. How can I not praise Him as I feel the power of the ocean He made under my board pushing me to shore? You should try it...'

Mr Fortnum snorted with laughter. 'Worship or wave-sliding? You make it look easy, Kainalu, but I am sure with my plump frame on the board it would rather sink than slide!'

'Not so, my friend, let me teach you!'

'One day, one day...' Mr Fortnum promptly moved the conversation away from recreation to business.

Chapter Eleven

New Zealand, December 1880

Isabella's body was still sore from the ride to the farm. Her legs and back ached, but it was the ache of exercise; her back pain from home had not returned.

The guesthouse had a new visitor. Isabella sat next to Mr Marty Holland Jr at the supper table, an American man in his late fifties. He was a handsome, vigorous-looking man with tanned skin. He told Isabella he had been working on contracts in Auckland for a year.

'I am planning on moving back to America, to be with ma wife and children. Been sailing round the Pacific for too long now.'

'Do you know much of the Polynesian islands?' Isabella asked, with interest.

'Yes, ma'am, I know 'em all.'

'I am wondering if I should visit one, maybe Fiji or the Tonga archipelago?'

'With respect, ma'am, I wouldn't bother, they're never the paradise which at first they appear. The natives are very different from the civilised society you will be used to.'

'What do you mean?'

'Well, for one, many don't wear clothes, like we would know clothing...'

Isabella was frustrated by the blush that she knew was rising on her cheeks.

'What you must do,' he said, 'is return home via the United States. You can find passage on a steamer that will take you to

San Francisco, and you're warmly invited to stay with my family.'

He spoke with such authority and assurance, Isabella felt she couldn't continue asking about the Pacific islands. She was still unsure at the thought of travelling alone, but she did not have a choice. There was no chance to wait for a chaperone and perhaps it wasn't needed. Mr Holland did not seem at all concerned by her lack of travelling companion for her journey to America.

As the grandfather clock chimed nine, the men stayed at the table to smoke their cigars and talk politics while the women withdrew.

'You seem distracted,' Elizabeth said quietly to Isabella as they sat on the veranda.

'It's the American, he has given me some ideas.'

'What do you mean, ideas? I hope this doesn't mean you are leaving New Zealand?'

'I will eventually, but I am not in a hurry.'

'Yes, no hurry at all!'

'I am only delaying a decision to go because I don't want to leave you and Eleanor. It's heartbreaking to think of not seeing her again.'

'Don't be silly. We will return to England to visit, and one day soon perhaps you will come back here.'

Isabella nodded in agreement, but doubted she would ever have a chance to travel so far again.

The next day, Auckland continued to shimmer and wilt under the furnace of the sun. The city's residents lived at a slower pace of life, most business and socialising happening in the early morning or late afternoon, when it was cooler.

Perhaps if the heatwave had not been quite so debilitating, Isabella would have chosen to stay in New Zealand as Elizabeth had hoped, but as she woke in the morning, the way ahead seemed clear.

'I have made a decision. I like the idea of visiting some of the South Sea islands. The American, Mr Holland, tried to put me off last night, but I feel I must see them, being that I am so close, relatively,' she said to Elizabeth. Eleanor was napping, and they were sitting on a blanket in the shade of the sprawling knotted and misshapen branches of a huge Pūriri tree in the guesthouse garden. Isabella was finishing off the portrait of Elizabeth. As it was so warm, the oils were drying quickly, so she had to work fast. It was a joy for Isabella to really study a face and try to replicate it on canvas. Elizabeth's features were now etched in her memory.

'Oh, can't you stay and visit them with us another time? We could employ you as Eleanor's governess until you find something else you want to do!' Elizabeth said, while staying still for her painter.

Could she? Isabella paused, testing this new option, but as soon as the offer was proffered, she knew she must not take it, however serious it was.

'I don't think she'd want me as a governess, or rather I don't think you'd want me. I much prefer to play with children than to teach them.'

Elizabeth laughed. 'That sounds perfect for Eleanor. Come on, what do you say?'

Isabella was torn. Why couldn't she stay? To spend time with Eleanor, and be paid for it, would be wonderful. But there was still a sense of urgency that she could not explain. A feeling that she had to be moving, to get to the place she was supposed to discover.

They were interrupted by the sound of Eleanor crying. She had woken from her nap on a chair on the veranda and tripped and fallen down the stone steps. Both women ran to her aid.

After much discussion, Isabella officially declined Elizabeth's offer, and decided to return home via Fiji and the Navigator Islands.[1] She would take two months visiting the islands, and then sail on to America. It would be a month-long journey to arrive in San Francisco and then another few months

[1] Samoa.

to cross the States. Perhaps she would stop at the Rockies, and then visit New England before sailing home. She calculated that it would take about six months to get home from the time she left Auckland, and the thought of this adventure left her brimming with excitment.

The next morning, Elizabeth and Hubert planned to ride out to the land where they would be building a home. Hubert had already been on a preliminary expedition, but now wanted to take his wife.

'The road will be too difficult for a buggy. We'll need to go on horses.'

'Oh, that is a shame. Eleanor won't be able to come,' said Elizabeth. 'Maybe I should stay with her and see the land another time?'

'Why can't I come?' Eleanor asked, looking up from where she was sitting on the floor, playing with her doll.

'Nonsense, you need to see it. I am sure we can ask Isabella to watch Eleanor,' said Hubert.

Isabella looked up from her book and smiled.

'Would you mind watching her while we are gone?' Elizabeth asked apologetically.

'It would be a pleasure.'

'Thank you. We don't want to take you for granted, but Eleanor will be overjoyed!' said Elizabeth, and Eleanor, in agreement, jumped up to sit on Isabella's lap.

'That's settled, then. Much obliged, Isabella,' said Hubert, leaving the room.

Although it was early, the day once again promised to be blisteringly hot. Isabella, hand in hand with Eleanor, went outside to bid farewell to her parents.

'It seems absurd that it will be Christmas in only a few days; this heat makes it seem quite incongruous,' Elizabeth said while mounting her horse, and wiping the beads of sweat from her neck with a hankerchief.

Hubert's face was already flushed. 'It'll break soon,' he said. 'Goodbye, all, we'll be back for a late lunch.'

'See you soon, darling,' Elizabeth called to Eleanor, and Isabella and Eleanor waved until they were lost from view.

'Are you ready for your own adventure today?' Isabella asked as they turned to walk inside.

'What is it?' Eleanor asked, looking up eagerly.

'We are going for a walk down to the sea. That will cool you off.'

'Yes, please!' she replied with a hop, skip and jump.

Isabella paid for a bottle of chilled sweetened lemon juice and some biscuits, freshly baked by the cook.

Eleanor was full of conversation on their slow walk down to the water, protected from the sun by a parasol.

'You know what, Isabella, my brother will be called Barney, and he'll be my *best* friend.'

'Really…' Isabella replied. Recently, having a brother was Eleanor's main topic of conversation. Elizabeth had said she might have to settle for a stuffed animal, but Eleanor was not convinced.

'Well, you will have to just have me as your friend until he comes.'

'I *know*,' Eleanor said, with a comical sigh. She squealed with delight as they turned off the road to the path leading to the beach.

Isabella found a tree with large branches to sit under, and took off her own and Eleanor's shoes so they could paddle in the ocean. Isabella had to squint to protect her eyes from the bright sunlight reflecting off the water.

After a while they went back to the tree and drank the lemonade. They ate a biscuit each, then Eleanor lay her head in Isabella's lap and Isabella made up a fairy tale for her until she fell asleep. When Eleanor awoke, she headed to the water and played until her cotton dress was wet and covered in sand.

'Time to go,' Isabella called, eventually.

'Not yet,' begged Eleanor.

'We need to get you cleaned up. Mama and Papa will be back soon, and we want to hear what your new home is going to be like, don't we?'

'Oh, yes!' Eleanor replied, remembering the reason for their absence.

They slowly walked back up the hill, but when they arrived at the house, Elizabeth and Hubert were not back.

'Come and have a drink before they return. I am sure they won't be long,' suggested Mrs Hunt.

Isabella quickly changed Eleanor and washed the salt and sand off her, and then she and Mrs Hunt sat in rocking chairs on the veranda looking out on to the parched garden while Eleanor played with her doll on the floor next to them.

'It's lovely to have a child in the house again. I miss the days when my five were young,' Mrs Hunt said.

'Where are they all now?'

'They have all left home and married; two are living in Auckland and three are further afield in New Zealand. We try to see each other as often as possible. I never see my family in England.'

'Where were you from?'

'I was originally from Ambleside, and moved to New Zealand with my husband soon after we married forty years ago. I still have two brothers and nieces and nephews in the Lake District.'

'What do you miss most about England?'

'Family. When we first arrived there were only a handful of European families in the whole of Auckland. It was a lonely time.'

As she was speaking, the clock chimed two o'clock. Isabella assumed Elizabeth and Hubert must have taken a rest out of the sun, and would return shortly. She hoped Elizabeth was finding enough strength for the ride. Mrs Hunt suggested they have something to eat and save some food for Hubert and Elizabeth when they returned.

By four o'clock they were still not back. Mr Hunt had arrived home from his appointments, and sent out Sharkey to see if he could discover what had happened to them.

'Why aren't Mama and Papa here?' Eleanor asked.

'They must have been waylaid, but they'll be back soon, I'm sure.'

Eleanor seemed happy with Isabella's explanation, and carried on playing with her doll on the veranda. Mrs Hunt and Isabella took tea under the shade of the Pūriri tree and waited. Isabella tried to distract herself by reading to Eleanor after she tired of playing alone.

Two hours later Sharkey returned. His face was tense and strained and he wouldn't look Isabella in the eye as she ran out to his horse.

'What is it?'

'Let me talk to Mr Hunt, ma'am,' he said, and jumped off his mount. He skirted past her and into the house, heading for Mr Hunt's study.

A few minutes later Mr Hunt came out to the veranda.

'Miss Buckley, we've had some very sad news; there has been an accident.'

'What happened?'

'It seems that Mrs Cornish's horse lost its footing and slipped down the side of a hill behind their land. It is almost a vertical drop.' Mr Hunt talked slowly. Isabella felt her heart beating faster in her chest.

'How is she?'

Mr Hunt paused, trying to find the right words. 'Elizabeth is unconscious, but she is alive…' He put his hand on Isabella's arm, as if to steady her. 'My dear, I have to tell you, Mr Cornish's body was found. He is no longer with us. Sharkey thinks he fell while trying to save his wife.'

Isabella's mouth opened in shock. Her skin prickled with panic. She felt as if she had been struck in the stomach and could be sick at any moment.

'A doctor is with Elizabeth now, and she will be taken to the hospital as soon as they can safely transfer her.'

Isabella sat down, put her head in her hands and wept.

The next few hours were a blur; Eleanor was put to bed after being given another excuse for her parents' absence. Isabella and Mr Hunt then took the buggy to the Auckland Hospital. It was early evening when they pulled up to the large Italianate-style building. The hospital was three storeys high, with outward-facing balconies. An elaborate stairway led them to the entrance.

Even though they had not arrived in visiting hours, they were taken straight to Elizabeth's bed on a ward on the second floor. The room smelt of disinfectant and lavender.

Elizabeth, who had a curtain around her bed, was still unconscious, lying with a thin cotton sheet over her. There was a bandage around her head and some dry blood on her left cheek. Isabella was shocked at how fragile she looked.

While Mr Hunt stood, Isabella sat on a chair next to the bed and took Elizabeth's hand.

'Everything is going to be alright. Just hold on,' she whispered.

Chapter Twelve

New Zealand, December 1880

'It doesn't look good, I'm afraid; they are just trying to keep her comfortable,' said Mr Hunt, returning from a conversation with the matron and placing his hand gently on Isabella's shoulder. She was hot and flushed, but his touch seemed to pervade calmness into her body.

After what seemed like an age of watching Elizabeth's unresponsive face, there was a movement. It was almost imperceptible, but Isabella saw it. Elizabeth's eyes began to flicker, and she gave a groan of pain from somewhere deep within.

'Elizabeth! It's me, Isabella. Can you hear me?' she asked, holding her hand and staring intently at her face.

There was no reaction, but after a few minutes her eyes slowly opened, trying to focus.

'Elizabeth!'

'Where am I?' she asked groggily.

'There was an accident… you are in hospital.'

Elizabeth's face winced in pain. With her lips dry and cracked, she asked, 'Where is Hubert… and Eleanor… are they here?'

'Eleanor is at the Hunts'. It's going to be alright…'

Elizabeth closed her eyes and fell back into a deep sleep. Mr Hunt called the nurse on duty, and a thickset woman with wiry grey hair under her nurse's cap came to check Elizabeth's pulse and temperature. She smiled encouragingly.

'It's a good sign she has come round; you can leave her to rest now.'

Isabella's head ached, and she felt drained; however, when she eventually got to her bed, sleep evaded her. Her thoughts went over the accident again and again, imagining Hubert falling, thinking of Elizabeth fighting for her life. She grieved for Hubert. Over the weeks on the ship, she had come to realise that he was, in fact, a good man. All his bluster and pompousness were just a show; she felt a deep and sudden sadness as she thought of little Eleanor having to grow up without a father.

The next morning Mrs Hunt invited her daughter and her two granddaughters to visit, mainly to occupy Eleanor. The girls were thirteen and eleven, and Eleanor was enraptured by them both. Isabella returned to the hospital, where she found Elizabeth awake and the nurse she had met before at her side.

'How are you feeling?' she asked Elizabeth.

'I am better,' she paused. 'Isabella, I know. He is dead, isn't he?'

Isabella's eyes immediately flickered to the nurse, annoyed that she must have told Elizabeth before she had regained her strength.

'She didn't say anything; I just knew,' Elizabeth said as tears slipped down her cheeks.

'I am so sorry.'

'Can I see Eleanor?'

'Of course. We will bring her this afternoon.'

Isabella went back to the Hunts' at lunchtime to find Eleanor full of life, playing with the granddaughters, oblivious to the fact that her world was about to be shattered.

After they ate, Isabella took her to the veranda on the pretext of reading a book together.

'Eleanor, before we read, I have something to tell you.'

'What is it?' she asked, placing herself on Isabella's lap and draping her arm around her neck.

'When Mama and Papa rode out to see the new land, they had an accident,' Isabella paused, trying to hold back tears. 'The

horse fell and your father fell too. It hurt him badly… and he…'
She paused, and then added, 'He is now in heaven.'

Eleanor scanned Isabella's face, trying to understand, as if hoping that what she was saying was a game. Then her face crumpled and her body slumped.

'Papa!' she cried out in tears. Isabella tried to soothe her, but no words could be sufficient for comfort.

'And Mama?' Eleanor asked after a while, wiping her nose with the back of her hand. 'Where is Mama?'

'Mama hurt herself too. She is in hospital being looked after so that she can get better.'

'Can I see her?'

'Yes, we can go now, if you like.'

'Yes, please,' Eleanor replied in a faint whisper. She looked so small, her eyes large and scared. Isabella's heart broke for her.

Isabella had already asked the Hunts if they could use the buggy again, and Sharkey drove them to the hospital, in his characteristic silence.

On arrival, they walked onto the spartan ward, with its gleaming white walls and a strong smell of disinfectant, to find Elizabeth awake, but obviously in pain.

'My darling!' she managed to say as Eleanor ran towards the bed.

Eleanor buried her head in Elizabeth's arms and cried. 'I'm so sorry,' her mother whispered.

Nurses came and went, allowing the little girl to stay curled up next to Elizabeth. In time they both fell asleep and Isabella went outside to get some air. When she came back, Elizabeth was awake.

'Isabella, I have something to ask you.'

'Yes…?'

'If anything happens to me, I want you to take Eleanor as your own. I want you to adopt her. Will you do that?'

'Nothing is going to happen to you. Don't be silly, you are on the mend,' Isabella said.

'But if it does,' she insisted, 'will you promise me?'

Isabella saw that she needed a serious answer. 'But what about your family?' she asked. 'Or Hubert's?'

'My mother is dead and my father old, and my brother is not married yet. He would not know how to look after Eleanor. My husband's parents are no longer alive. Eleanor loves you, and I know you love her. Please say yes.'

'Of course I will, yes.'

Elizabeth breathed a sigh of relief, but before they could talk more, Eleanor woke up. She was hungry so Isabella said she would take her back to the Hunts' for supper.

'Goodbye, Mama,' she said, giving her mother a kiss on the cheek.

'Goodbye, my darling, I love you very much,' Elizabeth replied, stroking her daughter's hair. When Isabella got to the door she turned back to wave to Elizabeth and saw that fresh tears were spilling from her friend's eyes.

With a heavy heart, Isabella picked Eleanor up and carried her out of the hospital.

They were silent on the journey home, and Eleanor would not leave Isabella's side for the rest of the evening, only eating her supper if she could sit on Isabella's lap.

The next morning both Isabella and Eleanor slept late, but Isabella was woken with a knock at her door.

'Isabella? Are you awake?' whispered the voice of Mrs Hunt.

'Yes,' she replied softly.

The door opened and Mrs Hunt came in. 'My dear, we just got a message from the hospital.'

Isabella got out of bed and put her shawl around her shoulders. They both moved out of the room into the corridor.

'What is it?'

'I am so sorry, Elizabeth passed away in the night.'

'No! I thought she was getting better?' Isabella whispered, her whole body shaking.

Isabella felt as though she was dreaming. Instead of succumbing to her grief, however, she became instantly practical, just like her own mother in a crisis.

'What do I need to do?' she asked.

'My husband is taking care of the details. We will know more later in the day... I'm so sorry, my dear.'

Isabella slipped back into the room. She looked at Eleanor sleeping safely under her cotton sheet a few feet away. Her cheeks were pink from the heat and her hair was still tied in a blue ribbon from the day before.

Not knowing what to do, Isabella sat on the chair until Eleanor roused, crying for her mother.

'Mama is not here,' Isabella soothed. 'She is in heaven now with Papa.'

Eleanor looked at her with big serious eyes, swimming with tears. She buried her head in Isabella's lap and cried deep sobs at the news. Eventually, with a sniff, she looked up at Isabella. '*You* won't leave me, will you?'

'No, my darling, of course I won't.'

Later than morning Mr Hunt went to the hospital to retrieve Elizabeth's belongings and arrange for her body to go to the undertaker. There was a letter for Isabella. He handed it to her, squeezed her arm gently and then left her to read it. Eleanor was playing with some foliage she had picked from the garden, taking off the leaves and arranging them in patterns, so Isabella took it back into her room and opened the letter.

My dear Isabella,

I have not the strength to write, so a kind nurse is my scribe. I have only known you for a short while but I feel as if it has been a lifetime. I am so grateful for your friendship. This letter is to confirm that if anything happens to me, I would want you to adopt Eleanor and to raise her as your own. I know you will do an admirable job, and I can't think of anyone better to raise my daughter.

With love and affection,
Your sister,
Elizabeth

Isabella rested her face in her hands. She was alone, in New Zealand, and now the guardian of a little girl. It felt overwhelming, and the grief of losing Hubert and Elizabeth made it hard for her to think clearly. She needed help to make some decisions, and guidance on how to go about her next steps.

She knew tears were close, but she could not give in to them now. Instead, she blew her nose hard with her handkerchief and looked at herself in the mirror. *Be strong, Isabella*, she told herself, and she left the room to find Mr Hunt.

He was in the sitting room reading a newspaper, and he looked up as Isabella came into the room.

'Can I be of service?' he asked, putting down the paper.

'Mr Hunt, I don't know where to begin with arranging guardianship of Eleanor and booking our tickets home. I know I am asking a lot, but could you help?'

'Leave it with me. Our son is a lawyer, and he can advise on the paperwork. It could take a little while, but I would be happy to help.'

'I am so grateful,' Isabella said, feeling a load lift from her shoulders. She could have hugged him.

It took a few days but the Hunt's son was helpful, and after the death certificates were produced, he arranged for Isabella to be made legal guardian of Eleanor. Mr Hunt had found out the timings for steamers leaving Auckland. The next passage to San Francisco was in just over a week. 'Would you like to take it?' he asked.

'Do you think it would be too soon for Eleanor?' Isabella asked, knowing it was impossible for him to say.

'I wonder if being here is more difficult for her. Heading home might be a helpful diversion,' he suggested. 'But it is up to you, my dear; we have space in the guesthouse for as long as you need. I'll leave you to think on it. Come and find me when you have made your decision.'

Isabella spent the next hour ruminating on what to do; going to the South Sea islands was now out of the question.

Eventually she decided to take the steamer home via America, so she would accept Marty Holland Jr's offer of a place to stay with his family once they arrived in San Francisco.

'Very well. I will make the arrangements,' said Mr Hunt.

It was only later that evening that Isabella realised what day it was: Christmas Eve. The Hunt family kindly invited Isabella and Eleanor to join in with what were now very low-key celebrations. Isabella accepted gratefully, for Eleanor's sake. They ate a roast in the heat, and Mrs Hunt gave Eleanor a new dress and bonnet for her doll.

Eleanor didn't say anything, but gave a faint smile when she opened the package. She dressed her doll up, and then stayed sitting on Isabella's lap, hugging Molly close.

Isabella wrote another letter home to her parents that evening, explaining everything that had happened and letting them know she was now the guardian of a little girl. There was no time to wait for their guidance and wisdom, she had to make her decision alone.

Eleanor and Isabella prepared to leave Auckland for America at the beginning of the New Year. Isabella found Elizabeth's address book and wrote to her father, introducing herself and explaining what Elizabeth had asked of her. Most of Hubert and Elizabeth's belongings would be left in New Zealand, to be sold or given away.

'Would you help me choose what to send back to England?' Isabella asked Mrs Hunt.

Together with Eleanor, they went into the large bedroom that the Cornishes had been staying in. They had unpacked very little, and their trunks sat side by side, pushed against the wall.

Eleanor flopped on the bed as Isabella and Mrs Hunt made judgements on what would stay and what would go.

'You can carry her jewellery with you, as it is probably safest. I think all the clothes should be sold or given away. What will you need of them in England?'

Isabella looked at Eleanor watching from the bed. 'I think we'll take her shawl with us – that will be a comfort... I would like to save one dress to go back with the books and diaries.'

Isabella picked up her portrait of Elizabeth; she was so glad she had taken the time to finish it. 'I wondered if I could fit this in our luggage.'

Eleanor came close to take hold of the painting. She sat with it on her lap, staring at her mother's face. Isabella went to sit next to her, kissing the side of her head.

'I want them to come back,' Eleanor said in a whisper, with silent tears streaming down her cheeks.

'I know,' Isabella replied, putting her arm around the little girl and holding her close.

That evening, Isabella sat alone on the veranda when Eleanor had at last gone to sleep. When Isabella had dreamed of adventure, this is not what she would have planned. She was now in charge of a little girl. She was a mother. How could she possibly fill the gaping hole left by Eleanor's parents?

Chapter Thirteen

The Nevada, January 1881

On the morning of Tuesday 4th January 1881, Isabella and Eleanor began their long journey back to England. Mrs Hunt held Isabella tightly without saying a word, and gave Eleanor a kiss on the cheek. Sharkey drove them to the docks and Mrs Hunt had tears in her eyes as she stood next to her husband and they waved their guests off. Isabella was humbled by the providence of staying at their guesthouse. She could not have got through the previous weeks without them.

When they arrived at the harbour which was busy with cargo being loaded and unloaded on to and from waiting vessels, Isabella got down from the carriage to find the *Nevada*. She approached a sailor coiling thick ropes in the sun, his weathered skin dark brown and glistening with sweat.

'Excuse me, which is the *Nevada*?'

Without words he pointed to a large, dilapidated paddle steamer.

The sun was beating down on the ship, but even the bright rays could not make the peeling paint and broken fixtures look any better.

'It can't be,' Isabella said in shock, wondering if it was too late to change her mind.

The *Nevada* had probably been beautiful in its day, with deck above deck, balconies, a pilot house and two jury masts, but now it looked exceedingly unfit for the voyage.

'She's seaworthy.'

Isabella turned and squinted in the direction of the voice. Standing near was a weathered sailor with a shirt too tight for his belly. 'How do you know?' she asked, somewhat irked by his familiarity and presumption.

'I'm the cap'n,' he said, looking her up and down before climbing up the gangplank to board his ship.

Isabella's heart sank. Eleanor was very quiet by her side, but as they walked closer to the *Nevada*, she pulled at Isabella's arm, stopping her from moving forward.

'What is it?' Isabella asked, bending Eleanor's bonnet back so she could see her eyes.

'I don't want to go; I want to stay *here*,' Eleanor said.

'We must go; we are going home. To England.'

'No!' said Eleanor, and started to sob.

Isabella tried to soothe her. She was aware that people on the dock were watching the commotion and, feeling exposed, she became increasingly uncomfortable.

'Please, Eleanor, stop your crying, this is no way for a lady to behave.'

'I'm not a lady; I'm a little girl,' Eleanor declared.

Isabella glanced at the small crowd that had gathered around them; some probably fellow passengers and some dock hands. Would they realise she was not Eleanor's mother and see that she was ill-equipped to look after a small child? She felt panic rising.

'Come, Eleanor, let's talk about it!' Isabella reasoned, trying to pick her up off the ground. Eleanor was fighting her now, squirming and tensing so she couldn't be held.

Eventually, Isabella encouraged her to sit on a bench in the shade.

'We must get on board, our trunks will be on there soon, and Molly is in your trunk. We can't have her travel to America without us, can we?'

Eleanor sniffed, her crying momentarily subsiding as she took in the information. Concern flickered across her puffy, tear-stained face. She could not be separated from her doll. Isabella took advantage of Eleanor's momentary reassessment of the situation.

'Come on, let's go and find our cabin. We can make sure Molly is tucked in for a good night's sleep.'

Eleanor's tears now turned to large sniffs and sighs. Against her better judgement, Isabella put aside her discomfort at the captain's demeanour and the ship's disrepair. She didn't know if she was being foolish, but she felt compelled to keep moving. She was relieved to have calmed Eleanor down. It was the first tantrum she had navigated, and it felt like some sort of victory.

Isabella said goodbye to Sharkey, who had been waiting patiently. He helped transfer their trunks onto the *Nevada*.

As Isabella and Eleanor walked gingerly on board, it looked as if the stewards outnumbered the passengers. From what Isabella could see, the men were varying degrees of riffraff. The captain, with a steely look in his eyes, said, 'Welcome aboard the *Nevada*, missus and little missy. You are privileged to be two of our nine passengers booked. You'll all be treated royally.'

'Bosun, show these ladies to their quarters,' he ordered a white-haired man with a scar across his cheek. Both Isabella and Eleanor's eyes widened when they saw him. Isabella hesitated.

'Can you carry me?' Eleanor asked. As she picked her up, Isabella wished there was someone to support her in the same way. Someone to lean on.

The small group of passengers congregated on the first deck to bid farewell to land for a few weeks. Eleanor wouldn't look at any of them, refusing to say hello by burying her face in Isabella's neck as the *Nevada* steamed away from Auckland, into the Pacific.

When Isabella saw their cabin, her heart sank once more. No polished teak here, but peeling paint and cracked wood, with lumpy mattresses that smelled of mildew and something else she couldn't quite pinpoint. She recoiled as she saw a cockroach scuttle under the bunk and knew there would be more where he came from. However, there was fresh, clean linen provided, so Isabella made up their beds, wishing she had a sprig of lavender or something to help with the odour.

The next morning, Eleanor rallied to life back on board. She charmed everyone with her inquisitive nature. She would stare at a passenger for a while as they were reading or sitting on deck, as if deciphering them. She then sidled nearer and nearer, until she was in close enough proximity to talk. They would invariably notice her and ask her a question, such as her name or how old she was. Eleanor blossomed with the attention, but once the interaction had ended, quickly ran back to Isabella for safety. This went on for most of the day, as the boat chugged towards America. The second evening, supper was late.

'I am ravenous; I hope we don't have to wait much longer,' said Mrs Scott, the only other female on board, as they sat waiting at the dining table. She seemed a robust woman, and Isabella was relieved by her presence. Isabella found out she was travelling with her twenty-three-year-old son, Michael. After a few gentle questions, Isabella ended up telling her a little of their story. Eleanor fell asleep next to Isabella while they were eating a stringy stew that eventually arrived. Isabella tried to rouse her, and when she awoke, she burst into tears.

'My darling, it's alright,' she said, pulling Eleanor into her lap and wrapping her arms around her. Eleanor didn't look up. In choked gasps she said, 'I want Mama. I want Papa.'

'I know, I know,' was all Isabella could say.

Isabella took Eleanor to their cabin. *Perhaps we should have stayed in New Zealand for longer?* she thought as she held the grief-racked child and silently prayed for help.

After a few minutes, there was a knock at the door.

'Are you alright?' asked Mrs Scott.

'I hope we will be, thank you.'

The woman smiled, and hesitated before coming into the cabin. She knelt down on the floor, next to the bunk, and with motherly concern gently stroked Eleanor's tangled hair and started singing a beautiful lullaby.

As Mrs Scott sang, Eleanor's breathing became calmer and she closed her eyes. After Eleanor had fallen asleep, Mrs Scott and Isabella quietly got up and returned to the table in the saloon.

'She will be alright,' Mrs Scott encouraged. 'Children are remarkably resilient. Your love will make all the difference.'

'I hope you are right,' sighed Isabella.

Over the next few days, Eleanor made a special friend of one of the stewards, a gentle giant of a Maori that the others called Kuki. He paid little interest to the rest of the passengers, but beamed as soon as he saw Eleanor.

'She is just like my granddaughter,' Kuki said to Isabella, as Eleanor skipped around the table.

After a week, Eleanor was content to play by herself or be entertained by Kuki or the other passengers. It gave Isabella time to sit and read, or simply try to contemplate her new future as a mother. She was sad to have missed the chance to visit Fiji or any other Pacific islands. She mentioned it to Mr Hackett, a retired English gentleman traveller, while they were both drinking black tea in the saloon.

'Oh, but we will be passing close to the Navigator Islands; this afternoon you should be able to view from a few miles out at least.'

He was right, and as the islands came into sight, Isabella and Eleanor leaned over the side of the steamer to see through the clear blue ocean to rainbow-tinted coral forests below. They were close enough to see a myriad of colourful fish moving in and out of the coral.

Palm trees and groves of banyan and breadfruit trees waved at them from the shore. Isabella's dream came back to her, and she felt frustrated that there would be no chance to explore the Pacific islands.

For the next fortnight, the unclouded sun blazed upon the crawling ship. The boiler tubes were giving way at the rate of ten to twenty a day, so the old boat dragged her 320ft length along. As a result, the voyage was slower than expected.

'We ought to have been close to San Francisco by now,' complained Mr Hackett to the captain, who shrugged his shoulders.

'Too much time in the damp inter-island region of the Tropic of Capricorn, not my fault.'

The passengers attempted to make the most of the slow, hot journey with early breakfasts, cold plunge baths and the ventilation from the portholes in their cabins, which only just kept them going. The nights were insupportably humid. Most days Isabella lounged on the bow with Eleanor lying next to her, torpid.

On the morning of day twenty-one, Mrs Scott came white-faced to the group at breakfast. Her son Michael had been coughing up blood.

There was a doctor among the passengers and he was called for.

'He's drunk,' Isabella whispered to Mrs Scott as the Scottish doctor stumbled to Michael's cabin, reeking of whisky.

'I know, but he still might be of help,' she said, desperately.

Isabella watched from the door as the doctor talked with Michael and took his temperature. He diagnosed the patient as having a ruptured blood vessel on the lung or a pulmonary laceration.

'He'll need to lie still in the deck house and will require careful nursing, constant fanning and the attention of two people night and day,' said the doctor, although his words were slightly slurred.

Mr Hackett and another gentleman stepped in to support Mrs Scott in looking after her son. They never left Michael by night so his mother could sleep, and they scarcely took a rest in the day. One or the other was always on hand to support him when he was faint, or raise him on his pillows.

But as the days went by, Michael became more ill. Many of the group thought he was dying, and it cast a great gloom over their circle. Isabella tried to hide it from Eleanor, but it was impossible.

'Will Michael die like Mama and Papa?' she asked.

'I don't think he will,' Isabella said, unable to be more positive.

'We are too far from San Francisco to help the boy. By my calculations, we should be passing the Sandwich Islands shortly. I think the only hope for his life is that we land in Honolulu so that Michael can get treatment,' said Mr Hackett to Mrs Scott as they were all sitting for dinner.

She simply nodded, her eyes full of fear.

Mr Hackett went to speak to the captain. He agreed that a detour to the Sandwich Islands was necessary.

Mrs Scott turned to Isabella, 'I do not know anyone in the Sandwich Islands and the thought of losing Michael is overwhelming. I cannot think clearly. My dear, would you disembark with us, just for a few days? I would so much value your company and help.'

'Of course, don't think any more of it, I would be glad to.'

Isabella was happy to get off the steamer, and knew it would be good for Eleanor too. The journey had been uncomfortable for both of them. Despite the captain's declarations that the vessel was seaworthy, equipment seemed to break daily, and Isabella was doubtful they really would make it to San Francisco in one piece.

They were a few days off from the Sandwich Islands. Before they got to Honolulu, Kuki realised that Eleanor was not sleeping well. He suggested fashioning a hammock for her in the saloon, where the open windows made it the coolest room, and the lack of a mattress would mean fewer cockroaches. He attached one for Isabella as well.

Eleanor loved her new bed. She let Isabella gently rock her to sleep each night. She still wanted to be near Isabella at all times, and would often talk about her parents. Isabella wrote down what she knew of Elizabeth to give it to Eleanor when she was older. She wanted Eleanor to know how loved she was. On day thirty, Isabella and Eleanor went to sit in the hammock.

'I am scared I will forget,' Eleanor said quietly.

'Forget what?' Isabella asked.

'Mama's face. I am losing her face.'

Isabella took Eleanor in her arms and rocked her gently.

'You won't forget her face, don't worry. She will always come back to you. And remember the portrait that I painted? It is in the trunk. When we get back you will be able to see her face every day.'

Eleanor's face registered relief; she lay clutching Molly, as Isabella made up a story to entertain her. The tale was of a young girl who landed on a paradise island with parrots and palm trees and who made friends with a little native girl called Coco.

'I want to go to that island,' Eleanor declared sleepily, closing her eyes.

'We are going; we'll be there soon.'

Isabella shut her eyes too. It was a happy and unexpected diversion to be stopping at the Sandwich Islands.

The day before they arrived, Isabella was up early. Checking Eleanor was still asleep in her hammock, she went out to the deck. There was no one about, and she was enjoying the stillness, until she heard someone behind her. She turned to see the captain lighting his pipe. He looked up, and blew the smoke in her direction.

'Hope he makes it,' he said, ominously.

Isabella felt riled at his pessimism. 'Yes, but what a relief the Sandwich Islands are so near... there will surely be a proper hospital for him to go to?'

'The Hawaiians are civilised people, Miss Buckley. It's not all grass skirts and mud huts. Business is booming in Honolulu. Wouldn't be surprised if it becomes a metropolis like any other capital in a few years' time. And then there's the royalty. I think it was in the 1820s that the Hawaiian king and his queen travelled to London...'

'They came to London?'

'The king's father, Kamehameha the First, palled up with the British Captain George Vancouver. But the agreement was never officially acknowledged by the British government. The king and his wife sailed to England in an attempt to finalise his father's negotiations with King George IV to provide some protection for the islands.' The captain paused, made a retching sound in his throat, and spat a bullet of phlegm into the water. Isabella winced. 'They arrived in England, good on them, but both the king and his queen contracted measles. The queen died and six days later her husband croaked.' He paused and then laughed. 'They hadn't even met King George.'

Isabella looked at the captain with both disgust and interest. 'What a tragic story.'

The captain took his leave and headed back to the bridge.

Isabella sat pondering what he had told her. How sad; the island king and queen would have travelled for months to a foreign country so different from their own island, and instead of gaining protection for the lands they ruled, they had both died. She couldn't imagine what the couple, having grown up on a Pacific island, would have thought of the strict traditions and confinements of polite society in England.

Isabella's thoughts turned to home, and she wondered what her parents would think of her new role – having a daughter. They would be shocked at first, but she hoped that as soon as they met Eleanor, they would welcome her into their hearts. Catherine would do the same without reservation. Isabella tried to imagine herself living back in Norfolk. It felt very far away.

Chapter Fourteen

Hawaii, January 1881

The winds of change were calling Kainalu. He could sense it. The feeling was strongest in the sunken hours of night as he lay awake in the darkness. Life continued as he knew it, and from the outside at least, all was as it had been. But inside Kainalu could feel a new current coming and he did not know when it would arrive

'Ey? You the leper-catcher?' called a Hawaiian man, thickset and with greying hair, as Kainalu walked, hot and sweaty, towards the ocean, his board under his arm, ready for an afternoon wave-ride.

'Could be,' Kainalu replied, stopping to look at the man.

'What you doing, banishing your people to Moloka'i? You cruel, brutha.'

Kainalu wedged his board vertically in the sand and kept it steady with one hand. 'You want to see *Ma'i pake* all over the island?'

'What you know about it? What you know about losing all you love?' The man spat on the sand at Kainalu's feet.

'*I know*,' Kainalu replied, standing his ground, prepared to explain more if the man was ready to listen. It appeared he was not. He simply sneered and trudged away, his outburst ended.

This kind of encounter was becoming more and more common for Kainalu. There had to be someone to blame for all these families being torn apart, and it seemed that he was the one bearing the brunt. With a sigh, he picked up his board and continued walking towards the water.

He thought of Maima. Did she see him as a 'leper-catcher'? Her parents surely did. Kainalu had fought to keep Maima in Kalihi for as long as possible so that she could have contact with her parents, but Kalihi was closing. A new hospital and holding station was opening up. The time was coming when Maima would have to make the journey to Kalaupapa. She was such an independent child, happy with her own company; often when Kainalu arrived at Kalihi, he would find her involved in some game, laughing easily, enraptured by a flower or playing chase with the other children. Her face lit up when she saw Kainalu. Maima seemed to have taken her lot in life with unquestioning acceptance. If she cried for her family and the freedom she had lost, Kainalu did not see it.

He was at the water's edge now. The ocean was his temporary escape; it always refreshed his tired mind and body. He made a decision to visit Maima the next day. He'd take her and the other children something sweet to eat. He had made a proposal for a girls' home to be built on Kalaupapa and was busy raising funds for it. He wouldn't let Maima go until it was ready.

Kainalu surrendered his thoughts to the ocean to rid himself of the heaviness he was carrying. He would be happy never to see another leper, never to have to tear families apart, but he knew he would lose his peace if he walked away now. He owed it to Lokelani.

Kainalu's daily habit was to wave-ride at Waikiki beach every afternoon at about five o'clock, after his working day was finished. He would then spend the evening with Aolani and Fili, playing with Leilani as if she was his own daughter.

'I want Leilani to learn some British manners, and speak like Emma Fortnum. Her accent is so refined,' Aolani said to him later that evening.

Kapuna Wahine scoffed, and Kainalu laughed.

'Is a little island girl not good enough?' remarked Fili, with a twinkle in his eye.

'Leilani would sound so beautiful with an English accent,' Aolani continued, ignoring his comment.

'You can always send her to school in England,' suggested Kainalu, knowing his sister would never agree.

'I don't want her to *leave* me, but I want her to benefit from the refinements of the British. Kai, it will be good for her.'

Fili went inside to find some food, shaking his head.

Kapuna Wahine stood behind her daughter and stroked her long black hair.

'My daughter, don't be impressed by these *haoles*. The English are more pompous than their actions warrant. Leilani does not need any English influence.'

'What about Miriam?' Aolani asked.

'I am sorry the princess married that Scot. She should have married an islander, a son of a chief, like Kainalu. Our bloodlines must be protected.'

Aolani rolled her eyes, but said nothing.

Chapter Fifteen

Hawaii, February 1881

At half past six the next morning, Isabella woke to cries that 'the islands' were in sight. With a rush of excitement, she sat up and dropped her feet onto the unpolished wooden floor.

Exchanging her cotton nightgown for her well-worn linen day dress, Isabella roused Eleanor.

'Wake up, dearest, we have arrived at the Sandwich Islands.'

'Is that good?' Eleanor asked, rubbing her eyes.

'Very good! We will soon be able to stand on dry land. Perhaps you will be able to play on the beach today?'

At that suggestion, Eleanor grinned and pulled back her thin cotton sheet. They were both very soon out on deck viewing the island for the first time. With all the anticipation over the last few days, Isabella was disappointed. Oah'u looked to her like a group of grey, barren peaks rising out of the blue sea, and was not at all the lush picture of a tropical island. In her more fantastical moments, she had wondered if these islands might be the very place she had dreamed about; now she realised they couldn't be.

'It's not an exception to the rule that the first sight of land is unimpressive,' said Mr Hackett, who was standing nearby.

'Perhaps as we get closer it will improve?'

'No doubt,' he agreed. 'The Sandwich Islands are said to be one of the most beautiful places on earth. Interestingly, they have a connection with our homeland – their flag even has a Union Jack in the top left-hand corner.'

Isabella thought he was joking, and laughed.

'No, no, it is true, the Hawaiian monarchy had a close relationship with the British Navy.'

They continued watching the horizon, the breeze from the boat's forward movement taking the edge off the heat. Eleanor, quickly bored, left to find Kuki. She used him as a human climbing frame. He would patiently comply and swing her up in the air or let her climb on his back like a monkey, giggling away. Soon, Isabella and Mr Hackett also retreated to the saloon.

As the sun rose higher in the sky, the deck was almost too hot to stand on. The sea and sky were both magnificently blue, and the unveiled sun turned every minute ripple on the water's surface into a diamond's flash.

As the *Nevada* approached land, the island changed in character. Isabella saw lofty peaks, both grey and red, sun-scorched and wind-bleached, glowing here and there with traces of their fiery origin. They were cleft by deep chasms and ravines of cool shade and entrancing green. Falling water streaked their sides. After weeks of the desert sea and the dusty browns of Auckland, it was a most welcome vision for Isabella. Nearer still, the coast came into sight, fringed by the feathery coconut palms and marked by a long line of white surf. The *Nevada* was close to the coral reef before a cry of, 'There is Honolulu!' from one of the crew made the wilting passengers alive to the proximity of the capital of the Island Kingdom.

Isabella saw simple wooden huts with deep verandas. The homes were nestled under palms and bananas on soft green land in front of the bright sand. She spied two church spires and a few grey roofs amid the trees.

'How long will we be on this island?' Eleanor asked Isabella, taking her hand and resting herself into the curve of her side.

'Probably a week. We want to help Mrs Scott and her son.'

Michael was still in a critical condition and was being prepared to disembark. The *Nevada* needed quite desperate repairs – it was listing portside so badly that half the stern was out of the water. The detour to the Sandwich Islands was necessary in more ways than one, and all the passengers now had to leave the boat on anchoring. There would be no more sailing until it was mended.

A few moments later, the captain called from the deck that they were nearly at the harbour.

Mrs Scott and Isabella were careful to stay in the shade but moved out of the saloon to have a clearer view.

'I cannot thank you enough for helping me,' Mrs Scott said.

'It is my pleasure; it will be a relief to get off this boat!' replied Isabella.

Eleanor was back with Kuki, now at the bow of the ship, spotting fish in the clear blue water below. The shallows were filled with islanders in their canoes, travelling to and from an American warship and other large steamers.

By noon they were moored in the impressive harbour. Looking down from their high deck, Isabella could see a huge crowd of a few thousand people; Europeans, Chinamen with their long, braided hair, and local islanders. They were greeting the *Nevada* crew and passengers with smiles and shouts of '*Aloha!*'

As soon as they anchored, a mass of people boarded the steamer, communicating in a language that sounded different from anything Isabella had ever heard. All were talking and laughing; an immense amount of gesticulation emphasised and supplemented their speech.

In the air was a sweet, fragrant aroma that Isabella could only describe as heavenly. A soft smell of blossoms travelled along the waters and enveloped them with its delicious perfume.

As they left the boat, the *Nevada* passengers were each given a garland of orchids to put around their necks, which meant that the flower's fragrance was never far away from their senses.

Eleanor was quite captivated by the new sights and sounds, but kept her hand firmly in Isabella's – who felt hot and sticky compared to the serene and cool women they saw on the wharf. She watched two European ladies with simple muslin dresses and white straw hats. They, like all the others, followed the native custom of wearing natural flowers around their hats and necks.

'They are perfectly beaming with cheer and kindness,' remarked Mrs Scott, wiping the beads of sweat from her brow with a dainty handkerchief.

The group were taken in three buggies to the Hawaiian Hotel. Michael was carried by the men on and off his carriage, and leaned, pale and weak, on his mother until they got to the hotel.

The staff greeted the new guests with a warm *'Aloha'*.

'It is like stepping into some sort of utopia!' Isabella whispered to Mr Hackett, as she took in the hotel. The Hawaiian appeared to be a great public resort in Honolulu, the centre of activity, a club house and drawing room in one. The group were led down a wide corridor leading out to a veranda, alive with English and American naval uniforms. On booking in, Isabella was told that the establishment was run by a German. His manager was American, the steward was Hawaiian and the servants were all Chinese, dressed in spotless white linen.

A cool and comfortable room was provided for Michael and a local doctor was sent for. After examination, he said there was hope that the invalid would rally in this temperate atmosphere. The group took turns in watching and fanning Michael, and Mrs Scott stayed with him, reading in a chair by the window as he slept. Isabella and Eleanor sat with Mrs Scott for a while, until Eleanor began to get fidgety.

'I'm very comfortable and Michael is resting. Why don't you take Eleanor to the beach before supper?' suggested Mrs Scott.

'If you are sure you are content to be alone?'

'Of course. Off you go.'

Eleanor ran out of the door, so eager to be near the water. After a short walk, they came to a path leading to Waikiki beach. The water was the most beautiful and inviting colour of turquoise. Eleanor stood still as she watched the islanders playing in the ocean.

'What are they doing in the water?' she asked, as about ten men on wooden boards used their arms to push out to the breakers.

'I'm not sure. Let's watch,' Isabella said. She took off Eleanor's shoes and then her canvas slippers, and felt the warm sand beneath her toes as they walked to the water.

The men would paddle with their arms out towards the breakers, and as soon as a wave was about to break, quickly turn their boards around. As the power of the water took the board, they would jump and stand up on the board, riding the wave into shore, to shouts of praise and exuberance from themselves and the other surf-riders.

At first, Eleanor was content to watch and play in the sand, making trips down to the water to wade in the shallows.

It was all so relaxing and idyllic that Isabella didn't want to leave. She sat down on a rock, closed her eyes and took a deep breath of warm, fragrant air. Her relaxation was momentary, as something cautioned her to check on Eleanor.

Isabella opened her eyes, scanning the beach for the girl. She was nowhere on the sand. Isabella stood up, using her hand to shade her view from the low sun. At last her eyes rested on a very wet little girl in the water, holding on to the wooden board of a native man.

'Eleanor!' Isabella cried, running down to the shore.

'I was swimming!' She had a broad smile on her dripping face.

'But... you are all wet...' Isabella said, exasperated, not knowing whether to be cross or to laugh.

'I didn't mean to. A big wave came and I fell...' Eleanor paused, looking up to the smiling Hawaiian holding his board steady in the water. 'Then this man helped me.'

Isabella had felt the man's eyes on her as she was speaking to Eleanor. He was tall with almond-shaped eyes. His short black hair and thick sideburns were still wet with salt water. His smile showed a row of perfect white teeth.

Unsure of whether he would understand, Isabella slowly thanked him for his help, and held a hand out for Eleanor to take.

'It was my pleasure; I always enjoy rescuing a damsel in distress,' he replied, and Isabella tried not to look surpised at his perfect English.

Eleanor looked up at him and grinned.

'You must be visiting our island… are you here for long?' the man asked Isabella, as he carried his board onto the sand.

'We just arrived today, from New Zealand,' Isabella said, feeling conscious of her proximity to his unclothed torso. The man did not seem to be aware of how uncomfortable his state of undress was making her.

'And is this little fish your daughter?'

Isabella was about to say no, but she realised that would require an explanation, which she did not want to give. Eleanor was now twirling around on the sand, her dress sodden and glued to her body.

'Yes, yes, she is.'

'My sister has a child of a similar age and wants her to learn good English. Would you be happy to allow your daughter to play with my niece?'

'We are only visiting; we won't be in Honolulu long…'

Apparently sensing her uncertainty, he smiled again. 'I understand. I will be at this beach again tomorrow about this time and I will bring my niece. If your husband approves, come with your daughter. It would be an honour for my niece to play with her.'

Isabella opened her mouth about to explain that she was not married, but shut it again. 'Thank you, I will.'

'Until tomorrow. *Aloha!*' he said with a chuckle, before walking off along the sand.

'Who was that?' asked Eleanor when he had gone.

'I don't know,' Isabella replied, realising they had not even exchanged names. They turned and walked back to the hotel,

Eleanor chatting all the way, the ocean adventure having truly invigorated her.

Isabella and Eleanor saw Mrs Scott standing on the veranda as they got to the hotel.

'Oh, Eleanor! Your dress is all wet. And what happened to your shoes?' Mrs Scott said, looking at the barefooted girl.

'She had an unplanned swim! I have her shoes, her feet were too sandy to put them back on.'

'A man came and saved me with his wooden board,' Eleanor interjected excitedly.

Mrs Scott looked at Isabella with eyebrows raised.

'He did, a native, and he offered for Eleanor to play with his young niece.'

'How wonderful! Eleanor needs some friends to play with.'

'Yes, she does,' Isabella said, surprised by Mrs Scott's enthusiasm, and questioning her own judgement. She had meant to decline his offer.

'Well, what an adventure, I do declare!' Mrs Scott said.

'How is Michael?'

'He is sleeping again, but his breathing is clearer. I believe he is already improving, thank the dear Lord.'

Chapter Sixteen

Hawaii, February 1881

That evening, the *Nevada* party enjoyed fried *mahi mahi* fish as they watched the sun set. Eleanor fell asleep on Isabella's lap, and she carried her to bed before rejoining the group. She heard her table before she got close, as the relief of being off the rickety *Nevada* and the luxury of the hotel had roused their spirits. The doctor was inebriated again, and Mr Hackett, who was sitting to his left, had to stop him from bursting into war songs. Isabella took her place at Mr Hackett's other side.

'What a place. I can see why our doctor friend is so happy,' she said as she sat down.

'I think we have all been saved by Michael's illness. But it is the island too; there is something different about it,' he replied. 'I have spent a good deal of time in the Caribbean, and although the climate and beauty can be matched there, the history of slavery and suffering causes a strange atmosphere. I find it means true relaxation carries something of guilt with it. Here there is no such feeling. The *kanakas* have such nobility about them, don't you think? I am sure I would like to have been born into an islander family!'

'I think we are going to stay here for longer than a week,' Mrs Scott said as they were about to retire for the night. 'I don't want to move Michael until he is completely better, and this place is heavenly.'

'Yes, that sounds wise,' Isabella added in a moment of spontaneity. 'Perhaps Eleanor and I should remain also?'

Mrs Scott clasped her hands together with pleasure. 'Do stay! It would be good for you both to be on dry land for a while.'

Her response confirmed it for Isabella; she felt impetuous with the decision, but they would stay.

The melodic sound of the waves rolling gently into shore lulled her to sleep on their first night in Honolulu. The only blot on this seeming paradise were the mosquitoes, whose hunger had evidently been satiated from the look of the tiny welts on her arms and legs. They had truly feasted on her.

After breakfast, Isabella sat with Eleanor in the shade of the wide veranda. They were surrounded by hotel guests and visitors sitting nearby, chatting happily. The smart Chinese waiters were popping in and out, deferentially seeing to the needs of the guests.

Even though this was the height of relaxation and luxury, Isabella knew Eleanor could not sit still for long – she had done that enough on the *Lyttleton* and the *Nevada*. If they were going to be in Honolulu for a little while longer, she needed to entertain her, and she hoped to explore more of the island.

While Isabella was wondering on the next course of action, she recognised a figure from the day before. Walking into the hotel was the surf-rider who had helped Eleanor. This time he was dressed very respectably in a dark suit, tie and hat.

As he walked past Eleanor and Isabella, he stopped and gave a little bow and a smile.

'Good morning! How wonderful to see you both again. How are you today?'

'Very well, thank you,' Isabella replied, aware of how differently she reacted to him now. He was obviously a prosperous and educated Hawaiian, and not a simple native as she had presumed him to be.

'I was very rude yesterday and never introduced myself properly. My name is James Kainalu Okalani, but my friends call me Kainalu.'

'I am Isabella Buckley, and this is Eleanor,' Isabella said, shaking his hand.

He winked at Eleanor and then addressed Isabella: 'Have you thought more about my offer? My niece, Leilani, would very much appreciate an English playmate.'

Isabella was uncomfortable at being put under pressure to make a decision so instantly, but in light of his new appearance, she felt confident enough to say yes. 'We would be happy to take you up on your invitation, thank you.'

'Perhaps this afternoon? I will bring Leilani to the hotel and take you all to Waikiki beach? I will bring my sister too.'

Isabella was relieved to hear his sister would be joining them. She looked at Eleanor, who was still smiling up at their new acquaintance. It would be good for her to have another little girl to play with.

'Yes, we can be available this afternoon,' she replied, thinking, *What better way to get to know the island, than with a local?*

'We will be here at two. Good day,' he said with a smile, bowing again before walking on into the hotel.

True to his word, Kainalu arrived promptly at two o'clock. Isabella and Eleanor were waiting on the veranda. He walked up to the hotel holding the hand of a beautiful little girl with long, wavy, black hair. She looked about four, the same age as Eleanor.

'Good afternoon, Eleanor. I would like to introduce you to Leilani,' Kainalu said, hunching down so he was the same height as the girls.

Eleanor looked shyly up at Isabella, as if asking for confirmation that it was alright to make this new acquaintance. Isabella smiled and nodded. The girls looked at each other and then Leilani reached out for Eleanor's hand and said, 'Come see horse.' Eleanor nodded and they both ran giggling down the path.

Kainalu smiled as he watched them. Turning back to Isabella he said, 'I am sorry, my sister, Aolani, was held up with preparations for a little party this evening. I hope it will not offend you that we are alone?'

In truth, Isabella did feel unsure of herself. *What would Mama advise?* she thought, but ignored what she knew would be the answer. *The girls will be our chaperones.*

'My sister would like to invite you and your husband to the *paina* – the dinner party – this evening, and of course, Eleanor.'

Isabella realised she had to tell him the truth. 'Mr Okalani, I am not married; I am Eleanor's guardian. Her parents died only a short while ago in New Zealand. I met them on the steamer out from England, and her mother asked me to look after their daughter.'

He looked surprised at the news. 'I am so sorry to hear that. Eleanor is blessed to have you, as I see you love her like a mother.'

'Thank you; that is kind of you.'

'Not at all. It is the truth!' he replied, before turning to follow the girls. 'Come, let us go to the water!' he called.

Isabella followed him, holding herself back from saying something matter-of-fact in response. He was right, she did feel she loved the little girl as if she was her own. It felt vulnerable to admit it, even to herself.

They arrived at a grove of hundreds of coconut trees surrounding what looked like fish ponds.

'The beach is this way,' Kainalu said, motioning a way through the wetlands. The girls ran ahead. Isabella smiled as she watched Eleanor follow Leilani's lead and embrace her confidence.

The sandy soil squelched beneath her feet.

'We have three main valleys *mauka* of Waikiki: Makiki, Manoa and Palolo. Their streams water this marshland. I apologise for your shoes.'

'What is *mauka*?'

'It means mountainside, or left, and *makai* is oceanside. You will hear them used for left or right on the islands.'

When they got to the shore, the water looked so inviting. Isabella longed to swim, but she would never do so in front of Kainalu.

There were a few Hawaiian families sitting in groups on the grass just before the sand started. Kainalu directed Isabella to a large palm tree. It provided some shade, and Kainalu laid down a mat for her to sit on. She had brought a book that she had found in the hotel on the etymology of the Hawaiian language, and began to read while the girls played.

Time seemed to slow down. Eleanor's face shone with happiness under her sun bonnet. She held hands with Leilani constantly, and they giggled as they ran up and down the beach together. Isabella only skimmed the first page of her book before leaving it aside. She spent most of her time watching the girls play. Kainalu had gone to the water's edge with them, but then he saw someone he knew and went to talk to him. When the man left, she observed him walk up to the coconut grove where there was a lady selling watermelons. She watched him buy one and carry it over to her. As he got close, she pretended to be engrossed in her book, but blushed as she realised it was upside down.

'Ever tried watermelon?' he asked.

'Not yet.'

He took out a knife, sheathed in his back pocket, and cut and sectioned the melon, giving a slice to Isabella. Leilani and Eleanor came running to him, and he handed them a slice each.

'You can eat the pips, or spit them out,' he said.

Isabella could not bring herself to spit in front of him, or anyone.

The girls ate ravenously, the juice dripping down their chins. Isabella felt she had never tasted anything so delicious.

'Come, it's time to go!' Kainalu said, when everyone had finished eating. The girls protested at first, but eventually they returned to the hotel, sandy, salty and sunkissed.

'Dinner will be at seven o'clock. I will send a carriage to collect you at half past six,' Kainalu said, when he dropped them off at the hotel.

'Thank you,' Isabella replied, grateful for the serendipitous meeting that was opening up the world of the Hawaiians to her.

'Hello!' greeted Mr Hackett as Isabella and Eleanor walked up to the hotel. He was reading a newspaper on the veranda. 'Good time?'

'Wonderful, the beach is beautiful.'

'Lucky you. Come and have a drink and tell me all.'

'There is nothing I would like to do more, but I think we need to check on Michael first, and Eleanor needs to get the saltwater out of her hair…'

'Don't worry, Michael is doing well, and Eleanor can bathe soon enough.'

Isabella conceded and pulled up the chair next to him, with Eleanor on her lap.

'It's wonderful that Michael is improving so fast. I and the other chaps will be leaving tomorrow, but definitely not on the *Nevada*. She still isn't fit for sailing. What are your plans?'

'I think we will stay a little longer, at least to support Mrs Scott.'

'Jolly good. It's very tempting to prolong my time here, but I sadly have commitments at home,' he said.

Isabella stayed talking a while longer, and then, bidding Mr Hackett good evening, took Eleanor's hand and went to their room to change.

While Eleanor splashed in the free-standing bath, Isabella looked at herself in front of the mirror. Strands of her hair had been lightened by the sun's rays and her eyes looked a brighter blue against the rosy glow the sun had given her skin. *What can I do with my hair?* Elizabeth had had pretty curls, and Catherine's hair appeared to do exactly what she wanted, but Isabella was at a loss with her own locks. She tried to brush them into a swoop and a high bun, but it didn't seem to work. Frustrated with her inability to make her hair the way she desired, she reverted to the same arrangement that she had always had, pulled back at the sides and held in a low knot at the nape of her neck. Isabella remembered the women praised for their beauty at home, and momentarily wished she was beautiful. She sighed.

Why am I caring about my appearance now?

Isabella assertively put her hairbrush down and walked away from the mirror. Nothing good ever came from worrying about her looks. At least she was healthy and well. The back pain that had once tightened her features had still not returned; she dared hope that perhaps it was gone for good.

She was brushing Eleanor's hair when they were interrupted by a knock at the door.

'Yes?' she called.

A Chinese servant entered.

'Your buggy, it arrive, ma'am,' he said, with a humble nod of his head.

They left the hotel, and Eleanor ran down the steps to the waiting buggy. The Hawaiian driver helped her up into the seat and she and Isabella left the hotel as the sun was sinking in the sky and the air was heavy with the scent of gardenia and tuberose. Sitting high on the back of the horse-drawn carriage, they had a tour of Honolulu, their driver calling out places of interest along the way. They drove along sandy roads with overarching trees through whose dense foliage the setting sun trickled in dancing, broken lights. Many of the dwellings straggled over the ground without an upper storey, and had very deep verandas. Isabella caught glimpses of cool, shady rooms with matted floors.

'Look left, here is the finest garden of all in Honolulu. It belongs to a Chinese merchant, Mr Ah Fong,' called the driver.

'Beautiful,' murmured Isabella, her eyes feasting on the colour and design. 'It is difficult to tell what the architecture looked like – what is house and what is vegetation – as all the lattices and balustrades are hidden by jasmine or passion flowers or the flame of bougainvillea.'

'Yes! Yes!' The driver nodded and then pointed to another house with extensive grounds, a perfect wilderness of vegetation.

'It is the summer palace of Queen Emma, or Kaleonalani, widow of Kamehameha IV. She visited England some years back,' he said, proudly.

The contrast of the neat grass houses of the islanders with the more elaborate homes of the foreign residents was pleasing to Isabella. The Hawaiians had not been crowded out of sight or into a special quarter, and she saw groups of natives sitting under the trees outside their houses on mats. Everyone seemed to intermingle with ease.

After fifteen minutes of travelling behind and above the city, they drew up to a large wood-frame house. It had coral stone walls and a two-tiered veranda wrapping around the home with Tuscan columns on the front. The house was set up on a hill with a spectacular view of *Le'ahi*, the volcanic rock formation jutting out into the ocean. Honolulu was below them, sparkling with the lights from the houses. There were flaming torches lighting the garden. A young Hawaiian girl ran out and without a word led Isabella and Eleanor towards the house. She called out something in Hawaiian, and in answer Kainalu came to greet Isabella on the *lanai*. He was wearing a white shirt, red neckerchief and a long, tailored jacket.

'Miss Buckley, Miss Eleanor, welcome! Our party have eagerly been expecting your arrival.' Isabella felt unsure of herself. She saw the room behind him full of people. A tall, striking Hawaiian woman came towards Isabella with a broad smile. She was wearing a Eurpoean dress, but her long brown hair was loose around her shoulders, with an orange hibiscus blossom behind her left ear.

'Let me introduce you to my sister, Aolani,' said Kainalu.

Eleanor, peering from behind Isabella's skirts, looked up at the woman.

'It's wonderful to meet you,' Aolani said, grasping both Isabella's hands. 'My daughter cannot stop talking about your little Eleanor.'

Isabella felt as if she glowed in Aolani's warmth.

'Come, let's go and see the *keiki* before I take you to meet the others,' Aolani said, taking Isabella's hand.

'*Keiki?*'

'That's our word for children.'

Isabella would normally have felt uncomfortable holding a stranger's hand, but here, it felt natural. She followed Aolani through another door to where Leilani and her cousins were.

'Eleanor!' Leilani squealed, and the two girls were reunited like old friends.

'We will give them food now, and they will be tired from the sun and ocean. Eleanor can sleep here, and we can wake her when it is time to leave,' she said with kind authority, before leaving the girls and leading Isabella back to the party. Isabella looked back to see Leilani giving Eleanor her doll to hold, and Eleanor hugging it tightly to her chest with a smile on her face.

Aolani took Isabella back into the main room, and introduced her to Emma Fortnum.

'She is English, like you,' Aolani said.

'How do you do?' said Isabella, shaking her hand. Isabella thought she looked a similar age to herself. She had pale skin and a rosy, smiley face.

'How very nice to meet you. Welcome to Honolulu!' Emma said.

The party ate on the *lanai*, sitting on a long table decked with candelabra, and were waited on by a Chinese servant.

'How do you find the island?' asked the man sitting to Isabella's left, when they were seated for dinner. He had introduced himself as Archibald Cleghorn.

'I have only been here a few days, but I have never been anywhere so lush and vibrant. It seems so far from the pains and trials of life in the overcrowded industrialised cities in England. I should imagine it is much easier to be poor on an island like this than in a colder climate,' Isabella said.

Archibald smiled. It was a kind smile, but with a hint of pity, or was it cynicism? He had a long, greying beard and a thick head of brown hair. 'Don't be deceived – there are pains and trials here. I don't know if those with very little would agree it is easier being poor on the islands than anywhere else. I am sure it is difficult being poor in any climate.'

Isabella felt herself flushing and regretted her generalisation. Archibald did not seem to notice, and continued.

'I was born in Scotland, but came here when I was sixteen, after my mother died in New Zealand in '45. After a year in Honolulu my father also died.'

'I'm so sorry,' said Isabella.

He batted off her concern. 'It was years ago. I decided to stay. My father started a dry goods shop, and I kept it going. That was when I was nearly seventeen and I am now fifty, although you may not know it,' he winked.

Isabella smiled politely.

'I became a Hawaiian citizen in 1870, and as you see, have married into the royal family. I quite recommend it.'

Isabella's eyes followed his to his wife. 'She is part of the royal family?'

'Yes, my wife is sister to the king, and cousin to Kainalu and his family.'

Isabella had never been in the presence of royalty, but there was no pomp and ceremony at this dinner; she did not feel overawed.

The princess sat at the other end of the table and looked substantially younger than her husband. Her skin was a beautiful dark olive, and she wore her brown hair up and with a fringe.

'Do you mind my asking how you have fared being Scottish and marrying into the Hawaiian people?' Isabella asked.

'Well, in many ways I feel Hawaiian. Now we have a six-year-old daughter, Victoria Kaiulani, I think I can stake my claim to be an islander. I consider it to be my home rather than Scotland.'

'You found yourself a warmer home,' Isabella smiled.

'Oh, but I do romanticise the misty glens and peat-filled locks…' Archibald, now in the flow, sat back. 'My wife, Miriam Likelike, is a wonderful, wise woman. She grew up on Kona as the *hānai* of a chief and his wife. When I met her, I knew I wanted to marry her. It took some persuasion, though.' He paused, taking a side glance at Isabella to see her reaction. 'I am a divorced man, you know. I already had three daughters from my first wife.'

While Isabella listened to Archibald, she stole glances at Kainalu, watching him laughing and talking with his guests.

When the women left the table at the end of the meal, Emma Fortnum came to sit next to Isabella in the sitting room.

'How did you enjoy talking to Mr Cleghorn?'

'Very much.'

'He is an interesting man; I like him not simply because he is from the British Isles. It is said he will be the next governor of Oah'u, and now serves in the House of Nobles and the Privy Council. So he's very important! Tell me, how long are you staying in Honolulu?' She was brisk and to the point, but Isabella also saw kindness in her.

'I am not sure… probably a week or so. I do love it here, and Eleanor – the little girl to whom I am guardian – seems to be enjoying it too. We have no fixed date to return to England.'

'How long has she been with you?'

Isabella meant to give only a few details, but she ended up telling her the whole story, of how her parents had died and that Isabella and Eleanor had been travelling to California, but had had to come to Hawaii because of illness on board.

Mrs Fortnum listened intently; her eyes glistened when Isabella talked about the death of Hubert and Elizabeth.

'That poor girl, she has been through so much…'

The evening came to an end but before Isabella left, Aolani came to sit with her. 'Please come and visit us tomorrow. I would like to have tea with you, and Eleanor and Leilani can play.'

'We would be delighted,' Isabella replied.

Kainalu came to tell them his driver would return them to the hotel. A sleeping Eleanor was carried to the carriage, but its movement woke her up.

'Did you have a nice time?' Isabella asked.

'Yes, Leilani is my very best friend! She said her name means "flowers from heaven". What does my name mean?'

'I happen to know it means "gift from God". I think that is very appropriate, as you are that to me.'

'I am a *hānai* girl. That is what Leilani said.'

'I don't know what that means, but what I do know is that you are very special to me.'

Eleanor gave a contented smile and rested her head on Isabella's shoulder.

On arrival at the hotel, the driver carried Eleanor inside, transferring her to Isabella outside their room. Isabella then lay her now sleeping charge on her bed, and changed into her nightgown. But after an hour of tossing and turning, sleep still eluded her. She decided to get up and write to Catherine.

Quietly she gathered pages of paper and ink from the small table at the other side of the room. By the light of a flickering candle, she wrote to her sister. Isabella told Catherine all about the party, especially of meeting the princess and Mr Cleghorn. 'Who would have wagered on a marriage between an older Scottish man and a Hawaiian princess being a successful match, but it evidently is!' she wrote.

It took Isabella about an hour to finish the letter. Her fingers cramped and she stretched them out, blowing on the fresh ink to dry it. Now ready for sleep, she put her pen down, washed the residue ink from her fingers and quietly got into bed. She lay still, covered only by a cotton sheet. A gentle breeze wafted through the open latticed windows. She had felt invigorated meeting such a diverse group of people at the party; they stimulated her with their opinions and experiences of the world, in a way the staid society of north Norfolk never had.

The lack of restrictive social rules on the islands, the laughter-filled, easygoing attitudes of the Hawaiians... It warmed her soul, and she didn't want to leave. Not yet.

Chapter Seventeen

Hawaii, February 1881

Isabella and Eleanor returned to Aolani's house the next day. As they arrived, heavy clouds were moving over the mountain ridge behind the house, but the sky above the ocean was now a deep, vibrant blue. The air was moist after a recent soft rain. It had fallen when they were in the open buggy on the way, but it was so light and the air so warm that it had felt like gentle kisses on the skin. The roadside foliage glistened brightly in the sunlight and a faint rainbow appeared above them in the sky.

'Aloha!' Aolani greeted them from the *lanai* as they arrived in the buggy.

'Good morning,' replied Isabella, noticing how the English welcome seemed substantially less convivial than its Hawaiian counterpart.

Aolani walked to meet them and bent down to kiss Eleanor, before Leilani, in a ball of energy, ran from the house. She embraced Eleanor in a hug before fully stopping and the force toppled them both. The girls collapsed into giggles. Isabella was about to tell Eleanor to get off the ground and to be more ladylike, until she saw that Aolani was laughing too. Two women who had been with Aolani left as Isabella arrived. They were full of smiles, and both wore hats with blossoms around the rim, in a sort of 'hat *lei'*.

Instead of the corset and silk skirts she had worn the night before, Aolani now wore a long, loose-fitting red dress, with a single white blossom tucked behind her right ear. She took Eleanor by the hand and led them into the cool of the house, her strong brown limbs moving slowly and gracefully.

'Aolani, thank you for this invitation. We have been looking forward to it all morning.'

'You must call me Ao,' she said to Isabella. 'And you,' she said, bending down so that she was at eye level with Eleanor, 'you must call me Aunty. Come, we sit, the girls can play outside,' she said, beckoning Isabella to chairs on the *lanai*, before going off to fetch refreshments. Eleanor ran down the coral stone steps with Leilani into the tropical garden.

Isabella felt she could be content just to sit and look at the spectacular perspective from the house. Being elevated meant there was a panoramic view of Honolulu below, the turquoise ocean glittering like an iridescent blanket. Here, it stretched out for as far as the eye could see and took Isabella's breath away. She made a silent prayer of thanks for being allowed to see such beauty on earth.

Aolani came back with water and a plate of cut pineapple.

'What does *aloha* mean? It appears to be more than just hello,' Isabella asked as they ate, the juicy yellow fruit feeling so exotic to her tastebuds.

'Oh, it is our word for everything. It can mean hello, goodbye or love, depending on the situation. It's like this: *Alo* is a word for experiencing and *ha* is the soul. So when we greet each other in love, with *aloha*, we are sharing our spirits. Do you understand?'

'I think so.'

'When my father was dying, he summoned Kainalu, as his firstborn and successor, and passed on his wisdom with his breath, the *ha*.'

Isabella wondered at how painfully sad that moment must have been for Kainalu. 'When was that?'

'He died five years ago. I will always miss him.'

They were both quiet for a while; Isabella did not feel the need to fill the space with conversation, as she did usually.

There was a little brook behind the house and she could hear the shrieks of joy from Leilani and Eleanor paddling in the water.

'Shall we go see?' Aolani asked.

'I think we should,' Isabella said with a laugh, and together they walked down to find the girls. Isabella was tempted to take off her shoes like the children, but refrained. She bent down to touch the thick grass. It was coarser than the English variety, but just as green.

'She is an enchanting little girl,' said Aolani, watching Eleanor.

'Yes, she is. She looks like her mother.' Isabella paused awkwardly. She didn't mean herself, of course, but she hadn't told Aolani about the death of Eleanor's parents.

'She is *hānai*, isn't she?' Aolani asked.

Isabella was about to ask the meaning, but Aolani explained. 'We call adoption *hānai*. It doesn't matter what age the person is, but a family who gives their child to another, that child is then called *hānai*.'

'Now I understand, yes.'

'Eleanor is your *hānai* child, and you can be ours – our English *hānai* princess!'

'I'd like that,' Isabella said, touched that Aolani had accepted her so immediately. Perhaps it was just the Hawaiian way, but it felt so welcoming and free, so unlike the formality of home.

'I was very glad to meet the Fortnums last night,' Isabella said.

'The Fortnums are *haole* like you, but they are loved here as if they were Hawaiian. I like the English very much, that is why I like you and little Eleanor. You English are good, but quiet.'

Isabella laughed. 'It's not so much my nature as my taught sense of propriety. Perhaps we have an ingrained belief that a female is to be quiet... submissive?'

'That is not the Hawaiian way... we women know our voice! But I still want to visit England one day. My family have all been to America, to California, but I would like to make the journey to visit your country. Can we stay with you when we come?'

'Of course, it would be an honour. I live with my parents in a place called Norfolk. We are by the sea too, but the water is very different, or should I say colder, than the Pacific Ocean.'

'I will look and not swim!'

After a while Eleanor and Leilani returned from their games, and the buggy arrived to take Isabella and Eleanor back to the hotel, but not before another invitation was issued for them to come again whenever they wanted.

Aolani's home was a community more fluid than Isabella had ever experienced. The house was always open to visitors, but not in the prescribed way she knew in England. For the Hawaiians, it didn't seem a burden having guests; rather, they were embraced and welcomed to join in normal life, without formality.

In a land where there were no carpets, no fires and no dust, and where there was no need for windows to open and shut, Isabella observed that people seem to live very happily indeed.

There was a note waiting for Isabella back at the hotel. It was from Emma Fortnum.

Dear Miss Buckley,

My husband and I would like to extend an invitation to you and to Eleanor to be our guests and to stay with us in rural Manoa Valley. We miss English company, and it would be wonderful for our sons to have Eleanor to play with, and hopefully teach them to become more gentlemanly. We have a peaceful guest bedroom, and a horse at your disposal. If you can stay, send a note to the address above, and we will come and collect you.

Very best wishes,
Emma Fortnum

Isabella was taken aback at the offer. Her natural inclination was to refuse, embarrassed by the generosity of someone she had only just met. But she had taken an instant liking to Emma, and the hotel was expensive at $3 a night: two reasons why it was tempting to accept. This invitation meant they could remain in Honolulu.

Mrs Fortnum had the familiarity of home with her English sensibilities, and Isabella was sure she and Eleanor would be happy staying with her and her family. So she sat down to write a note accepting the invitation when Mrs Scott and Michael had left Honolulu. Until then, she felt she must stay with them. She also wrote to Elizabeth's father, hoping he had got her first letter. She explained their uncomfortable journey on the *Nevada*, and the feeling she had that it would be good for both of them to stay on a little longer in the Sandwich Islands.

A week later, Isabella and Eleanor went to the harbour to say goodbye to Mrs Scott and Michael. Michael was almost back to full health, although much thinner and weaker than when he had stepped onto the *Nevada* more than a month earlier.

Even though she was sad to see her new friends go, Isabella was relieved not to be getting on the boat with them. She packed Eleanor's and her things and moved to the Fortnums'.

Emma was hungry to hear news from England. It seemed that in her memory it was perpetually bathed in spring light, with only green fields and trees full of blossom.

'Remember the rain? The moody skies? The cold and *drizzle*?' Isabella laughed.

'Yes, but the changes of seasons are wonderful! We don't have that here.'

'You have forgotten what it feels like to be so cold that you have to huddle close to the fire to warm up your numb fingers!'

'Perhaps,' agreed Emma, 'but I still miss it.'

Isabella wondered why she didn't.

Isabella felt at home very quickly with the Fortnums, and Eleanor adored Harry. The Fortnum boys, Horace, Wilbur, Leonard and Harry, ranged from ages fifteen to six. Harry, the six-year-old, was a sensitive child, and while his brothers played rough and tumble, he would happily favour Eleanor. Together they were content to spend hours in make-believe games. They would sit under the shade of the banyon tree and produce a 'food shop' for animals out of leaves, mud, petals, berries and water from the stream. They found old plant pots in which they made the concoctions that probably would have poisoned any animal that had cared to taste them.

As the Fortnums' home was near a stream, there were many mosquitos. Eleanor had welts on her exposed limbs, and they occasionally made her cry in frustration. All Isabella could do was make sure she wore long sleeves, and ensure that they slept under netting. Emma Fortnum produced an oatmeal compress when the bites were particularly itchy. It relieved the discomfort and stopped Eleanor's tears.

Carefree, happy days staying with the Fortnums turned into weeks. Isabella worried that they were outstaying their welcome. She told Emma that they must leave soon.

'Why? Your company is a blessing to us. We have the room and provisions. We love having you both. Honestly, your presence in a house of boys has been a light relief!' said Emma.

Eleanor had made a friend of a bright green gecko that seemed to live in their bedroom. It shyly darted behind the thin cotton curtains and Eleanor patiently waited for it to inquisitively come close.

Most afternoons were spent with Aolani, Leilani and their wider family. Isabella would paint or sketch; there was inspiration all around her. She had been focusing on a series of miniatures of the flora. She loved painting the pink and cream frangipani flower from the tree in Aolani's garden, with its delicate yellow centre; it seemed to grow in every garden in Honolulu, even though Emma, with her interest in gardens, informed Isabella it was not indigenous, but had been brought to the islands by a German twenty years previously.

One morning at Aolani's, while Eleanor was with Leilani, Isabella put up her easel on the *lanai*, to paint the panoramic vista. The valley was surrounded by a mountain ridge with the blue ocean filling the horizon. She spent the whole morning on it, and was only disturbed by Aolani calling her for lunch.

Aolani stood behind Isabella, looking at her work. She was quiet for a while. Isabella tidied up her brushes and threw the paint water over the *lanai* into the grass.

'Loke could paint like that,' Aolani said eventually.

'Who is Loke?' asked Isabella, wondering if it was a cousin she had met already but forgotten the name of.

'Kainalu's wife.'

Isabella fumbled with the brush she was cleaning. 'Kainalu is married?'

'He was... she died.'

'Oh, I am sorry! Was it recently?' Isabella was surprised Kainalu had not mentioned his wife before.

'No, it was a long time now... but he still misses her.'

Aolani sat down on a wicker chair and Isabella sat next to her, cleaning her hands with a cloth.

'What was she like?'

'Lokelani? She was a beautiful person,' Aolani said with a wistful sadness. 'They were friends from childhood and were really like children together, laughing and playing. But it all changed when...' Aolani looked at Isabella, and took an intake of breath. 'Lokelani was suffering from leprosy. We call it *Ma'i pake*. They found out after they were married. We tried to keep it hidden and her death was nothing to do with the disease. Lokelani had problems in childbirth; she lost a lot of blood.' Aolani shook her head at the memory.

'And he never got sick?'

'No, some people don't, I don't know why. He is one of the blessed ones. Kainalu was so helpless when she died... he would walk around with a glazed expression on his face. He went away by himself for many weeks to Maui. When he came back, he had made peace with what had happened. He had an experience on Maui that I know little about. He does not talk of it much, but he was a different man when he returned. His life changed dramatically: before he had been concerned with making money and having as much fun as possible. But after his time in Maui he was focused on others. It is because of this that Kainalu wants to help the lepers on the islands.'

'I had no idea,' Isabella said in a whisper.

'Ladies, we are falling asleep out here,' called Fili from the table at the other side of the house.

Aolani sighed. 'Please don't talk about what I have said.' She stood up, 'Come, let's eat!' She took Isabella's hand, called for Eleanor and Leilani, and they went to join Fili for lunch.

Before the meal was finished, Kainalu arrived at the house. He stood in the frame of the door, smiling at the assembled group.

'I came at the right time,' he said with a laugh.

Aolani smiled at her brother, 'Come, eat!'

'No, I have eaten. I am here to relax. I was up early this morning, and my working day is now done.'

'Can you read to us?' asked Leilani, jumping up to embrace her uncle.

'Later, my little Lei, first let me sit in this chair and close my eyes.'

As lunch disbanded, the *lanai* emptied. Eleanor was with Leilani, and Isabella returned to her painting. She was setting up her easel and paint board when Kainalu came out and joined her.

'Mind if I sit?' he asked.

'Not at all, if you don't mind me painting here?'

'I like it... reminds me of someone. Please carry on.'

Isabella did so and quickly became totally engrossed in her art, but she felt Kainalu's presence near her. His eyes were closed, his head resting on a cushion. He looked asleep, but Isabella knew he wasn't. Neither of them said a word.

Chapter Eighteen

Hawaii, March 1881

Self-conciously, Isabella modelled new Turkish-style riding trousers she'd had made by Emma's dressmaker on Fort Street.

'What do you think?'

'Much better,' Emma said as she pulled the fabric so it hung straight, and then stepped back to admire them again, murmuring her approval. 'What would be scandalous in Norfolk is perfectly acceptable in Hawaii.'

'My mother would be shocked to see me in such an outfit,' Isabella said with a wry smile.

'Well, you can thank the good Lord that she will never see you in it, then, and you'll be much happier being able to ride astride.'

Isabella was about to go inside to change, when there was a call from outside. Kainalu ran up the steps leading to the Fortnums' *lanai*. He appeared, the sun behind him, framed by the wooden pillars holding up the *lanai* roof. Eleanor immediately lept up and ran to him, and he swept her into the air.

'*Aloha*, my English flower!'

When he put her down he smiled at Isabella. 'Very fetching.'

'Thank you, I was about to change.' Isabella blushed, and slunk into the nearest rattan chair, keeping her legs together.

'Where is Leilei?' Eleanor asked.

'Leilei is going on a little holiday, and that is why I came to see you. I wondered if you would like to go too?' Kainalu asked her, and then to Isabella: 'My sister has to go to the Big Island today. Our mother lives in Kona, a small fishing village. I thought it might be an opportunity for you to see more of our islands, and for Eleanor to keep her playmate? I am sorry, it's last minute…'

'Oh, Isabella, you must go,' encouraged Emma.

'How very kind.'

'The inter-island ferry will take you. It will be a three-week trip there and back. I sadly won't be able to join you.'

'Thank you, that would be wonderful. Once again I am in debt to your kindness,' Isabella replied, and realised she was disappointed he was not joining them.

The ferry was leaving in four hours, so Isabella had to hurry to get their things together. She wrote a letter to her parents to explain. She felt guilty postponing her return home and knew these excuses to stay would eventually have to end, but until then she and Eleanor would remain.

The Fortnums were relaxed and accommodating with the new plans, and Emma assured Isabella that they would welcome the two of them on their return.

Watching Isabella pack the small trunk for the journey, Eleanor suddenly understood they would be going on a voyage again. Bursting into tears, she sat on the floor and crossed her arms. 'I don't want to go on a boat!'

Isabella sighed, knowing there would be many more boat journeys to come.

'You want to go on holiday with Leilani, don't you?' she soothed, but Eleanor was not to be won over. She flung herself on the bed and wailed, not letting Isabella come close.

Frustrated and realising she was getting annoyed, Isabella decided to leave her with her tantrum. She shut the door to the bedroom, sat in a chair and waited for the sobs to subside.

Emma heard the commotion. 'Is she alright?'

'I think I just need to wait for her to exhaust herself.'

'Very good, I'll bring you a cup of tea!'

After twenty minutes, Eleanor's cries turned to sniffles, and then silence. A meek voice called out, 'Isabella?'

Isabella opened the door, and peered in to see Eleanor on the floor; her face was red and tear-stained, and her hair was no longer tied neatly in a bow.

'Are you feeling better now?'

'Yes,' came the whispered response. Isabella joined her on the floor.

'Eleanor, will you trust me that this journey will be fun? We will soon be on another island that has a volcano,' she said, pulling the little girl onto her lap.

'Can Harry come?'

'Harry has to do his lessons, but he will be waiting for you to play with him when we get back.'

Eleanor sniffed. 'Very well.'

When they arrived at the wharf a few hours later, there was a dense mass of islanders effusively taking leave of their friends and family. Aolani said the ferry, called the *Kilauea*, was slow and sure, but capable of bearing an infinite amount of battering. This was just as well, as Isabella had heard of swells that could come in and cause the waves around the islands to grow to monstrous heights.

'There are many inter-island schooners, but the *Kilauea* is the only sure mode of reaching the Windward Islands in less than a week. We'll be there by Friday,' Aolani said with a smile of assurance as they boarded. The steamer's deck was already thronging with men, women, children, dogs, cats, mats, calabashes of *poi*, coconuts, bananas and dried fish. Everyone leaving was wreathed and garlanded with beautiful flowers. There was a softly spoken Malay steward on board, who, with infinite goodwill, attended to the comfort of everybody and directed them to their sleeping quarters.

Aolani was still saying goodbye to Fili, with a show of emotion that embarrassed Isabella. She tried not to watch as Aolani was held and kissed by her husband in a way that Isabella's upbringing said should only be done in private. At the same time, if she was honest, her heart longed for the very thing she judged.

'Would you like a mattress on deck or below, madam?' a steward asked Isabella.

Thinking there would be a ladies' cabin, she was surprised at his question. In unhesitating ignorance, she replied severely, 'Below, of course, please.'

Isabella followed him below deck to inspect the berth. Almost immediately her eyes alighted on a cockroach the size of a small mouse occupying the pillow. A companion, not much smaller, was roaming the quilt.

The steward looked at Isabella expectantly, and she was about to accept, thinking it was the only real option, when Aolani appeared.

'We will sleep under the stars,' Aolani whispered into Isabella's ear. She called for the steward to bring mattresses on deck for the four of them.

That evening, Isabella lay sandwiched between the side of the boat and Eleanor as the ferry moved through the night. She saw three shooting stars within minutes of each other, come and gone before she had a chance to wake Eleanor. They felt like an encouragement, a sign from above, perhaps. She was in the right place.

Their first anchor was on the island of Maui, where there seemed to be endless delay. Goods had to be discharged and many islanders disembarked along with their paraphernalia of pets and belongings. The ferry transported post and supplies for the islands, so it was awaited with much excitement. Aolani and Isabella watched the cacophony of noise and movement, to a backdrop of the island's dramatic high-peaked mountain range.

As Aolani had predicted, the *Kilauea* arrived in Kona the following Friday, to the usual greeting from brown bodies in outrigger canoes, islanders swimming in the turquoise ocean, and cheerful welcomes and calls from the wharf. Aolani and Isabella watched the activity from the deck.

'It's good to be in Kona again,' said Aolani. 'My mother will be moving to Honolulu soon, even though she dislikes all the *haoles* there…' She looked at Isabella with an apologetic smile. 'Kona is where her heart is, but three years ago there was a lava outbreak from the Mauna Loa volcano, and it flowed through here. Her home was safe, but five people died and many were made homeless. Then there was a great earthquake wave in Hilo over the other side of the island. It went miles inland and destroyed so much. Mama said she feels my father here, but it's right she comes to live with us.'

Isabella was about to ask if they would be safe on an island with an active volcano, but was distracted by Leilani jumping up and down shouting as she recognised her cousins and grandmother waiting on land.

'Kapuna Wahine!' Leilani cried, pointing to a group who had spotted them too and were now waving. Isabella made out a large and elegant woman. She was dressed formally in a silk dress and had a garland of flowers around her neck.

When they disembarked, Isabella was introduced to her as a traveller from England with her daughter.

'Welcome to Hawaii,' *Kapuna Wahine* said in perfect English. She smiled, but the smile did not reach her eyes. *She doesn't have the same warmth as her daughter and son*, thought Isabella.

Kapuna Wahine didn't ask Isabella any questions; instead, she proceeded to make a fuss of her daughter and Leilani, turning her back on her English guests.

Isabella took Eleanor's hand and smiled at her, feeling confused by the frosty greeting.

They were taken by buggy to a whitewashed wooden house above Kona on Mount Hualalai. The elevation meant the air was cooler, and coffee was being grown on the surrounding hillside. It was a roomy, rambling, wood-frame house with a *lanai*. The door, as was usual, opened directly into the sitting room.

'Mrs Buckley, you and your daughter can stay at my brother's house. It is empty but should be comfortable; it is not far,' said *Kapuna Wahine*.

'No, Mama, they are staying with us!' insisted Aolani.

'There isn't room,' replied her mother, firmly.

Aolani then said something in Hawaiian, and with a shrug of her shoulders, *Kapuna Wahine* said, 'Alright.'

Aolani put her arm around Isabella and said with relaxed good nature, 'It's much better if we're all together, isn't it? Then we can stay one big family.'

She showed Isabella where she and Eleanor would sleep. Isabella was rather alarmed to see that the stairs by which she would get to her bedroom had been removed three inches from the wall.

'We had an earthquake,' Aolani said in explanation, following Isabella's gaze. 'It also brought down the tall chimney of the boilerhouse at the neighbouring plantation. But don't worry, we are not expecting another one tonight!'

As Eleanor clambered up the stairs, Isabella silently hoped that there would not be another tremor, or it would surely remove the stairwell altogether.

'We eat!' called *Kapuna Wahine*, when everyone's things had been brought inside.

As if in agreement, Isabella heard her stomach rumble. They hadn't eaten since breakfast, and it was now four o'clock.

The meal consisted of sweet potato and *poi* with fried fish. '*Poi* comes in various consistencies and is given a name from the number of fingers needed to eat it – three finger, two finger, or the thickest, one finger *poi*,' Aolani explained as Isabella ate.

'This must be three finger *poi*?'

'Exactly!'

Isabella ate with the girls and cousins all chirping like little birds. When they had finished eating, Aolani and her mother went out on the *lanai*. Isabella was conscious that she could still hear their conversation, and tried not to listen in.

'Why did you bring a *haole* tourist?' *Kapuna Wahine* said in an audible whisper.

'Mama, she is a *friend*,' Aolani replied.

They started speaking in Hawaiian, but Isabella recognised her name. She looked away as they both came into the room, afraid the expression on her face would give away that she had heard their conversation.

'We are going to pick coconuts, come and watch!' cried Leilani, unaware that she had defused whatever tension was growing between *Kapuna Wahine* and her mother.

Isabella, grateful to leave the room, followed Leilani and Eleanor to a tree outside the house. Kahaia, a nimble cousin, climbed up a curved trunk with a knife in his mouth. He cut off a coconut and then threw it to the ground to shouts of joy from the children. Kahaia climbed down and opened it up. He sliced the top off and let everyone sip the cool coconut water. The children then feasted on the coconut flesh.

Isabella was thinking how lucky Eleanor was to experience such a thing, when Aolani appeared at her side.

'Come, let me show you where the horses are, so we can go for a ride,' she said, taking Isabella by the arm. Isabella was grateful, ready for some exercise and eager to see more of the island.

'Can I come with you?' asked Eleanor, who had overheard.

'You will have much more fun here, Eleanor,' Isabella paused, then added, 'And it would be very uncomfortable for you sitting on my horse.' She bent down to push a strand of hair behind Eleanor's ear, and kissed her forehead.

'Alright, but can you tell me a story afterwards?'

'Of course. I'll be back shortly, my darling.'

On the way to the stables, Isabella had a change of heart. 'Aolani, do you mind if I don't go for a ride? I feel that I should stay with Eleanor.'

'She is happy with the *keiki*. Come! It will be good for you to have a gallop…' Aolani replied, picking up a heavy saddle.

Isabella still felt uneasy. She wanted to please Aolani, but there was something nagging at her.

'I know, but she is so attached to me, and her parents' death was so recent. I know it is silly…'

Aolani placed the saddle back on the post. 'You are her mother, so you know what is best for her. We can ride another time.'

When Eleanor saw Isabella returning, she left the other children and ran to her, putting her arms around her waist and pressing her cheek against Isabella's stomach.

Later that evening, Isabella put Eleanor to bed.

'Can I have a story?' Eleanor asked.

'Of course, what would you like it to be about?'

'Mama and Papa,' Eleanor said quietly.

So Isabella reminded her of her mother's kindness and how her father had loved her. She recounted memories Elizabeth had told her of when Eleanor was born, how she was such a tiny baby they wondered if she would survive the cold winter of her birth. She told Eleanor about England and the things she loved about home. Isabella had already talked a lot about Catherine and her parents. She hoped it would mean that when Eleanor finally met her family, she would feel as if she knew them.

Eleanor was almost asleep when Isabella finished whispering tales from her past. The child had a smile on her face as she dozed off. As Isabella watched Eleanor's sleeping body, her cheeks flushed and brown hair ruffled, she felt overwhelmed by a feeling of love and protectiveness for the little girl.

The next day, a large party went to a beautiful little cove. The light was dappled between palm fronds, and the gentle breeze meant it was comfortable to sit in the shade. The sea was a transluscent turquoise, and although they were surrounded by black volcanic rock, the little bay had a sandy path into the sea. The Hawaiians all took to the water straight away.

'Your people are truly amphibious,' Isabella laughed to Aolani. 'Both sexes swim so naturally.'

'This ocean is our playground,' Aolani said, looking at the children splashing in the shallows. Even though Isabella had her bathing dress and trousers with her, she watched the swimmers from the shade of a palm. Aolani and *Kapuna Wahine* sat with her. She breathed in the warm sea air and laughed as she watched Eleanor and the children enjoying themselves. It felt like a dream; life in Hawaii seemed to be one long, relaxing afternoon; the sea was so blue, the sunlight so soft, the air sweet. There was no toil or rush.

Aolani went to lie in the shallows with the children, letting the gentle waves push the water over her body like a blanket. She wore a long loose dress, not a woollen bathing costume like Isabella had, but had not yet worn. Isabella did not feel the same freedom as the Hawaiian women, and stayed under the tree, wishing she was braver. She had tried to articulate her feelings in a letter home to Catherine:

> *I still feel the ingrained need to keep up appearances. It is not an easy thing to shed a lifetime of training about what is and isn't acceptable behaviour for a woman.*

It was only Isabella and *Kapuna Wahine* left under the shade of the palm. *Kapuna Wahine* was a woman of few words and Isabella felt uncomfortable in her presence, so she filled in the silences with whatever she could think of to say.

'You have lovely children; you must be very proud of Aolani and Kainalu.'

Kapuna Wahine gave a slight nod in reply.

Isabella wished she had brought a book with her. Without anything to occupy herself, she felt she must try harder with conversation. 'Do you miss them when they are not with you?'

Kapuna Wahine sighed, as if the question tired her. 'Yes.'

They lapsed into silence again. As a final offering Isabella deferred to an English person's favourite topic, the weather. 'Lovely sunshine you're having.'

There was another long pause. Isabella felt more and more uncomfortable.

Eventually *Kapuna Wahine* spoke. Her voice was low and precise. Her words were like stones thrown into the ocean as they came out of her mouth. 'The weather must be an interesting topic of conversation in England. Not here.'

'Yes, of course...' Isabella glanced at *Kapuna Wahine*'s face. It was impenetrable.

Silence reigned once more.

Chapter Nineteen

Honolulu, April 1881

When it was time to return to Honolulu, *Kapuna Wahine* travelled with her daughter and Isabella on the *Kilauea* – preparing to move permanently to Oah'u. She showed some softening towards Eleanor, and even smiled when the little girl sang a Hawaiian song Leilani had taught her. There was no such grace with Isabella, and she felt a weight of pressure lift as Fili drove her and Eleanor back to the Fortnums'.

Emma Fortnum came out to meet Isabella and Eleanor as the buggy drove into her driveway. Eleanor was so excited to see the boys, she jumped down from the buggy and ran past Emma straight into the house calling, 'Harry!'

Emma raised her eyes at Isabella. 'Someone is pleased to be back!'

'I'm sorry, I must teach her some manners.'

Fili laughed. 'If you are worried about her manners, you'll need to teach the whole island your English ways.' He flicked the reins and the horse trotted on. 'Let her be free!' he called over his shoulder.

'Eleanor is just fine,' Emma said, and then looked Isabella up and down. 'You look wonderful, full of health… Now, some post has arrived for you.'

Once they were inside, Emma gave Isabella a pile of letters that had been stacked on a side table. Isabella's heart leapt. Although she wrote to them, her parents and Catherine had in truth been far from her mind recently. She was preoccupied with Eleanor and content in Hawaii. But now the letters had arrived, she suddenly felt a surge of homesickness.

There were six letters in all, all of them months old. Three were from Isabella's parents, three from Catherine. They had been sent weeks apart but had been delivered together, having travelled from the Hunts' guesthouse in New Zealand to the Honolulu Hotel. Isabella had sent a telegram to the Hunts with the address to forward mail to.

The first letter Isabella opened was from her parents; it had information about Aunt Emily and Uncle Hamish. Although they were not home by the date the letter was written, they had given news that they were on their way, and would be back on English soil in a couple of weeks.

> *This is wonderful as it means your hasty return to us. We are sorry that you had to make the journey for a wasted reason, but our hope is that it will have been of some benefit to you. Please let us know the steamer you will be on, and the time of your intended arrival.*

Isabella's heart sank as she realised she was disappointing her parents by not getting on the next boat home. Her family did not know about Eleanor yet, as there was no mention of her in the letters. Isabella wondered afresh how they would take the news. Putting her mother's letter aside, Isabella sliced open Catherine's letters with the Fortnums' silver letter opener. They were each pages long, telling her in detail what had been happening in her life. The last letter brought tears to her eyes:

> *William kindly went for a walk with me on the weekend. It was a sunny day and we went to Holkham beach. My dear sister, he told me of his love for you, and that his heart is yours. I know you think I will be devastated to hear this news, but in truth I was not so surprised, and I couldn't think of a better man to be with my sister. I don't know if you love him too, as you never gave anything away, but I want you to know that you have my blessing. You cannot make someone love you, and William does not love me. I will have to learn to live with it.*

There is still so much good in my life. I am so looking forward to your return.

Isabella felt pained. Catherine made light of the situation but Isabella knew this was her way. She would have put the rejection aside and told herself she was not good enough for William anyway. Isabella hated that she was not there to tell her sister that was a lie.

Thinking about how she would reply to Catherine, Isabella followed Eleanor's calls into the garden. The air was rich with the peaty smell of soil and wet foliage after a brief rain shower. As she was walking outside, she bumped into Mr Fortnum coming from his study.

'Isabella, I wonder if it would be an idea for you to register your passports at the British Consulate, as you are staying for longer, we hope? It is not the law, but the British consul to Hawaii recommends it.'

'Yes, of course. When should I go?'

'Why not now? I can accompany you if you like; it won't take long.'

'If Emma doesn't mind watching Eleanor...'

'Doesn't mind? She'd adopt that little girl herself if she could!'

Isabella went back to the room to get the two single-sheet, hand-drafted paper documents from the secret pocket her mother had secured into her canvas holdall. Eleanor was with Harry, so she had a word with Emma, and left them playing. Mr Fortnum was already in the buggy.

Isabella enjoyed the journey into town, sitting in the buggy and travelling between the palms that lined the streets of Honolulu, a couple of miles from the meadowy Manoa Valley. The trees towered over everything except the church spires in the town, and the streets were a hive of activity with horses and carriages. As they were nearing Iolani Palace, 'the hallmark of Hawaiian Renaissance architecture', Mr Fortnum told her, there was a loud boom.

'Ah, there's the cannon. Must be for an approaching mailboat. Just you wait, in a couple of hours there will be a crowd at the post office on the corner of Merchant and Bethel Streets. The roads will be deserted for a few hours while everyone reads the foreign newspapers and correspondence that has come through!'

Isabella's heart leapt. She knew she had just received post, but maybe more would come on this boat?

There were a few clouds in the sky to shelter them from the sun. Isabella had given up holding her parasol and sat with hands on her lap, enjoying the view.

Once at the consulate, the business of administration was quick and easy. As they were coming out of the two-storey stone building, Isabella looked left down the street and realised Kainalu was walking towards them. He seemed lost in thought. Mr Fortnum saw him too. 'Mr Okalani! Whatever are you doing at the British Consulate?'

Kainalu came back from wherever he was in his reverie, and smiled when he saw them.

'*Aloha!* I am actually about to ride to Kalihi. I am trying to find a solution to something.'

'Can we help?' Isabella asked.

'I don't know…'

'Well, how about we have a drink at the Hawaiian Hotel and discuss the matter?' Mr Fortnum suggested.' We're in no hurry, are we, Isabella?'

She shook her head.

'*Mahalo*, friend, but I don't have long. I will need to get to Kalihi by three o'clock.'

'There'll be enough time,' said Mr Fortnum with confidence.

Kainalu smiled and nodded.

As soon as they were settled with their drinks, Mr Fortnum asked, 'So, tell us, what is happening at Kalihi?'

Kainalu stretched out his legs and rubbed his eyes wearily. 'It's not so much what is happening. My concern is not only for the welfare of the lepers, but also for their families. It's like this:

once the sick person goes to the colony on Moloka'i, their families, in all likelihood, will never see them again. They can't afford a photograph or a portrait to remember them.' He sighed. 'I know it seems a small thing, but being able to remember the face of the one you love is significant.'

Mr Fortnum was silent. Isabella was fascinated.

'I have been mulling it over, how best to help remember the lepers. Our world calls them outcasts, cursed, but to their families they are obviously as precious as the day they were born, perfect and free from the disease.'

Isabella heard herself speaking. She wanted to stop herself, to think more on what she was offering, but the words came out. 'Kainalu… I can paint portraits.'

'I saw your landscape, and that was impressive. I did not know you could paint portraits as well.'

'Albeit not as the Old Masters, but I am able to copy a certain likeness.' She paused; his eyes were on her. 'Would you like me to paint the portraits of the lepers before they leave?'

What am I saying?

'First-class idea! Get Isabella to paint them. That is… if it's safe?' Mr Fortnum said.

Kainalu played his fingers on the table and looked at her. 'Thank you, Isabella. It will be safe. I have to get permission, but I think this is a wonderful turn of events. How serendipitous to meet you both today.' He stopped, and to Isabella's surprise he closed his hand over her own. 'Isabella, I will confirm by tomorrow, but I am most grateful for your offer.' Perhaps sensing the anxiety behind her smile, he said, 'The mechanism of transmission of leprosy has yet to be fully made clear, but malnutrition, prolonged close contact and transmission by nasal droplets all seem to be causes for the transference of the disease. Isabella, you won't be close enough to them or with them long enough to be in danger.'

'That is reassuring, thank you,' Isabella said.

They talked a little longer, until their meeting had to disband, each returning to the duties of the day.

Mr Fortnum went to the post office and came back with post for the family, and with a letter for Isabella. She saw from the handwriting it was William, and did not want to open it straight away.

The next day the Fortnums prepared a celebration lunch for Isabella and Eleanor's return. Their cook baked bread made from Californian flour, along with stewed beef, sweet potatoes and boiled *kalo*. Island coffee was served after sliced guavas eaten with milk and sugar, which Eleanor declared were 'scrumptious'.

After a little while Isabella went out to take Eleanor for a nap, and decided she would have a rest too. The sun was high in the sky but there was a gentle breeze in the air, which made the heat comfortable. Their room was light and airy, and the covered *lanai* around the house kept out the direct sunlight from the windows.

As Eleanor slept, Isabella sat in an armchair in the bedroom and opened William's correspondence, pulling out a two-page letter on thick, cream-coloured manila paper.

My dear Isabella,

I was not going to write to you, as after declaring my position, I felt there was nothing more to say. However, recently I was made aware by your father that Catherine might be holding a light for me. I am sure you know all about this, and I wondered if your refusal to me was because of it. If so, I respect you all the more. I hope you will not be angry, but I felt I had to tell Catherine of my feelings for you, so as to let her down gently. I do admire her greatly, but I feel you and I have a likemindedness that is rare among people. I am sorry to burden you with this, now that you are so far away, but I think it is important you know: I will be here on your return, and my heart will not have changed.

Isabella left the letter on her lap and looked out of the window, the view at one moment hidden and at the next revealed by the white curtain fluttering in the warm breeze. She knew that her heart had also not changed.

While still thinking of William, she wrote to Catherine to let her know the truth.

Dearest Catherine,

I am so very sorry for how the situation has turned out. I never loved William as you love him, and it was very hard for me when I knew his feelings. I still believe you two are better suited, but he does not see it, so I must put away the desire to see you both as husband and wife. I pray you will find happiness with another, and that your friendship with William will still be a blessing, he is such a dear man.

My time in Hawaii is opening up horizons that I have never known before, ways of living that seem so free and exciting. I am relishing the new experiences, and Eleanor is very happy too.

Just as she finished her correspondence to Catherine, Eleanor awoke. Isabella put down her pen and took her outside to read a book on the *lanai*.

Chapter Twenty

Hawaii, April 1881

Isabella entertained and was entertained by Eleanor the next day. She watched the little girl dance and play, and answered her innumerable questions, but her mind often wandered with a certain amount of anxiety to the appointment at the leper station with Kainalu.

He arrived with news after lunch. He didn't get off his horse, but called for Isabella.

'This is just a brief visit. Are you still happy to paint the lepers?'

Isabella looked up at him, shielding her eyes from the sun. 'Yes.' She was about to add her concerns, but he replied too quickly.

'I am indebted to you. I have three at Kalihi I would like you to work on, before they go to Moloka'i. Two are children, and their families will be so grateful for the gift. I can collect you tomorrow morning at eight, if that is not too early a start?'

Kainalu's horse was frisky and wouldn't stand still. He held the reins tight, turning the gelding back to face Isabella.

Eleanor ran out from the house to join them and took Isabella's hand as she looked up at Kainalu.

He smiled at her, and then said to Isabella, 'I wanted to give you more clarity on leprosy; is it alright if I explain?'

Isabella looked down at Eleanor and then back at him, and nodded.

'We believe the disease is transferred through bodily fluids. It is estimated that owing to genetic factors, only 5 per cent of the population are susceptible to leprosy. This is mostly because the body is naturally immune to the bacteria.'

'What is bacteria?' Eleanor enquired of Isabella.

'I'll explain later,' she said gently, and then to Kainalu, 'That is good to know. I will check that Eleanor can be looked after, and if so, tomorrow it is.'

'I admire you choosing to help. I will bring Leilani to play with her while you are working.'

'Leilani!' Eleanor brightened at the name of her friend.

'Do you need any paints or paper? I can get you supplies as well.'

'I am running low on blue and white oils – if you could get those colours, I should have sufficient,' she replied, grateful that he had asked.

'Isabella, let me give you my thanks now for offering to paint our forgotten ones.'

She was about to interject, and tell him it was nothing.

'There is one child in particular… she is very close to my heart; I feel responsible for her. Her name is Maima. To give her parents a portrait of their daughter would be a wonderful thing.'

'Of course,' Isabella said, thinking how special this girl must be – she had his love.

That evening Isabella stayed up with the light of a flickering candle, finishing the letters that she wanted to send on the next mail boat. As it was the hardest, she left William's letter till last.

Dear William,

Thank you for your kind and candid letter. I am well, and as you may have heard, now have a daughter! Eleanor is four years old and very sweet. Despite the tragic circumstances of my guardianship of her, she is a gift to me, and I love her very much. I heard from Catherine the news of your conversation; she wrote a letter and was very gracious. William, please do not wait for me. I do not know when we will be home and I am sorry to say that my heart will never be yours in that way, although in friendship you will always be held in my highest esteem.

At present we are happily ensconced on the Sandwich Islands – or Hawaii – in the Pacific, and have not set a date to return. I wonder if you might reconsider your affections towards my sister? Catherine is one of the most wonderful people on this earth, selfless and kind. She would make the most companionable wife, and her heart, I am sure, is still yours. Please think again.

Affectionately yours,

Isabella

Isabella left the envelope unsealed so that she could reread her words in the morning. Exhausted, she fell asleep as the hallway clock struck two in the morning. She woke just before six and, although heavy with tiredness, went to the light of the window to reread her letter to William. Satisfied, she sealed the envelope.

Eleanor was still asleep, so Isabella got dressed and walked through the quiet house and out the front door. The day was already beautiful; it had rained in the night, and the air was filled with the scent of frangipani blossoms from the trees surrounding the house.

Isabella decided to take a walk down the Manoa lanes. As she walked, she felt a sudden desire to pray. She prayed for William and Catherine and for Eleanor, that she would have a blessed life, and that she herself would be the best mother she could be.

She turned back to the house feeling lighter and more hopeful, and went to wake Eleanor for breakfast. Eleanor was up already when she entered the room, sitting on her bed playing with her ragdoll.

'Are you my mama now?' she asked when she saw Isabella. Isabella sat on the bed and gently stroked the hair away from Eleanor's forehead.

'Your mama is in heaven, and I am going to do the best job I can to fill her shoes. But she was very wonderful, and I have never been a mother before, so you have to help me.'

Eleanor crawled into Isabella's lap and put her arms around her neck. 'I think you are doing very well, Mama Isabella.'

Tears welled up in Isabella's eyes and she kissed Eleanor's head.

The whole Fortnum family were up for breakfast, which was unusual as Mr Fortnum had normally left for work before they ate.

'Are you portrait-painting today?' he asked Isabella.

Emma interjected, 'My dear, Charlie said about your painting. How very noble of you.'

'Not at all. I am a little nervous, actually,' Isabella said.

'You'll have Kainalu with you; you won't have to worry,' Mr Fortnum encouraged. 'But I hope you will not find the lepers too shocking. There is a reason they are called outcasts of society. Often their form is so disfigured it is quite disturbing.'

When the call came that Kainalu had arrived, Isabella was already wearing her riding clothes. Her painting equipment was strapped to the Fortnums' chestnut mare that she had been lent. She said goodbye to Eleanor as Leilani came running to find her. The girls sat down to play with their dolls on the *lanai* with Emma nearby. Satisfied they were content and had all they needed, Isabella went to meet Kainalu on his horse.

He was looking up at a bird circling overhead, but turned as he heard her footsteps. He smiled when he saw her.

'Are you ready?'

'Yes,' Isabella replied, but could not hide her uncertainty.

'Don't be afraid, Isabella. Their sores will be bandaged, and most of the worst cases are already in Moloka'i, so you won't see anything grotesque.'

How did he know? She mounted her horse and followed Kainalu out of the gate.

As they rode past the harbour, the *Kilauea* was waiting at the dock, taking passengers. There was the usual hustle and bustle of trade and activity with the loading-up of the ferry, but amidst the noise, Isabella shuddered when someone let out a loud, heart-wrenching cry of mourning. A group of Hawaiian men and women were howling in despair on the dockside. They seemed inconsolable.

'What is going on?' Isabella asked Kainalu.

He sighed, shaking his head. 'There's a group of forty lepers from Kalihi going to Kalaupapa on the boat today; those people you see are their families saying goodbye. The lucky ones have a *kōkua* to go with them, but it is rare.'

'What is a *kōkua*?'

'It means helper – they can be a spouse or family member. They have to willingly go into isolation with the leper. It is the ultimate expression of love, the ultimate sacrifice. I am humbled by them.'

Isabella felt voyeuristic witnessing such raw declarations of loss and grief. She hadn't seen anything like it before, and it caused a heaviness on the top of her chest, a pressure that she wanted to flee from. She didn't want to see this pain, feeling so helpless to do anything.

'Can we walk on?' she asked Kainalu.

'Of course. It doesn't get easier to see,' he said, as he kicked his horse into a trot away from the commotion.

Isabella followed. 'Are they all alone? Will anyone help them when they get to the colony?' she asked when they had gone about mile, and the horses fell into a walk side by side.

'They take supplies with them and the government sends food, but they are encouraged to grow their own crops. Because of the lack of general oversight and medical support, alcoholism has taken over and there have been some sad reports of goings-on. Many say they feel they are in a prison with nothing to live for because Kalaupapa is cut off from any other civilisation. Sometimes I think I should live there for a time, as how else can I make a difference?'

Isabella looked at him aghast.

Kainalu smiled at her reaction. 'There is some encouragement, though; a noble instance of devotion has been given by a Belgian priest. His name is Father Damien. He came nearly ten years ago to spend his life on Kalaupapa to remarkable effect.'

'And is he well? Has he contracted the disease? Surely he is at terrible risk?'

'From what I know, the priest is disease-free. Some nuns have been sent to work with him as well; they are stringent with hygiene. They have not contracted the disease.'

Once they got to the Kalihi receiving station, the gate was opened by a guard who recognised Kainalu. He stared unabashedly at Isabella, but let her pass. The receiving station was a series of small buildings with tin roofs.

'Here, why don't you set up under the tree, and I will collect Maima,' Kainalu said.

As he left, Isabella looked around. The place seemed eerily quiet; she could only see two men sitting under the shade of a *lanai* on one of the buildings. Their bodies did not appear to show the disease. Isabella wondered if they were staff. They did not seem bothered by her. Kainalu was right, she saw nothing grotesque, but she did not want to enter the buildings and see what was in their dark halls.

Kainalu reappeared, carrying two chairs and followed by a lively looking girl, skipping next to him in a long red dress. Her brown, silky hair was down to her waist.

'Let me introduce, Maima,' he said, once they were close. 'Maima, this is Miss Buckley. She has come all the way from England to paint your portrait!'

'Me, Uncle?' Maima's eyes widened.

'Maima, it is very nice to meet you. You can call me Isabella.'

The girl was shyly watching her, still about ten feet away.

Maima did not seem like a leper. Her face was perfect, her skin a beautiful copper colour, and her eyes large and dark.

'Now, I am going to paint you, so you must stay very still. Do you think you can do that?' Isabella said, smiling at her.

Maima looked at Kainalu and ruffled her nose. He laughed. 'I will read to you as Isabella paints, then you won't get bored.'

162

Kainalu fished a book out of his jacket pocket, and Maima sat on the floor, resting her head on the chair. Isabella prepared the paper, smiling encouragingly at Maima. From the Fortnums' she had bought a jar of water to clean her brushes, but decided to start with some charcoal sketches first.

Kainalu sat with his back against the tree trunk and began to read. He spoke clearly and slowly, and soon Maima was engrossed in the story. Isabella watched her and sketched. She stole glances at Kainalu, and laughed as he spoke in a high-pitched voice for a female character in his story. They were together for more than an hour, when Isabella realised Maima had fallen asleep. She caught Kainalu's eye and they both smiled.

'I think that is time for today,' he said quietly, walking over to inspect her work. 'You don't mind, do you?' he asked, before looking.

'Not at all.'

'Isabella, these are excellent. I don't think you need to do a painting. These sketches are such a good likeness I can give them to her parents, if you are happy with that decision?'

'Yes, of course.'

Kainalu gently woke up Maima, and Isabella showed her the sketches. She asked to keep one.

'Which one would you like?'

'This one,' Maima said, pointing to the one sketch where Isabella had coloured in her red dress. They said their goodbyes, and Kainalu took Maima back inside.

Isabella had enjoyed sketching again, and Maima was a beautiful subject. *To feel useful is a wonderful thing*, she thought.

'Now, you must need some refreshment; are you hungry?' Kainalu asked, when they were back on their horses. She was both hungry and thirsty.

About a mile from Kalihi, they dismounted and tied their horses at a little stall on the roadside selling pineapple. Kainalu paid the vendor more than he was asked, and the man looked overjoyed at his profit.

'Pineapple was introduced by the Spanish a few decades ago, and we are forever grateful,' Kainalu said as he gave Isabella her portion. The fruit was so ripe that they were left with sticky fingers, and pineapple juice dripping down their chins.

'My, it's even better than the watermelon at the beach!' Isabella said as she wiped her face with the back of her hand.

They returned to the horses and were quiet for the remainder of the ride home.

'Thank you for being willing to draw Maima. I am grateful,' Kainalu said, as they arrived at the Fortnums'. They both dismounted, and there was a moment of silence between them. They stood with their horses, Isabella waiting for Kainalu to say something, but before he could, Leilani ran from the house.

The moment was gone, and Kainalu jumped back on his horse. He lifted Leilani into his saddle to sit in front of him. Isabella looked up at Kainalu, but his face was set, as if deep in thought. He gave her a nod and wave, and then was off down the road they had just come by. Isabella was disquieted by his quick exit, and wondered if she had offended him in some way.

Chapter Twenty-one

Hawaii, May 1881

On Isabella's second visit to Kalihi, the day was overcast and humid. Thick cloud gathered over the mountains and the air was heavy with expectant rain. It was Isabella's birthday, but she hadn't told anyone. She was now thirty-eight. At her age she had felt so long on the shelf as to be gathering dust. But now, in Hawaii, it was different. She had lived a lifetime in the last few months, and having Eleanor to look after meant she had someone else to focus on, and it was a blessed relief.

Maima sat watching Isabella as she painted a boy of about fifteen. His brown hair was long and loose around his shoulders, and he had the beginnings of a moustache. His left hand was bandaged, and there was another on his neck. The boy would not look at Isabella as she set to work, which she found disconcerting; he would avert his eyes. Maima, sitting near her, seemed captivated by how Isabella's brushstrokes could come together to form such a likeness to the sitter.

Kainalu stayed with them at the beginning, sitting behind Isabella and watching her work. She felt self-concious initially, but then the painting absorbed her, and she forgot his presence. So much so, that when she turned around to ask how much longer they had, she was surprised to see he had gone.

'Did you see where Uncle went?' she asked Maima.

The girl shrugged her shoulders and shook her head.

Isabella returned to her painting, but noticed two men who had come in through the front gate. They staggered drunkenly together towards one of the houses, until one of them saw Isabella under the tree.

'Ey, *haole*, what you doin' here?' he shouted, leaving his friend and walking towards her.

Isabella felt a flush of nervous anxiety, but ignored him, carrying on with her painting as if she hadn't heard.

'Ey! I'm talkin' to you!' he persisted.

Isabella pursed her lips and turned to look at the man, her heart beating faster.

'You a leper too? Can't be here if you not,' he snarled.

He was close now. Isabella saw he was probably in his fifties. His hair was unkempt and he walked with a limp. She felt the boy and Maima tense up, both looking at her.

'Please leave us be. I am working,' she said primly, her voice a little too high, and not at all as commanding as she had hoped.

'Working? Let me see your *work*.' The man picked up the canvas, now standing inches from Isabella. She could smell the liquour seeping out with the sweat from his pores. He looked at the picture, and then spat in her direction, spittle hit Isabella's cheek. She recoiled in horror. The man turned and laughed. Maima jumped up, hiding behind Isabella; the boy had already run into one of the houses.

For a moment Isabella thought he was going to spit again, but she saw Kainalu walking fast towards them.

'Hey!' he shouted.

When he got close, he stood face to face with the drunk. Kainalu was a good few inches taller, and used his height to his advantage.

'What's going on?'

'What do you care?' the man sneered, but with less confidence than before.

'It's time for you to go inside. *Now*.'

The man stood his ground, challenging Kainalu's authority, but then he seemed to think better of it. He dropped the canvas at his feet and it fell face down on the sandy soil.

'Fine by me, I'm hungry anyway; got to eat some *haole* food,' he said, turning to Isabella with a look of disdain, but he walked away, turning back when he got close to the building and laughing in a mocking way.

'I'm sorry, Isabella. Maima.'

Isabella was shaking.

'I think that's time for today. Maima, let me take you back.'

Maima waved goodbye, and Isabella began to pack up her things. As she gathered the paper, she watched Maima follow Kainalu closely until they entered one of the houses. Isabella scanned the area around her; she was alone, which made her uncomfortable, but she knew Kainalu would not be long. When he returned, he had a look of concern on his face.

'Isabella, again, I am sorry. Come, let's take you to the water.'

He put his hand on her lower back to guide her towards an outside tap. Pulling a hankerchief from his pocket, he turned on the tap and rinsed the cloth. Gently he took Isabella's face in his hand, and slowly wiped her cheek, cleaning off any residue from the man's outburst. She felt self-concious at such intimacy, but her surprise stopped her from refusing his care. All she knew was that her whole body was responding to his touch. If felt as if something had awoken in her and she did not know where to look or what to say when he had finished. He seemed to feel it was completely natural. Isabella smoothed down her skirts, hunting for something to talk about.

'I was thinking…'

'Yes?'

'Can I get some paper and paints for Maima, in order to teach her as I paint?'

'Of course.' Kainalu rewashed and wrung out his hankerchief. 'We can bring them next time.'

The thought of 'next time' made Isabella happy but nervous. She could see the visits to Kalihi with Kainalu becoming the highlight of her time in Hawaii, but with the man's outburst, they had lost a sense of safety.

On their ride home, Kainalu kept his horse at a walk.

'The man you met today is a perfect example of the problem we are facing. He keeps running away and infecting people. We can't lock him up in chains, but something needs to be done. It's not working here at Kalihi...' He looked across at Isabella. 'Do you mind me speaking to you about all of this?'

'Not at all. I am interested. Now I have met the people you are talking about, it makes it easier for me to understand.'

'It is one way to humanise the lepers – to get to know them and their stories. It is the way of compassion, and that is the direction I want us, the Hawaiian people, to take.'

'We often prefer the sick to be out of sight, and therefore out of mind. If we can't see, then we don't have to act,' Isabella reflected.

'We have to move the lepers to quarantine; the result is that they are out of sight, but it is not because we want them out of mind.'

'I know, I didn't mean that...' said Isabella, berating herself for not explaining what she meant better.

Kainalu looked ahead, but kept his horse close to Isabella's. Their feet and legs sometimes touched as the horses walked parallel.

'You are right. Human nature is not naturally altruistic. We need grace to put others first.' He laughed self-deprecatingly. 'Here I am talking like I have mastered this, and how far off I am...'

'If *you* are far off, there is little hope for the rest of us!'

'Would you be available to return next Friday? I think I can get the supplies for Maima by then.'

'I will check with Emma. Could Eleanor perhaps visit Aolani and Leilani while we are gone?'

'Of course, I will arrange it all, and be with you on Friday morning.'

Their horses fell into a trot, and Kainalu left Isabella at the driveway to the Fortnums' with a wave.

For their third visit to Kalihi, Eleanor had said she wanted to come.

'It is not safe for you, and you will be bored.'

'I *won't* be bored. I want to paint with you,' insisted Eleanor.

When Kainalu arrived, Isabella asked him if Eleanor would be allowed to come with them.

'To get permission for a healthy child to go onto the grounds would be impossible. Shall I explain to her?'

'If you would like to, but you don't need to...'

'I'll do it,' he said with a smile. 'Where is she?'

'In the garden.'

Kainalu walked down to meet Eleanor. When she saw him she came running.

'Can't I come with you?' she asked, flinging her arms around his legs.

Isabella watched from the back *lanai*. Kainalu sat down on the grass, and Eleanor sat next to him.

'I am afraid not, my princess, there are strict rules and regulations I have to follow. The people in Kalihi are sick and the sickness is contagious, which means it is easy for others to catch. We have to have special permission to go in, and to keep Isabella safe she has to follow their guidelines. It's not very fun for a little girl.'

Eleanor pouted, but she did not argue.

'Would you like to go to the ocean with Aunty Aolani and Leilani?'

'Now?'

'Yes, but you'd better be quick, they will be here soon!'

Eleanor jumped up. 'I am ready!'

Kainalu laughed, and stood up. Taking her hand, they walked back towards Isabella.

Isabella's heart swelled as she watched the interaction. For a moment she allowed herself to wonder at Kainalu being a father to Eleanor and a husband to herself. She blushed at the thought as the two walked towards her.

Once Eleanor was with Aolani and Leilani, Kainalu and Isabella set off for Kalihi. The sun was already hot, and Isabella was grateful for the shade of the banyan tree to paint under, and the breeze coming in from the ocean.

Maima ran to them as soon as they arrived.

'Can I watch?' she asked, quietly.

'Of course,' Isabella said.

'And we have something for you,' Kainalu announced, taking out a package from his saddlebag and handing it to Maima. The girl's eyes grew large as she opened it up and found the paper and paints. 'For me?'

Kainalu nodded.

'I can give you a little lesson as I paint, if you like,' Isabella said.

Maima hugged the open package to her chest.

Two chairs were found for them, but Maima preferred to sit on the ground. This time the subject was a man in his forties. He had a black beard and a bulbous growth on his nose. He had lost his left foot to the disease and so walked with crutches. He did not speak much, but he carried an air of hopelessness and depression that made Isabella want to weep.

'I am sorry, I will have to leave you for a moment, as I have a meeting with the superintendent. Will you be alright?' Kainalu asked, when she had started painting.

'Of course,' Isabella replied.

Maima sat with her new pad of paper, experimenting with the paints. Isabella, aware of any movement from the buildings, was distracted by the fear that she might be accosted again.

However, she was not disturbed, and when she finished her work, she laid the painting out on the ground for her sitter to see.

He looked in silence for a long time.

Isabella waited, and then realised that tears were running down his cheeks.

'I am sorry,' she said falteringly.

'Don't be sorry, lady. I cry for this picture will go to my wife and my children, and I will not.'

'Are you going to Kalaupapa soon?' she asked.

'Yes, next boat out.'

They continued to look at the painting, with nothing more to say, and Isabella was relieved when Kainalu came back.

'Finished?' he asked cheerfully, and then seeing the work on the floor he stooped down to take a closer look. 'Exceptional. We'll make sure your family gets this, Kanoa. You won't be forgotten.'

Kanoa sniffed, and looked away.

Kainalu put his hand on Kanoa's shoulder, and Isabella picked up the canvas.

'Would you like to ride over to *Le'ahi* before we get you home today?' Kainalu asked when they had said goodbye to Maima and Kanoa. 'Eleanor will be occupied with Ao and Leilani all day.'

'I would love to.'

She knew it was quite a way across the valley, but the thought of a longer ride and feeling the wind on her face held much appeal. She wanted to rid herself of the heaviness she felt from painting Kanoa.

When they were out of Kalihi, Kainalu kicked his heels and set off at a canter, and Isabella followed. They came to a meadow, Kainalu led them off the road into the grass and with a cry he kicked his horse into a gallop. Isabella, startled, followed his lead. When they had ridden for a few minutes, Kainalu stopped with a 'Whoa' to his horse and laughed heartily.

'I am impressed! You ride like a Hawaiian!'

'Thank you... I think!'

They trotted back to the road and continued in a walk. Kainalu turned to her. 'I am glad to have met you, Isabella. What a difference you have made to our lives.'

He seemed sincere, not flirtatious, but Isabella felt his words were weighted, like they were leading to something.

'I might say the same to you; spending time with your family has been wonderful for both Eleanor and me.'

'Good, we'll make Hawaiians of you yet! In fact, we can do something now,' and he rode over to a frangipani tree on the side of the road, picked a white flower and brought it back to Isabella. 'Here, let me help you.'

Isabella held her breath as he leaned over from his saddle. She felt his fingers touch her skin as he gently tucked the flower behind her ear. A nervous laugh spilled out of her.

'How do I look?' she asked with feigned confidence.

'Not quite Hawaiian, but it suits you... I know you are a refined Englishwoman, but if you were Hawaiian, we would now race to those trees ahead...'

Before he had finished his sentence, Isabella kicked her horse forward and cantered to the trees, laughing as Kainalu tried to catch up.

'Touché,' he smiled as she beat him.

Eventually they got to the base of *Le'ahi*. In single file, Isabella followed Kainalu up the hill. They had to tether the horses on wooden posts before they got to the summit and walk the rest of the way.

Despite being hot and out of breath from the twenty-minute climb, Isabella gasped when she saw the panoramic view that she had heard so much about. It was majestic: before them was the ocean for miles, to the right the buildings of Honolulu and its illustrious harbour, everything shimmering in the sunshine.

'Aren't you tempted to stay?' Kainalu asked, as they stood looking out at the horizon.

'It will be hard to leave this paradise, but for Eleanor's sake, I know we cannot remain here forever.'

'Why not?'

'Eleanor's family are in England. My family are in England. It is where we belong,' she replied, but her words felt empty.

'It may be your home, and being English is who you are, but it does not mean you have to live there.'

'Well, it is also hard to be on the receiving end of hospitality, even when it is such a blessing.'

They sat in silence on a rock. Isabella tried to ignore Kainalu's hand, resting so close to her own. She had a sudden desire to touch it, to feel his fingers clasped around hers.

Instead, she moved and sat on her hands, trying to maintain her equilibrium.

Kainalu seemed oblivious to the battle inside her. 'I want to tell you my story, Isabella. Why I am who I am. You know I was married?' he asked, turning to her. Isabella nodded. 'After my wife and baby died, I thought life was over for me. I was angry with *Ke Akua*, even though I had never truly worshipped Him, for taking my wife and child. I had professed to be a Christian growing up, and went to church with my parents. In truth I was just giving lip service: my life was dedicated to pleasure, in whatever way I could find it.' He paused, playing with a stone under his foot.

Isabella looked ahead, waiting for him to continue.

'I was broken and desperate, and left for Maui to be away from everyone I knew. I raged to the skies. I had no reason to live. I spent my days hunting in the forest, eating what I could catch and kill, and sleeping under the trees. During a majestic thunderstorm I challenged *Ke Akua* to kill me with a lightning bolt, to prove His existence. He ignored me. Then on the third day I was out in the ocean on my *o'lo* board. The waves were high, too high for me, but I battled through. I paddled out to catch one more wave. I caught it, but not for long. I fell from the board into the pounding waters. I was pushed and shoved in every direction. I accepted that I was about to drown as I had no breath left in me. Before I could let go completely, a hand grasped me and pulled me up and out of the water. A surf-rider I did not know balanced me on his board and paddled to the shore. He risked his life to save mine. He left me on the beach but then came back with his wife. They were Hawaiian Christians, having been converted by missionaries years before. The man told me he had been working on his plantation when he heard the voice of *Ke Akua* telling him to go to the beach where there was a man in danger. Because of his obedience my life was saved. As I sat with the couple, I told them what had happened to me – how I had been widowed. I was unable to keep the anger and self-pity out of my voice.'

Isabella's eyes were now fixed on Kainalu. He glanced at her. 'You know what he said? He said, "My boy, your life is not over, there is a purpose and a plan, or God would not have told me to come and save you. It is your decision now to choose life."

'His words hit me. I knew it was a miracle my life had been saved. I had asked God to strike me with a lightening bolt to prove His existence, but instead He had caused someone to grab me from the deep.' He paused, raising his face to the sun and closing his eyes, as if reliving the moment.

'What happened to you then?'

'I stayed with the couple for many months and learned from them. They would pray for me and teach me from the Bible. As I read about the life of Jesus in the Gospels, I was compelled to help the poor and needy. I read the book of James, which said true religion is "To visit the fatherless and widows in their affliction",[2] and I knew that was now my purpose, to help the widows and orphans, and the sick, the leprous in Hawaii.' He stopped and gave the smile of someone who had just laid themselves bare and did not know how they were going to be responded to.

'Kainalu... I... Your story is extraordinary.' Before she could try to express how moved she was, a group arrived to watch the sun set.

Kainalu smiled and greeted them, before rising and helping Isabella up. The moment was gone and she felt disappointed.

They had to turn around as the sun began to sink in the sky. The deep blue was blushed with peach and fuchsia pink. Darkness came quickly in Hawaii, and Isabella needed to be back at the Fortnums' for Eleanor.

'Thank you for listening to my story. I hope I didn't overstep propriety by speaking so intimately...'

'I feel honoured that you told me, and only think of you more highly.'

---

[2] James 1:27.

He held out his hand to lead her down the steep section of the path. She took it, and he curled his fingers around her hand. Nothing was said, but Isabella could almost hear her heart – it was beating so fast.

As they got to a wider section of the path, he let go of her hand, and they walked back to the horses. They were both smiling as they rode home.

'My dear, you look radiant,' exclaimed Emma, when Isabella and Kainalu arrived back.

'We rode fast,' Isabella said quickly, before Eleanor rushed to her, enveloping her in a hug.

'What have you been up to?'

'I missed you,' Eleanor said, hugging her tighter. Isabella felt a pang of guilt that she had been gone so long.

'Aolani is here, too,' said Emma.

'I have to meet Fili, so I will take my leave,' said Kainalu. He turned to Isabella, 'Thank you for a most enjoyable day.'

Isabella smiled, and watched as he jumped back on his horse and rode away. All the while, Eleanor and Leilani chattered away about their adventures.

Chapter Twenty-two

Hawaii, June 1881

'Today we must swim!' Emma Fortnum declared. It had been two months since Isabella's first visit to Kalihi and four months since she and Eleanor had arrived in Honolulu, but she had not yet swum in the turquoise ocean. Eleanor had spent many happy hours in the water with Leilani and Aolani, while Isabella would sit watching from the beach.

Emma continued, 'Even though my bathing gown is so cumbersome and most of the weights have come out of the hem, I will swim! I should really just get a *holoku* dress like the Hawaiians, but I feel a desire to float in the clear blue sea today. There are times when donning my parasol and being respectable seems extremely unamusing. Do say you will come too. The boys will always say yes to an excursion to the water, especially now Horace is trying to emulate those wave-riders.'

Although Isabella had jealously watched the Hawaiians as they swam and surfed the waves, she felt a reticence about going into the ocean herself. Her parents had never outwardly said a lady should not swim in public, but she knew there was some disapproval. And the rigmarole of changing and sitting in her wet bathing dress and pantaloons, it all seemed too difficult and, frankly, embarrassing.

'It will just be us and the children; we'll find a private spot,' Emma said, as if reading her mind.

'Very well. I know Eleanor will say yes, but I agree, it is a good day to swim in the ocean!'

'Splendid, I know just the place. We will go straight away, so it's not too hot. The midday sun causes my skin to go dreadfully red.'

Isabella went to find Eleanor, and to change into her black bathing gown. It was brand new, having been bought for the trip, but was as yet unworn. It came with a bathing cap, which Isabella left behind. She had never seen the Hawaiian women wear anything on their heads in the water, so she would forgo it as well.

The boys and Eleanor all squashed into the buggy, along with Emma and Isabella. It was a beautiful day; blue sky, a gentle breeze, and the calls of birds in the trees above them.

After driving for a while, they stopped at a pathway flanked by a thicket of lantana bushes.

With a cheer, the older three boys jumped out of the buggy and ran towards the sound of waves. Harry waited, and sweetly held Eleanor's hand as they followed.

Isabella felt a rush of excitement at the thought of entering the Pacific. They set up camp with a few wicker mats, and Horace called his brothers to some rocks where they could jump into the water. Eleanor and Isabella, together with Harry, walked towards the waves.

'You swim first, and I will remain here until you come back,' Emma called, placing herself in the middle of one of the mats.

Eleanor stayed in the shallows with Harry, digging holes in the sand and laughing as the water filled them. Isabella had put her feet into the water many times, and knew it was warm, but now she was wading up to her waist she felt embraced. It was wonderful not to have to tense every muscle and gird herself for the chill, as she would have done in England.

She dived under water, so she was fully submerged, and pulled her body forward with two strokes of her arms and a kick of her legs. Her eyes were shut tight, and the sensation of the salty water on her face made her skin tingle. She came up for air, feeling invigorated. She could stand, her woollen bathing gown heavy around her, hugging her body. The water was so transparent that she could see clearly for quite a few feet. Isabella lay back, floating with her hair underwater, eyes closed, a wide smile across her face. How had she waited so long to swim? This was the most glorious feeling. She wanted to laugh aloud; joy emanated out of her, and a spontaneaos internal cry of thanks to her Creator.

She swam some more, and just as she was about to return to Eleanor, Isabella noticed a dark shape in the water near her. Her heart flipped and, making a small yelp, she splashed away from it, trying to see what was swimming so close to her. It came up to the surface, seeming to catch the wave that was building behind it. Isabella gasped. *A turtle*!

She was nervous, as she did not know if it might bite, but after a while her nerves dissipated as the gentle reptile glided through the water near her. She wanted to call Eleanor, but also did not want to ruin the moment. She felt such a deep peacefulness, being in the water, so close to nature.

She could have stayed lazily swimming around for hours, but was alerted by a cry from the beach. Isabella saw two figures walking down the path through the lantana bushes.

'Kainalu!' Isabella heard Emma cry.

Kainalu and Fili had walked onto the beach. She could see them saying something to Emma, who pointed to her in the water. Isabella waved back self-consciously, keeping her body hidden underwater. Both men came down towards the shore carrying their huge 15ft-long wooden boards. They floated them on the water with one hand to guide them as they walked into the ocean.

'Our English rose in the ocean!' Kainalu exclaimed when he got close to Isabella.

'It was about time!' she said, trying to swim away a little so they were not too close. He did not seem to be deterred.

'What are you doing in the water so early?' she asked.

'It is Saturday, the day we play! Are you coming to ride the waves?'

'One thing at a time,' Isabella laughed.

'I'll take you. Aolani has come many times…'

'No, no, honestly I don't know how to do it.'

'You will do nothing, just sit and I will do the rest. I promise you, you will love it.'

Isabella looked back to the beach, unsure.

'Come,' Kainalu commanded, his arm outstretched before her. He brought his board closer.

Against her better judgement, but with a thrill of excitement, Isabella pulled her body onto the board, her soaking bathing gown dripping water in streams back into the ocean. She knelt on the front half of the board, and Kainalu jumped on behind her.

'Yuuweeee!' Fili called out, and paddled off.

Isabella felt their board slice through the water, as Kainalu used his arms like paddles to move them forward. As they got nearer to where the waves were breaking, Isabella held tightly to the sides of the board, wondering if the next wave would wash her off. But as the swell came towards them, Kainalu expertly turned the board so they were facing the shore. He was lying behind her, paddling fast. She hunched low, trying not to get in his way, or make them lose balance. The power of the water lifted them, and then they accelerated forward as they caught it. She could feel Kainalu jumping up behind her, but she didn't dare turn around. To her left she could see Fili on the same wave; his arms were in the air and he was grinning.

'Yuuuueeee!' cried Kainalu, as he moved the board along the wave in a horizontal direction to the beach, where Emma was standing, watching them.

They were carried close to the shore as the wave petered out.

'How did you like that?' Kainalu asked, jumping off the board into the shallows.

Isabella shook her head but could not stop smiling.

'I now see why it is so popular. I felt like I was a bird!' She slid off the board and held onto the side.

Eleanor, who was on the sand, called, 'Can I have a turn?'

Kainalu looked at Isabella. 'Do I have your permission?'

'Yes, you do.'

He went to pick Eleanor up, carried her onto the board and then paddled out. Isabella reluctantly swam to shore and sat on the sand to dry.

'That looked simply glorious!' Emma laughed, as she came to sit next to her. 'I think Horace will ask for a ride next. Was the water sublime?'

As Emma took her turn to swim, Isabella dried quickly in the sun, her skin flecked with salt from the water, and her hair loose down her back.

Eleanor shrieked with joy as the wave brought her and Kainalu in.

After a few more rides with the children, Kainalu and Fili took to the waves alone.

They did not come back to the beach in time for Isabella to say goodbye, so she just waved to them in the distance. The sun had risen high in the sky, and there was not enough shade to keep the party from burning.

'What a successful morning,' Emma said, as they piled back into the buggy. 'I think I might try that wave-sliding next time.' Horace and Wilbur burst into laughter. Isabella just smiled, thinking back to the feeling of being on the wave with Kainalu.

A few days later Emma was up early and sitting on the *lanai* drinking tea, when Isabella and Eleanor got up.

'There is breakfast on the table inside, but come and eat out here with me, it's lovely today. The boys have gone fishing. They left a few minutes ago, so you've missed them… oh, and you have just missed Kainalu too.'

'Kainalu?' Isabella felt her stomach flip at the mention of his name.

'Yes, he dropped off a note for you.'

Isabella took the missive as if it was some clandestine love note. She opened it quickly, chiding her imagination. It was an invitation for Isabella and Eleanor to come to a *luau* to celebrate the birth of a baby being born to his cousin. Isabella was surprised, as Aolani had invited her to the same event a few days previously, but then had reneged on the offer.

'I would love for you and Eleanor to come, but I don't know if it will be acceptable to everyone. It is a family celebration,' she had said, not able to look Isabella in the eye.

Isabella knew the only person it would not be acceptable to was *Kapuna Wahine*, who was still staying with Aolani. She had not embraced Isabella into the family in the same way as her offspring had. Isabella mentioned her fears to Emma when they were in the garden together. Emma had developed and nurtured an impressive vegetable patch that was swelling with produce. She asked Isabella and Eleanor to help pick some sweetcorn, but Eleanor had been distracted by the 'animal shop' with Harry.

Isabella had a wicker basket and was filling it with cobs. 'It feels very much like she does not like or approve of me.'

'I have only met her briefly, but what you describe is very unusual. Hawaiians are by nature warm and accepting. Maybe it is simply because you are English, and so different from her culture?'

'Perhaps,' said Isabella, picking up the basket and taking it inside, but she was not convinced.

Kainalu's note stated that the *luau* started at six o'clock, but Aolani had extended the invitation for the afternoon as well, and would expect Isabella and Eleanor after lunch. Isabella wondered what had changed for her now to be invited.

'What do you think, should we accept?' she asked Emma.

'Go, my dear, it will be an event you will never forget!'

So, despite some reservations, Isabella dutifully arrived with Eleanor at Aolani's at two o'clock. Aolani was full of warmth when they walked into the house, and Isabella felt more assured about accepting the invitation. The house had been descended upon by cousins and cousins' cousins. People were coming and going with pots and pans and cheerful welcomes; women were sitting on the floor, combing out their long brown hair, preparing flower garlands and sewing final changes to the trains and ruffles of their dresses. Eleanor stared open-mouthed at the industry around her; everyone was laughing and good-natured. It felt as if the celebration had already started.

'Isabella, you will get ready with us. I will make you like a Hawaiian princess,' Aolani said, taking her hand.

'My dress is at the Fortnums', and so is Eleanor's. I had planned to go back to change and then return before the *luau*.'

Aolani laughed. 'You are not wearing your English dresses today. Come.' When she saw Isabella's face, she laughed again. 'Don't be afraid!'

Isabella couldn't imagine what Aolani was envisioning. Surely she was not suggesting she wear one of her dresses? Aolani was both taller and broader than Isabella. Curious, she followed Aolani into her bedroom.

'Here, we have outfits for you both. Come and see,' said Aolani, pointing to a cornflower-blue *holoku* dress and a smaller pale-pink dress hanging over a chair.

'Aolani, where did these come from?' Isabella asked, picking up the blue cotton dress and measuring it against her body.

'We had them made. I wanted you to have them as a gift, and the *luau* is the perfect time to wear them. Try it on!'

'Wouldn't it be better to wait till later?'

'Put the dress on! I know it is not what you are used to, but you are on our island and you will become one of us when you wear it. It is blue, like your eyes, I made sure of that.'

'Very well,' Isabella gave in.

She went to the next room and changed out of her long skirt with its tight waist and long-sleeved cotton blouse. When she put on the *holoku* dress, she immediately felt more comfortable. It was a hot and sticky day, and with this dress there was no restricting corset or waistband. It hung loosely from her shoulders and fell into a train behind her.

Aolani came in to inspect. '*Ho'onani!* My sister, you look beautiful,' she exclaimed, coming forward to pull the ruffled material down to reveal her shoulders. 'We will arrange your hair too, and give you slippers and a *lei*.'

'Isn't this too much?' Isabella asked. Self-concious with so much flesh revealed, she pushed the material up closer to her neck.

'No, for you this is better,' Aolani replied, pulling it back down so her neck and shoulders were bare, without ruffle or pleat. 'You must take it off now, and I will give you another that you can wear while we will start on your hair.'

Isabella consented, wondering if she would look ridiculous, like a woman in fancy dress. However, she wanted to please Aolani, so relented. While Eleanor played with Leilani, she put the spare *holoku* dress on, and went to the *lanai*.

'Come,' Aolani said, beckoning Isabella to sit on a mat in front of the chair she was sitting on. As the sun flickered on Isabella's back through the leaves of the palm tree, Aolani proceeded to undo Isabella's bun, letting her hair fall down her back. Isabella didn't stop her or ask what she was doing, but relaxed into the feeling as Aolani methodically combed and smoothed, as if it was the most natural thing in the world. Isabella felt like a small girl again, and closed her eyes, enjoying the feeling of the wooden teeth running through her hair, which was now flecked with blonde from her months in the sun.

She felt completely enveloped in Aolani's *ohana*. Time seemed to stand still, and Isabella was caught in a comforting *déjà vu*, feeling like she had known Aolani before she had come to Hawaii. How could she feel so comfortable in a society and culture so different from her own?

'Lei, time to get ready,' Aolani called to her daughter, who was playing with Eleanor near the entrance of the driveway. The girls were trying to walk around the perimeter of the house without touching the ground, climbing from rock to fence post, and clinging on to any branch or bush that would keep them off the ground. They were so intent on their mission that it took another call from Aolani before Leilani took notice.

Isabella stood to go and help Eleanor. It felt good to have her hair loose down her back.

'Let me pin my hair up again, and I will get Eleanor dressed.'

'No, you must leave your hair long tonight. I will give you a flower for behind your ear.'

'I have never had it like this in public. I fear I will feel very self-conscious.'

Aolani laughed, and stroked her hand down Isabella's smooth hair. 'No one will think about it. You will just look like us. Your skin is not as dark, but the rest of you will be Hawaiian this evening.'

Leilani and Eleanor came running up to the *lanai*. Eleanor stopped when she saw Isabella, taking in her new look.

'You are beautiful, Mama Isabella,' she said. Isabella smiled, and wanted to believe she was right.

Chapter Twenty-three

Hawaii, July 1881

They arrived in the Fortnums' buggy at the site of the party as the sun was setting. The *luau* was held in a clearing surrounded by palm trees and illuminated by flame torches only yards away from the gentle rush of waves breaking on the sand. Fili and Aolani led the way. Two women stood at the entrance, greeting the guests and placing orchid *leis* around their necks. Isabella had a white frangipani blossom from Aolani behind her ear. She still felt conspicuous in her outfit, but the Hawaiian women had their hair loose and were wearing similar dresses. They did not seem to find her out of place at all.

There must have been about 200 people gathered. Aolani left Isabella almost immediately, to see to some problem with the tables, and Eleanor and Leilani ran off to the beach in front of the *luau*. But Isabella was not alone for long, as Mr Cleghorn approached from the crowd.

'Welcome to the *luau*! I see you are embracing Hawaiian attire, very fetching.' His face was rosy with sunburn. 'Let me get you something to drink. Then we must speak about your return to England.'

Isabella did not want to talk about leaving the island.

He returned with two glasses. 'My wife is occupied, but she will join us presently, I am sure. It's guava juice,' he said as he handed Isabella a glass. 'Of the islands, Honolulu is the only place where alcohol is allowed to be sold, but you'll hardly ever see it in homes.' He took a gulp, and then asked, 'So, when are you going home?'

Isabella felt uncomfortable. 'I am not certain of a date yet.'

'We have plans to educate our daughter in England, but not until she is older; for now, she will have tutors. As she is half-Scottish, I want her to have some idea of life in the United Kingdom.'

'Won't you find it hard being so far from her?'

He raised his eyebrows and nodded. 'No doubt I will, but I am more concerned about separating her from the ocean,' he chuckled. 'She would spend her life in the water if she could. She's even learning to be a surf-rider!'

Isabella watched Victoria as he spoke. She had taken Eleanor in hand and was leading her to play with the other children.

'My daughter is heir apparent, her uncle the king, but I fear we will have to fight to keep our monarchy here on the islands. There are greedy business people talking about an annex with America. If that happens, Victoria will never be queen.'

As Isabella was listening to Mr Cleghorn, who was now giving her the history of the islands, she noticed Kainalu standing under a tree. He was looking straight at her and smiling. She responded with a smile and nod. What would he think of her with hair down and in Hawaiian dress? He started walking towards her, so she quickly turned her attention back to Mr Cleghorn, trying to concentrate on what he was saying.

'... and as you know, we were named the Sandwich Islands after the Earl of Sandwich, by Captain Cook. He died on the island of Hawaii in 1779...'

'Isabella, I hardly recognised you. Ao has made you Hawaiian,' Kainalu said as he approached them. He nodded a greeting to Mr Cleghorn.

'Oh dear, is the outfit outlandish on me? Aolani convinced me to wear it, and keep my hair untied...'

'It was right that she convinced you. You look beautiful.'

'You do indeed, my dear,' confirmed Mr Cleghorn, but Isabella hardly heard, her heart was beating so loudly because Kainalu had called her beautiful.

The sun descended and the flickering fire from torches in the ground became the only light as they sat down to eat.

Kainalu took Isabella's arm and led her to a low seat. Eleanor, who did not seem to be at all worried about where Isabella was, was seated next to Victoria at another table. Bowls filled with *poi* and platters of meat were set out with sweet potatoes and salt-dried fish laid directly onto *ti* leaves.

'There is so much food,' Isabella laughed at the tables piled high.

There were no knives or forks, but by now Isabella was used to the lack of utensils when eating with Hawaiians. She watched proudly as Eleanor tucked in with her fingers.

There was a sudden hush and the guests turned to the entrance.

'King Kalākaua has arrived,' Kainalu whispered. He was so close to her as he spoke, she could feel his breath on her skin. Her whole body felt alive with his proximity.

Trying to focus, Isabella watched as the present king of Hawaii walked towards the people. He was dressed in European fashion, and had dark hair and heavy sideburns. He was escorted to a throne at the centre of the *luau*.

'He looks as smart and regal as any British sovereign, wouldn't you say?' Kainalu asked Isabella, and she had to agree.

As the evening continued, a group of women performed a *hula*, and the king, along with two other men, played ukuleles.

Kainalu again leaned close to Isabella to explain what was happening. He had not left her side, even when others came to speak to him or to call him away, he remained.

'This is the dance that King Kalākaua brought back to our people. In the recent past many complained the *hula* was too sensual, so with pressure from missionaries, the dance was banned. When King Kalākaua came to the throne he said, "*Hula* is the language of the heart, therefore the heartbeat of the Hawaiian people." And so *hula* was allowed to continue.'

Isabella was enraptured; the dance was beautiful and mesmerising. The women moved with a rhythmic sway as they smiled out at the audience.

'This *hula* is performed in worship to *Ke Akua*, as we call Jehovah. It's thanking him for the earth and sky, the fish in the ocean and the birds of the air. Watch the dancers' hand movements, everything is telling a story,' he explained, his face close to Isabella's as he translated the songs and the women danced. She wanted to pocket this moment in her memory forever.

Eventually the flaming torches began to splutter and fade, and the piles of food became discarded bones and remnants of *poi*.

Leilani and Eleanor played for a while with the other children, but as it got late Eleanor began to tire. She came to sit down next to Isabella, her eyelids closing as she rested her head on Isabella's shoulder. Isabella noticed *Kapuna Wahine* watching them. She could not read the expression on her face, but was sure it was not one of pleasure. With his strong arms Kainalu lifted Eleanor into his lap, where she promptly fell asleep.

'It is time to go, I think,' Kainalu said. He carried a sleeping Eleanor to the Fortnums' buggy. 'Isabella, I need to take care of some business in Hilo, but I will find you on my return,' he said as he helped her into the carriage.

'I look forward to it.' Isabella could not hide the affection in her reply. She wondered what business he had to take care of. *Probably something to do with the lepers*, she thought, and closed her eyes as the driver took them back to the Fortnums'.

The next day Isabella woke with the magical feeling of the *luau* running through her. She realised she never wanted to leave Hawaii, its warmth and ease, and its inhabitants. In the afternoon, Aolani came to visit with Leilani and two of the cousins from Kona.

'Kainalu has sailed to Hilo. He will be away for a few weeks,' she said as soon as she arrived. Isabella didn't think more of it, as he had already told her that he had business to tend to, but she was still disappointed not to see him.

Leilani and Eleanor were occupied in the garden, and Emma went to prepare tea. Aolani came and sat with Isabella on the *lanai* swinging chair. She opened her mouth to say something, and then closed it.

Isabella waited, knowing not to try to fill the silence.

'I just wondered...' Aolani said, and then stopped.

Isabella looked at her. 'What is it?'

'My mother thinks you have desires for Kainalu and she does not approve. She has arranged for him to marry a Hawaiian *wahine* and that is why he is travelling to Hilo: to meet the bride chosen for him.'

'He is getting married?' Isabella tried to disguise her shock, and, if she was honest, horror. 'He never told me.' She felt sick, then foolish and embarrassed all at once, and angry that she had been so judged by *Kapuna Wahine*.

'I'm sorry,' Aolani said, looking uncertain.

Choosing her words carefully, Isabella said, 'I respect and admire Kainalu very much, but I would never presume to have affection for someone who had not voiced the same towards me.' She paused, collecting herself. 'I enjoy spending time with him, but set your mother's heart at ease; I am not trying to ensnare your brother. I am happy that he will be married again.' There was an edge to her voice that she could not hide.

'I am sorry if I have offended you,' Aolani said, taking Isabella's hand. 'I wanted to explain the truth to *Kapuna Wahine*. She was the one who sent Kainalu away to Hilo. She is afraid he loves you, and you will take him to England.'

Isabella shook her head in frustration. 'Has he ever said anything to you?'

'He has not spoken to me, but he is different around you and *Kapuna Wahine* notices it. She has arranged a marriage for him with the daughter of another chief from Hilo.'

'So he is agreeing? He wants to marry the chief's daughter?'

'I think he does; he wants children. You see how good he is with Leilani and Eleanor.'

Isabella nodded her head silently. *Perhaps he thinks I am too old for children?*

'I want you to be happy, and I want my brother to be happy.' Aolani looked at Isabella as if trying to coax a smile out of her.

The conversation made Isabella's future plans suddenly very clear. 'I admire your brother, but I am sorry your mother feels as she does.' She then added impulsively, 'Anyway, we will be leaving shortly. We cannot stay here in Hawaii forever. My place is in England.'

Aolani looked pained. 'Please don't go because of what I have said. You are so special to all of us. Kainalu being married won't make any difference.'

But Isabella knew it would make all the difference in the world. She found it hard to keep engaged in conversation after she had been given the news of Kainalu's plans. She was relieved when Aolani eventually left, so she could have more time to think.

Isabella decided on a walk after supper. Eleanor was already in bed. The sun was setting and the sky was ablaze with beauty. She tried to force all thoughts of Kainalu out of her mind. She was resolute when she got back to the house, and walked into the large light sitting room with its wide-open windows to break the news to Emma and Charles.

'What is the rush? Our home is your home; you are welcome here for as long as you like,' said Mr Fortnum.

'We have already taken advantage of your generosity for too long, and despite what you say, I do not want to wear out our welcome.' Isabella tried to speak briskly.

'But we will miss you both so! You have become like family,' said Emma, coming to sit next to Isabella and placing an affectionate hand on her arm.

'Your hospitality and friendship have been such a blessing to us, but I have made up my mind.' Isabella stopped talking as her voice broke.

The next day Isabella purchased two tickets for San Francisco. The passage would take about two weeks. From there she would arrange travel on the Transcontinental Railroad which linked California on the Pacific coast to the east coast, and their ship home. It came together so clearly in her mind.

Isabella wrote a letter to her family informing them of her plans, and letting them know she would send a telegram from New York, when she knew which steamer they would be travelling on to England.

When everything else was done, all she had left to do was to tell Eleanor.

'I don't want to leave!' the girl said immediately.

Calmly, Isabella explained they had to go home to start their new life. She reminded Eleanor she was an English girl, and would be happy there.

Isabella knew that Kainalu would not be back before they left to say goodbye. She would write him a letter to explain, without actually telling him what her real motivation was for the swift departure. It took her a few versions until she found the right tone:

> *My dear Kainalu,*
> *I am sorry that I have had to leave before saying goodbye. I have realised I need to take Eleanor home. I cannot live this half-life forever, however lovely, without any real responsibility or roots.*
> *Kainalu, I am so glad that I met you on our first day in Honolulu. Your friendship has brought me much joy, and spending time with you at Kalihi has been very special. I hear you are to be married, and I wish you every happiness. You deserve the very best.*
> *Your friend,*
> *Isabella*

She sealed the envelope and put it on the table to give to Aolani in the morning.

Chapter Twenty-four

Sailing for America, July 1881

Isabella and Eleanor had been on Oah'u for nearly six months. Isabella marvelled at what they had both been able to accumulate in that time, as she attempted to repack their trunks. She held up the blue *hokolu* dress Aolani had given her. Of course she would never wear it in England, but something stopped her leaving it behind. She found space for it, and wondered if she would want a reminder of the enchanted *luau* evening when she was back in cold, dark Norfolk.

The day they were to leave was almost perfect weather, blue sky with a gentle breeze. As Isabella and Eleanor were taken to the steamer in the Fortnums' buggy, they drove past Hawaiians surf-riding and playing in the clear ocean. The steamer was departing at eight o'clock and the Fortnums' were giving them supper at the Hawaiian Hotel before boarding.

As the sun set, they were treated to a Samoan fire dance on the hotel lawn. Three burly men, wearing traditional *mahlos* and thin strips of material tied around their arms and legs, juggled torches of fire while shouting and ululating in a powerful fashion. Then a group of grass-skirted Hawaiian girls danced a *hula*. There was something both beautiful and worshipful in their movements. Isabella watched the bright smiles of the dancers; they looked so serene, each with a flower behind their ear. It was as graceful as any ballet she had watched in England.

Saying goodbye was more difficult than Isabella had expected, and she wanted it to be over as soon as possible. The Fortnums seemed to understand. Emma and Charles were almost formal in their farewells, matter of fact and unemotional, which helped greatly.

After supper, Aolani came with Leilani to say goodbye as the steamer left the harbour.

'We will miss you, my *hānai* princesses,' Aolani said, embracing Isabella. 'You are always *hānai*, even if you are not physically with us. We will wait for your return.' She picked Eleanor up, despite her being almost too big to be carried now. 'Eleanor, what will we do without you?' she laughed, as the little girl giggled with glee. She put her down and kissed her forehead.

'It is time, my English friends,' Aolani said.

Isabella took Eleanor's hand, and together they walked on board for their final voyage, bar one, until they were home again on English soil. They stood on the deck to wave goodbye, the warm air and smells of frangipani blossom filling their senses for the last time. Isabella could only dream that one day she would be back on this island. She guessed that it would not be until she was in heaven that she would again inhabit such paradise.

Eleanor cried for the first day of their journey, only stopping to eat. Her grief seemed to overwhelm her. Isabella held her, realising her pain at leaving her friends in Hawaii was surely compounded by the deeper bereavement of losing her parents. Isabella felt despairing, not knowing what to do. Eleanor had experienced so much loss in her short life, and there was nothing she could do to help her. Isabella frequently found her eyes filling up too, but would wipe the tears away quickly so that Eleanor couldn't see. She offered Eleanor some food to distract her and she accepted a slice of bread and butter in the saloon, but mouthfuls were punctuated with heavy tear-exhausted gasps of air.

'We are about to see America! It is probably a hundred times bigger than Hawaii and England put together, with mountains and deserts and *huge* forests. We'll be taking a train across the *whole* country. You are a lucky girl to be seeing so much of the world.'

Eleanor looked up at her and her solemn, tear-filled eyes were full of doubt.

'And when we get there, it will be your birthday! You will be five!'

Eleanor was more interested in this news. 'Will I get a cake?'

'We will make it special somehow, and if we can't get you a cake, I will ask Mrs West to make you a very big one when we come to England.'

Eleanor smiled, and her tears subsided.

At night in their cabin, sleep came in waves but was never sustained. *Why did I dream of this island that brought me such heartbreak?* Isabella wondered when Kainalu would get the letter she had left for him, and what his reaction would be. The words she had written were clear in her mind's eye. She worried that she had been too formal, or that she had revealed too much.

Eleanor had nightmares throughout the journey, always connected to the death of her parents. Isabella was often awake when Eleanor cried out, and would comfort the little girl, telling her she was safe now, and that they were going home.

As they steamed further away from Hawaii, Isabella and Eleanor mostly kept to themselves. Isabella made up stories for Eleanor, or they would stroll hand in hand around the steamer's top deck. Eleanor's conversation naturally focused on Hawaii. She talked about Leilani, and playing in the ocean. She talked about the *luau* and the trip to Kona. In all of it, it was as if she was trying to cement the memories in her mind.

'If I was a grown-up I would never leave.'

'You would if you knew that your life was supposed to be lived elsewhere.'

Eleanor shook her head fiercely.

They would have continued the journey in this uneventful way, awaiting the first view of the great land mass that was the United States of America, if it had not been for sickness striking the ship. Cholera broke out on the fifth day. No signs of it appeared among the passengers until a young Chinese girl was taken ill with severe cramp. This was not out of the ordinary, but the passengers were in shock when the news circulated that she had died a few hours later. The ship's doctor, who was accustomed to the disease, pronounced it at once as cholera of the most virulent type. After the girl died, several others were found to have contracted the disease. A few days out from San Francisco the cholera continued to rage with great fury. The deaths on board amounted to thirty.

The passengers had all been warned that cholera spread through contaminated food and water. They were confined to their cabins and told to wash their hands frequently. For the first day, Isabella and Eleanor bore the seclusion well enough, but during the second day of confinement they were both feeling frustrated.

'I want to go outside!' Eleanor begged continuously.

Isabella was fearful, but eventually relented. 'Very well, but I have one condition. You must hold your hanky over your mouth, as there are lots of germs and I don't want you getting ill.'

Eleanor nodded solemnly.

They stepped out of the cabin and looked up and down the corridor. There were no passengers about, except a steward walking towards them.

'Ma'am, you'd be advised to keep her out of the way of the sick,' he said, his eyes on Eleanor as he side-stepped them.

'We are just going on deck, briefly.'

The steward raised his eyebrows, but walked on.

Isabella and Eleanor got to the saloon, where only a man and woman sat together holding hands; both looked like they had been crying. Eleanor was staring at them.

'Isabella, why are they sad?'

Isabella bent to whisper. 'You know people have been sick on the ship? Well, some people have died, and that is why people are sad.'

'So they will be with Mama and Papa in heaven, then?' Eleanor said, not in a whisper.

'Yes...'

'Shall we tell them? Shall we tell them it will be alright? They are just in heaven,' Eleanor said, pulling Isabella back to the couple.

'Not just now; we can tell them another time. It is too soon.'

Eleanor reluctantly let herself be led forward, but looked back at the man and woman inquisitively.

Isabella opened the heavy exterior door out onto the deck, and the sun and fresh air hit them. It was like a tonic, and she immediately felt invigorated. They spent half an hour outside and then grudgingly returned to their cabin.

Once they were back inside and Isabella shut the cabin door, she leaned her back on it and sighed. The room now felt like a prison, and the gloom of death was becoming more and more oppressive.

'Wash your hands properly,' she told Eleanor.

'I am,' Eleanor insisted.

'Let me make sure.' She poured more water in the marble basin and Eleanor surrendered her wet fingers to Isabella, who scrubbed and agitated the soap and water until both their hands were red.

'Stop!' cried Eleanor.

'All done! It is important; it's how we won't get ill.'

Isabella sat on Eleanor's bunk and looked at the wall in front of her, slightly moving with the ebb of the water below. The cholera and death only deepened her sense of loss. How could she have put her hope in Kainalu so quickly? It was foolish, and she told herself to remember who she was. She would get over this.

'Can we play make-believe that we are in Y-ee?' Eleanor asked for the fifth time. She wanted to dress up in her *holoku* dress and pretend she was dancing the *hula*.

'Very well,' Isabella relented, and found her dress. To see the little girl with her now tanned skin in her Hawaiian dress, trying to dance the *hula* movements, was both sweet and funny. Isabella laughed and Eleanor giggled, and the atmosphere shifted momentarily.

The ship very quickly became a floating hospital. The staff on board were busy with the sick, and other passengers stayed in their berths. Most of the fatalities were among the steerage passengers, though several had died in the upper and lower cabins where Isabella and Eleanor were stationed.

Isabella peered out of the porthole continually, waiting for land to at last be in sight. But when they did arrive in San Francisco, they couldn't leave that easily. At the wharf, the passengers were quarantined on the steamer. The mayor of San Francisco despatched the best medical aid available to attend to the sufferers, but there were three more cholera cases on board, which the coroner asserted were likely to prove fatal. Two women died when they were at anchor. The steward who had been so disapproving earlier was reporting all of the information to Isabella.

Isabella did not want to hear any more sad news. Life felt unbearable with its sadness and disappointment.

The second morning at the port of San Francisco, Isabella was woken to the sound of Eleanor being sick. She was leaning over her bed, and the floor was covered in vomit. The odour made Isabella's stomach turn.

Not Eleanor! Fear gripped Isabella as she jumped down from her narrow bunk.

'Eleanor, I am here, it is going to be alright,' she said, smoothing the little girl's damp hair off her forehead.

Eleanor groaned in reply. She shed weak tears as she turned her head to and fro on the pillow, obviously in pain. Her forehead was hot and her nightdress already wet through with sweat.

'She cannot die. *Jesus*, she cannot die,' Isabella prayed fervently under her breath. She tried to clear up the mess on the floor with a towel and called for clean sheets for Eleanor's bed, getting a fresh nightdress out of their packed trunk.

Through the day Eleanor worsened. The ship's doctor gave Isabella some chamomile for her to drink, to get fluids back into Eleanor's body, but by evening she was barely conscious, and did not seem to hear Isabella when she spoke.

The cabin smelt heavily of vomit. Isabella kept the tiny porthole open. She had hardly dressed and her long hair fell unkempt down her back, half pinned-up earlier in the day and then forgotten. The hours ticked by slowly; Isabella was exhausted but could not sleep. Eleanor was so small and she knew it would take something extraordinary for her to survive. By evening there was little improvement.

Isabella tried to sleep, but found it impossible. At about four o'clock in the morning she eventually dozed off, sitting on the floor with her head resting in her folded arms on Eleanor's mattress. Then Isabella was awakened by a noise, but as she opened her eyes and got her bearings, all was silent. It was dark outside, except for a light in the corridor that seeped through the cracks of the door. Fearfully, she put her ear close to Eleanor to check if she could hear breathing. She sighed with relief when she could, and from the faint light she was able to make out Eleanor's pale cheeks and sunken eyes.

'If you are real, God, *please* heal Eleanor,' Isabella prayed in a whisper.

It was a desperate prayer, and one she was not sure would be answered. She remembered Kainalu's story; if he prayed, perhaps it would be heard.

Isabella watched and waited, hoping to see some sort of change. Two words were floating around her head – *'Talitha cumi'*. She had no idea what they meant, but she found herself whispering them into the dark silence of the cabin as she fell back to sleep.

A few hours later, it was Eleanor's voice that woke Isabella. She was calling her name. Dawn had arrived and the cabin was slowly brightening.

'Eleanor, thank goodness! How are you feeling?'

'Better,' she said in a tiny voice, and she did look different; there was colour in her face that had definitely not been there the night before. Isabella was stiff from her uncomfortable night on the floor, but she got up and washed her face, and gave Eleanor a drink of water.

As the day progressed, so did Eleanor's health. By midday, she wanted to get out of bed. Isabella called the stewards for food to be brought to the cabin, and Eleanor ate some bread and half a boiled egg. Isabella watched her in amazement; she had been so sure she was going to lose her. She remembered her prayer at the darkest hour of the night.

God had answered. God had healed Eleanor. Isabella laughed at this realisation.

'Eleanor! God answered my prayers!'

Eleanor looked at her, nonplussed.

Isabella searched for her childhood Bible that had been presented to her at her confirmation. She had packed it out of duty, and had started to read it in Hawaii, trying to find in its pages more of the reality of faith that Kainalu had talked about. She found it and started flicking through the chapters. She wasn't sure what she was looking for, but for some reason stopped at Mark's Gospel. Her eyes were drawn to chapter 5. It was the story of Jesus healing a little girl who was very ill, and then died. Isabella read the words Jesus spoke to raise her from the dead, and as she did, goose flesh appeared on her skin. He said, *'Talitha cumi'*.[3] She read on and discovered that the words meant, 'Little girl, get up'. They were the exact words that were in her head when she had prayed for God to heal Eleanor in the early hours.

'Eleanor, we have to say thank you to God, because He has made you better.'

'You say thank you,' Eleanor replied, with childish stubbornness.

---

[3] Verse 41.

Isabella laughed, and from her laughter came one 'thank you' after another. They tumbled out of her mouth as hot tears streamed down her cheeks. She would have continued had not Eleanor reached out and placed a finger over Isabella's lips to quiet her.

Isabella had thought they would stay in San Francisco for a few days, but when they were eventually allowed to disembark, she was ready to leave the city and its association with sickness.

They took a buggy to the train station and booked the sleeper going from San Francisco to Reno, Nevada. They would then be taking big jumps eastward across the States, and finish in New York for the steamer home.

Before their train left, they had time to visit a general store, and Isabella purchased a small globe and some ribbons for Eleanor's hair as a birthday present. She had been sick on the day of her birthday, so they would celebrate once they were on the train.

The San Francisco weather was brisk and cool. Having got used to the balmy Hawaiian air, Isabella had to take her woollen shawl out of her trunk, and make sure Eleanor was wearing enough clothes. She was busy encouraging Eleanor to put on her cardigan, motivated more by fear than necessity, when she suddenly realised, if God had healed Eleanor once, surely He could stop her from getting ill again? It was too easy to allow fear to keep snapping at her heels.

The train journeys gave a beautiful moving imagery of majestic mountains and wild prairies. Eleanor spent most of her time glued to the window, in awe of the landscape. She would study her globe and run her finger around it, as if to trace the long journey they were making. Isabella tried to paint, but it was too hard and messy with the movement of the train, so she succumbed to sketching Eleanor. Her hair was so much blonder than when they had first met, having been bleached by the Hawaiian sun. Isabella enjoyed drawing her large, inquisitive eyes as they watched silently through long brown lashes.

They got off at various stops along the way, usually small one-horse towns that the railway was bringing to life. Many of the bigger towns were new, according to Isabella's standards, having been established only forty or so years previously. Isabella would post her letters, and they would find a guesthouse before catching another train the next day.

Despite Isabella's sadness at her misplaced affection for Kainalu, something had changed in her heart while on the islands. She had seen a different way of living. She had flourished in the warm, open society, and for the first time she believed there was more to life than what she could see. She wrote to Catherine:

> *My experience in Hawaii was like someone dying and going to heaven, and now I have returned to the reality of earth. There is hope in knowing that there is a different way of living...*

Isabella sometimes allowed herself to imagine that Kainalu would come after her. But why would he? She had misinterpreted him and let herself fall into the trap of unrequited love. But then she thought back to their time at Kalihi, to his openness with her, telling her of his past at the top of *Le'ahi*. She had thought he was drawn to her, attracted to her even, but maybe he had just seen her as a sister, a friend. Perhaps on the islands it was normal to share more intimately with members of the opposite sex. But then she remembered his face when he saw her at the *luau*, dressed up in Hawaiian costume. His eyes had given him away, she was sure; he must have felt something. Perhaps it was not enough.

After three weeks of trains and a few stops to recuperate, Isabella and Eleanor arrived in New Haven, Connecticut, just over 100 miles from New York. Isabella found a hotel, but sent a message to friends of her parents who had moved from England many years previously. The husband, Professor Ferrier, had been given a position lecturing on ancient history at Yale University and Isabella hoped that they might have her and Eleanor to stay until they could find a passage home.

Within a few hours a message came back with a buggy saying that they would be welcome as guests. Their trunks were collected and they were driven to a large townhouse made of red brick, three storeys high.

'Welcome, welcome, what a lovely treat for us,' cried Mrs Ferrier as she ushered Isabella and Eleanor inside. She was a sprightly woman, full of energy, and seemed genuinely ecstatic to have visitors from England. A maid was called to show Isabella and Eleanor their room. 'Get yourselves settled, and then we will have a refreshing cup of tea,' Mrs Ferrier instructed, and then scurried down the corridor to give orders to the cook.

Professor Ferrier joined them for tea. He was the opposite of his wife, with slow movements and a contemplative spirit. Isabella told the couple about her journey. When she explained that she and Eleanor had been in the Sandwich Islands, the Ferriers informed her that there were some Hawaiian students at Yale.

'How would you like us to invite them to dinner?' asked the professor.

'That would be wonderful.'

There was a knock at the door.

'Ah, I think this might be for Eleanor!' said the professor.

Eleanor looked up at Isabella enquiringly, but Isabella was none the wiser.

'Here we are, Eleanor, could you help?' said Professor Ferrier, as the maid came in, followed by the cook. They were carrying four small black Labrador puppies. Bess, their mother, padded in behind and settled on a rug in the corner of the drawing room. 'Your remit, young lady, is to play with the puppies. Do you think you are up to it?' asked the professor seriously.

'Oh, yes!' Eleanor said with eyes wide.

Eleanor asked for the puppies to sleep with her when it was time for bed, but when Isabella explained they had to be with their mother, she seemed to understand. She tired easily with all the travelling, and having been ill, so that evening Isabella put her to bed early, saying prayers and singing her the same lullaby that her mother had sung to her.

Eleanor started singing it with her, but faded out for the last line, her eyelids heavy with sleep. Isabella kissed her forehead and tucked the sheet and blankets close around her.

Downstairs, Isabella met Mrs Ferrier in the drawing room, which was lit by flickering candles.

'How is Eleanor?'

'She's fast asleep,' Isabella said with a smile.

'You have a lovely relationship with that little girl. I watched you both this afternoon; it is a very special bond you have. You were obviously made to be a mother one way or the other.'

Isabella had not realised how much she had needed the encouragement. 'Thank you. I cannot imagine life without her now.'

'I can understand that.'

They were interrupted by an announcement that the Hawaiians had arrived. The men entered the drawing room.

'*Aloha!*' Isabella said in greeting.

'*Aloha!*' they replied simultaneously.

The men, James and Hani, joked and laughed, telling stories and asking questions. They were both in their early twenties and, Isabella thought, as cheerful and warm as their people back on the islands.

'How did you come to study at Yale?' she asked.

'We are following a long history of Hawaiians in New England. Have you heard of Henry Opukahaia?' James replied.

Isabella shook her head.

'His family were murdered by warriors, and he ended up getting passage to New Haven as a teenager. He met some kind Americans who enabled him to be enrolled in study. Through their influence he converted to Christianity. This was in 1815. He was a clever man, and in his short life he translated the book of Genesis into Hawaiian.'

'He also started work on a dictionary for our language. He was going to come back to the Islands to preach the gospel, but died of typhus fever in 1818. He was only twenty-six, just a few years older than us now,' Hani added.

'Because of Henry, the first missionaries arrived in Hawaii in 1820 from New Haven,' said James.

Mrs Ferrier was not interested in religious talk. 'Enough about missionaries! Let us hear more about Isabella's travels. She really has had quite a remarkable journey. You should write a book, my dear.'

When the students left, Isabella said goodnight to the Ferriers. The evening had been a welcome antidote to the weeks of travel, the horrors of cholera and the responsibility of looking after Eleanor alone, which had been so much easier with the community in Honolulu to help her.

The next day they awoke to rain and grey skies.

'You are being prepared for England!' Mrs Ferrier said to Isabella over breakfast. Isabella laughed, but with little joy.

The next steamer they could take was in a week, and Isabella went to the telegram office to send a message to her parents to inform them of the day they would arrive and the name of the ship. She also wrote to Sir Mark Winter, to ask if they could stay with him and Lucy in their London home, to break the journey back to Norfolk. She wanted to speak to him about Eleanor, to make the guardianship official.

When she had finished all the administration, Professor Ferrier kindly took her and Eleanor sightseeing around New Haven, and the impressive Yale University.

But to Isabella, its academic excellence, although formidable, was nothing compared to the simple natural beauty of the tropical island in the Pacific.

Chapter Twenty-five

Passage to England, September 1881

The steamer to England would take ten days. It cost £7 for both Isabella and Eleanor's tickets. Isabella was grateful she still had the means to travel first class. They had a small but smart cabin; the décor was red and gold, giving an opulent feel, like a floating palace. Isabella guessed it had been newly decorated as the smell of fresh paint was still hanging in the air. It was quite a change from the cockroach-infested *Nevada*.

In cloudy, inclement weather, Isabella and Eleanor stood on deck hand in hand and watched America fade into the distance. Isabella's heart sank, wondering whether this voyage marked the end of her travels.

Eleanor tugged at Isabella's sleeve. 'I think I remember England. I remember the farm and the cows and I have a cousin called Sybil…'

'I haven't heard about Sybil before. How old is she?' Isabella enquired, feeling uncomfortable that she wasn't taking Eleanor straight to her family.

Eleanor paused, tilting her head. 'She's bigger than me.'

'Well, we will see her and her family again soon, after we have settled with my parents.' Isabella inhaled the fresh, salty air, watching the white froth from the wake of the ship funnel out behind them.

'Where will we go in England?' Eleanor asked, looking up at Isabella.

'We will arrive in a town called Plymouth, and then we will travel to London. London is a big city, with lots of people and smoke and noise…'

'I don't think I like London.'

'You might, it's an exciting place... but don't worry if you don't like it – we won't stay long. My parents live in Norfolk, near the beach. That's where we are going.'

'The beach!' Eleanor immediately lit up.

'It's very different from the ocean in Hawaii. Where we are, there are beaches full of pebbles and the water is very cold.'

'How will I make a sandcastle?'

'We'll find a sandy beach for you, and we have dunes near my parents' home.'

'What are dunes?' Eleanor asked.

'Big mountains of sand, taller than you are!'

Eleanor smiled with anticipation and Isabella pulled her into a hug.

After a while it got too cold to be outside, and so they retreated to the saloon. Isabella decided that when they were home she would contact Elizabeth's father and brother to arrange a time for them to visit Eleanor. She knew there was a chance they might contest the guardianship – understandably so, as they had no idea who she was. She was gripped intermittently by fear at the thought of being separated from Eleanor.

The sea was choppy for the whole voyage east. When Eleanor was asleep, Isabella would wrap her shawl around her shoulders and walk out onto the deck. Even though it was night, the waves were illuminated by the steamer's lights, and were strangely hypnotising. Her thoughts would return to Hawaii and Kainalu. She prayed for the day he would no longer be uppermost in her mind. She knew time would help, but she was also sure that if she saw him again the desire would come rushing back. It had to be contained and forgotten. Isabella's future was in England.

'Penny for your thoughts?'

She turned around to see a grey-haired gentleman in a top hat, leaning on a walking stick. He had bushy grey eyebrows that almost hid his eyes. Isabella smiled politely and he came to stand next to her.

'It's beautiful, isn't it?' he said, looking up at the full moon revealing the peaks and valleys made by the clouds in the sky. 'May I introduce myself, with the lack of anyone present to do it for me? My name is Professor Adrian Withal.'

'I am Isabella Buckley.' They shook hands. 'At which university are you a professor?'

'I am based in King's College in London, but my wife and I have just been at Yale for a semester. Philosophy is my subject; I was invited to be a visiting lecturer on secondment.'

'You don't by any chance know Professor and Mrs Ferrier? We have been staying with them.'

'Well, I never! Of course I know them.' They talked of the Ferriers for a while, and then he concentrated on Isabella. 'What about you, my dear? Why are you travelling?'

As he asked the question, Isabella felt tears involuntarily come to her eyes. Embarrassed, she looked away and tried to compose herself.

He was not perturbed and waited for her to speak.

'I went to New Zealand to help my family, and have returned via the Sandwich Islands, where I spent a few months.'

'The Sandwich Islands... I have heard that they are paradise on earth. It must have been hard to pull yourself away.'

If only he knew.

'It was, but the green hills and forests of England were calling me home,' Isabella said, with a forced laugh.

They sat for a while in silence.

'It's late, and my wife will be wondering where I am. I bid you goodnight. Don't lose heart, my dear, circumstances always change when you least expect it.' He turned and went into the bright saloon while Isabella stayed outside. Watching him go, she was strangely comforted by his words.

After a few more minutes Isabella started to feel cold. With a sigh, she walked inside.

Isabella slept deeply that night, and both she and Eleanor were woken by the sound of a blast of steam coming out of the ship's engine. Land was in sight.

It was a beautiful day on the south coast of England; a clear blue sky reigned overhead. Being so close to those she loved, Isabella suddenly became impatient. She wanted to be off the ship and at home in the bosom of her family.

She and Eleanor went on deck to watch the land as it came closer, although Eleanor preferred to run up and down with a young boy and his sister. Isabella noticed their parents didn't seem to mind, and so she let Eleanor play. She wanted Eleanor to be as free as the children in Hawaii and she wasn't sure how this was going to work once she was home, where the norm was for children to be seen and not heard.

Eventually the green fields of Devon, and Plymouth's rooftops and church steeples could clearly be seen.

'It's England, it's England!' cried Eleanor as they watched the land draw near.

After a few more hours the steamer dropped anchor. Isabella and Eleanor said goodbye to the Withals before they disembarked. Isabella paid for a carriage to take them to the train station, where she purchased two tickets for London. The weather was sunny, and Isabella was grateful; it made coming home much easier. She was beginning to wonder what she had been so worried about, but as she watched the familiarity of the architecture and the people go by, she had a strange sensation of being out of place, as if she had put on a set of clothes that didn't quite fit her any more.

After three hours the train drew in at Paddington Station and Isabella and Eleanor caught a Hansom cab south to Cheyne Walk on the river in Chelsea, Sir Mark's London abode. She hoped he had received her letter and would be expecting them. The crowds, noise and grime of London felt overwhelming. Eleanor was silent, watching the people and buildings, her large eyes taking everything in.

A young red-headed maid opened the door to Isabella and Eleanor, and led them into a bright drawing room on the second floor. Within a few minutes Sir Mark blustered in. Isabella immediately felt her hackles rise, but knew she needed him on her side and would have to show patience and grace.

'Miss Buckley, welcome back to civilisation!' he barked, before seeing Eleanor perched on the sofa. 'Ah, you must be Eleanor; you've changed since I last saw you.' It was said briskly.

Eleanor was silent, looking to Isabella for assurance. Isabella smiled, and put out her hand for Eleanor to come and join her on her chair.

'Terrible business, all that happened...' he appeared unsure of what to say. 'I see you have quite a bond.'

Eleanor was nestling into Isabella's side.

'Yes, well, we have had quite a journey together, and I am now her guardian. That is what I wanted to talk to you about.'

'I see. You are staying the night, am I correct? We can discuss details over supper.' He stood up. 'Now I must take my leave as I have an appointment in the City.'

Isabella was grateful he did not ask too much in front of Eleanor. She didn't want her to get any inkling that there was a possibility she might be taken from her.

The maid had been told to put Eleanor in a smaller room a floor above Isabella's, but Isabella explained that she would prefer for Eleanor to be in the same room as herself. It meant she could comfort her if she awoke with nightmares. Arrangements were made, and a small bed was made up and positioned next to Isabella's four-poster.

Eleanor was given an early supper of shepherd's pie in the kitchen, and then Isabella put her to bed before changing for supper. In her short few hours in the capital, she realised fashions had moved on since she had been away, and she felt rather dowdy in her well-worn black silk.

'My dear!' cried Lucy, Sir Mark's new wife, when they met in the hallway. 'I am sorry I was not here when you arrived.' She looked Isabella up and down. 'You are looking... fresh.'

'Thank you, Lucy,' said Isabella, unsure if it was a compliment or not, but guessing the latter. Isabella had forgotten how small and mouse-like she was and bristled at her new superior attitude now that she was lady of the house.

They walked together to the drawing room and sat down on chairs opposite the fire.

'I've just come down from Norfolk in order to attend a few balls here. I do love London!'

'Yes.' Isabella couldn't think of what else to say about London, or the society balls for that matter. 'How are my family? Have you seen them?'

'They were at church on Sunday, all in good spirits and excited about having you home, no doubt. Catherine seems to be very well. When you first left, I dare say she found it very hard, and who could blame her? But Isabella! You are asking me about home, and I have so many questions for you. Tell me about the dear little girl I hear you are looking after.'

Isabella was desperate to hear more of her family, but politely acquiesced. 'She is named Eleanor, and she is now five years old. I got to know her parents on the passage out to New Zealand; your husband is their relative, if you remember?'

'Yes, I do remember. How tragic for her to lose both parents,' sighed Lucy.

Before they could talk more, Sir Mark walked in, and a few minutes later a maid announced supper. They went through to the dining room where they were served oxtail soup, followed by pork belly and then apple tart. Isabella brought up the subject of the guardianship over pudding. Sir Mark was businesslike about the situation.

'I will talk to Eleanor's family on your behalf. They may well contest the guardianship, you know. Perhaps, if you can agree to visit to make sure Eleanor knows her relatives, then they would be happy to give their blessing.'

'Of course, I want Eleanor to be close to her family and will do whatever I can to make that possible.'

'Good, glad to hear it. Well, let's see what happens,' said Sir Mark.

'Yes, let's see,' agreed Isabella.

Chapter Twenty-six

England, October 1881

The next morning, after a fortifying breakfast of smoked haddock kedgeree, Sir Mark's carriage took Isabella and Eleanor to Liverpool Street. A heady smell of oil and steam emanated from the station as they walked inside. The train to Norwich was waiting on platform one and Isabella found their compartment, making sure the trunks were safely stowed by a steward. Once seated, Isabella leant back on the headrest and gave a deep sigh. She was nearly home.

The train chugged out of the station and caught up speed as the smoky tenement buildings of east London became a moving picture outside their carriage. The steam from the engine was like a signal calling them home, with the noise of the tracks seeming to repeat, 'We're coming, we're coming.' Eleanor and Isabella watched the familiar undulating green landscape of Essex, Suffolk and eventually the flat fields of Norfolk go by. With passengers joining and getting off at different stops, their compartment was finally empty when, after nearly three hours, they arrived at Norwich station, where they changed for a slower train to Cromer on the coast.

'Here we are!' Isabella declared, when the train pulled to a halt with a loud screech.

'Is this my home?' Eleanor asked, looking up enquiringly to Isabella

'Nearly. We've just a short carriage journey to go.'

Eleanor looked weary, but she did not complain. Isabella held out her hand to help her step down onto the station platform. She looked to the entrance of the platform and saw the familiar silhouette of her father waiting, wearing his black top hat. The sight of him gave her an overwhelming sense of relief.

'Papa,' she called, waving her arm in the air.

With a look of joy, he walked towards them. 'My dear,' he said, giving her a kiss on her cheek.

Isabella wondered if she could detect a tear in his eye. This was most unusual, as Reverend Buckley was particularly restrained with his emotions.

'I'd like you to meet Eleanor, Papa.'

Lowering himself to be at Eleanor's eye level, and resting on one knee, Reverend Buckley took her little hand and shook it.

'I am very pleased to make your acquaintance. What an honour to meet such a charming young lady.'

Isabella was so grateful for him at that moment; she should have guessed he would know exactly the right thing to do. Eleanor's face flushed with pleasure, and she took his hand to be led out to their carriage.

It was a five-mile journey home, and when they eventually pulled into the driveway, Isabella thought the house and garden had never looked more lovely. It was early October, but England was evidently experiencing a particularly beautiful autumn. The trees were a collage of russets and greens, and the purple and white flowering hydrangeas around the side of the house were in full bloom. Even the rose garden boasted a riot of late blossoms. Isabella's heart leapt as she saw her mother and Catherine coming out through the open front door. They both picked up their skirts and hurried towards the carriage with expectant smiles on their faces.

'That is my mother on the left and my sister, Catherine,' Isabella said to Eleanor as they came closer.

The carriage came to a halt, the horses snorting and shaking their manes, ready for water and hay. Isabella stepped down from the carriage and her father lifted Eleanor out. Within seconds Catherine had enveloped her sister in a hug, and her mother was close behind.

'And you must be Eleanor,' said Catherine, bending down and drawing her into an embrace too.

Eleanor smiled shyly, but allowed herself to be hugged.

'My dear Isabella, how wonderful to have you back!' said Mrs Buckley. 'You'll be thirsty. Let's get some tea, and some of the elderflower cordial for Eleanor.'

'I am so glad you are home!' said Catherine, holding on to Isabella's arm as if she was afraid she would fly off again. Slowly they walked to the wooden chairs and table that had been brought to the flagstone area outside the drawing room, Eleanor's hand safe in Isabella's. A tablecloth was laid on the table and Hattie came out carrying a cake, and placed it on the table.

'Welcome home, miss,' she said with a smile.

'Thank you, Hattie. This is Eleanor. She will be living with us now.'

'Pleased to meet you,' Hattie said to Eleanor with a bob of her head.

After a while Eleanor became fidgety, so Catherine took her to the old swing at the end of the garden.

'She is very dear, but can you look after her by yourself?' Mrs Buckley asked as Eleanor was playing with Catherine out of earshot.

'I don't know, Mama, but I will try, and I would be grateful for any help,' Isabella said, peeved that her mother had detected her insecurity straight away. She wanted to be encouraged and told it would all work out well. The truth was, she didn't know if she alone would be enough for Eleanor.

Reverend Buckley, whom Isabella thought had been sleeping in the chair next to them, suddenly perked up. He changed the subject by telling her that Hamish, Emily and the boys had settled on an estate in Suffolk where Hamish had found a job as land manager.

'I've sent a message for them to come and visit.'

After Eleanor had had her high tea and Hattie had heated some water for a bath, Catherine and Isabella put her to bed together.

'Do you want to say prayers or shall I?' Isabella asked.

'I'll pray,' Eleanor whispered. 'Thank You, Lord Jesus, for Mama Isabella, my Aunt Catherine and my new grandmama and grandpapa. Thank you for looking after Mama and Papa in heaven, and please look after Harry, Uncle Kai and Leilei in Y-ee. Amen.'

'Amen,' Isabella agreed, giving her a kiss.

'Goodnight, Eleanor,' said Catherine, and they left the room quietly as she closed her eyes.

'She seems to have accepted us so quickly,' whispered Catherine as they walked down the corridor.

'I am so relieved; I wonder if it is because I spoke of you all so much that she feels she already knows you.'

As supper would not be for another hour, Isabella went to sit in Catherine's room.

'Who are Harry and Kai and Leilei?' Catherine asked as she closed the door.

'Harry Fortnum was the son of the family we stayed with. Leilei is Eleanor's nickname for the sweet Hawaiian girl called Leilani, who became her dearest friend while we were there, and Kai is Kainalu, her uncle,' Isabella said. 'Do you remember I wrote to you about them?'

'Oh yes, of course. She obviously loves them.'

Isabella didn't feel ready to talk about Kainalu and his family quite yet, so she changed the subject by asking about William.

'We are better friends than ever now that it is all out in the open. I know he does not see me in a romantic way, so I feel free to be his friend. Of course, it hurt at first, but I realised I had put all my hope in him, and so I just tried to transfer my hope back into something else. I feel surprisingly content.'

'I am so glad, Catherine. I am very sorry.'

'Don't say any more, it is not your fault he chose you,' she said, turning to sit at her dressing table and arrange her hair. 'You can still say yes to him, you know.'

'Catherine, I don't feel for him the way you do. I could not be his wife. It is unfair how it has worked out.'

'I am learning that life is not always fair.' Catherine looked at Isabella through the reflection in the mirror. Isabella could see the pain in her sister's eyes behind her acceptance of the situation, which she had no power to ease.

'Let's talk after supper; there is so much more to say, but I need to get changed,' Isabella said. As she walked to her room, she knew Catherine would understand more of why she would not say yes to William when she learned about Kainalu. Isabella peeped into Eleanor's room to check that she was asleep. This was the first time the child would be sleeping in a different room from herself... but they were home now.

'It is *so* wonderful to have you back,' said Mrs Buckley at supper. 'What was the food like in Hawaii? Were the natives dreadfully different from us?'

'The food was simple, but fresh. I loved the fruit they grow on the islands. The people are not so different; in fact, it is said the islands have the highest rate of literacy in the world, but they are not restricted by *Englishness*, or whatever you want to call it.'

'I don't know what you mean.'

Isabella knew her mother would not understand, so she did not attempt to explain more.

'Is there hardship there?' asked Reverend Buckley.

'There is sickness; leprosy is a big problem. I met a Hawaiian man who was working to help eradicate it from the islands.'

'How terrible. I don't think humanity will be free from hardship until we are in heaven.'

'What was the man called?' Mrs Buckley interjected.

'Kainalu.'

'What an extraordinary name...'

Isabella didn't expand, but instead talked about the Fortnums, and when her parents retired to bed, she and Catherine moved into the candlelit drawing room, the fire in the grate still burning strong. The shutters had been left open and the garden was illuminated by a harvest moon.

'From your letters, I wanted to come out and join you in Hawaii!'

'Oh, Catherine, it was paradise, like nowhere else on earth. The people are free from our social conventions that I find so restricting. There is a class system – with chiefs and royalty – but life appears to be a constant holiday, with the turquoise ocean a free playground for all. Life for many Hawaiians is very basic; they live in grass-roofed huts, built in small compounds or villages. They call it a *kauhale*.'

Catherine repeated the word, trying to pronounce it.

'They have houses for the men to eat and another for the women and children, and then a sleeping house. Life is lived outdoors, really. I spent most of my time with a Hawaiian family who were highly educated and very warm. They had servants and homes similar to the Europeans.'

'I think you must have caught something from these Hawaiians. You look different; something in your face has changed. You are beautiful,' Catherine said, before adding, 'But I see sadness in your eyes too. Has it been harder than you have let on? I imagine being close to Eleanor's parents and having them die must have been traumatic.'

'It was, but I am so blessed to have Eleanor. I never thought I would be a mother.'

Catherine nodded sadly and Isabella knew that she too had given up that hope.

The next morning Isabella awoke late to birdsong and the sound of the wind blowing the leaves in the cherry tree outside her window. Sleepily she got out of bed and splashed water on her face before getting dressed. Eleanor's room was empty and Isabella followed the sound of voices downstairs to find her dressed and sitting in the library with Catherine, who was helping her to make something with swatches of material.

'Ah, there you are!' exclaimed Catherine as Isabella joined them.

'We are making bunting!' Eleanor said when she saw Isabella.

'It's for the Sunday school party. Have some breakfast and come and join us.'

Mrs Buckley had asked friends not to visit while Isabella and Eleanor settled in, but by the weekend they had a stream of guests welcoming her home. Isabella recounted the same stories over and over as friends asked about her experiences.

For the first week William was noticeably absent from the rectory. However, he eventually gave word that he would be visiting and Mrs Buckley invited him to stay for lunch. Isabella was nervous, not knowing how things would be. She waited for him in the driveway while Catherine entertained Eleanor in the garden. As she heard the clip-clop of horse hoofs coming along the lane, she took a deep breath and straightened the front of her jacket, but when she saw his smile, she knew she need not have worried. As soon as he jumped off his horse, he walked over to her and took her hand.

'Isabella, welcome home!'

She smiled. He was his same warm, kind self.

'I have so much to ask you, but first, where is little Eleanor?' he asked.

Isabella pointed to the swing where Catherine was pushing her. He strolled over.

She watched as he greeted Catherine and then introduced himself to Eleanor. He must have said something funny, as they all laughed, and then he bent down to invite Eleanor on a piggyback ride. Watching the three of them together, anyone would have thought they were a happy little family.

At lunch, William was very polite and attentive to Isabella, asking her questions about New Zealand and Hawaii, but she noticed how he looked at her sister, and how they laughed at jokes together.

She felt a sudden, unexpected pang of jealousy.

Uncle Hamish and Aunt Emily came to visit with their sons, Titus and Freddie. There were hugs and tears from Emily as she greeted Isabella.

'I am so sorry you came all that way for nothing,' said Hamish. 'But I knew if anyone could survive it, and make good of the situation, it would be you.'

'We never got your father's telegram saying you were coming; if we had, we would have waited. I am so sorry,' added Emily, linking her arm in Isabella's.

'It wasn't a wasted experience; in fact, I was very glad that I was given the opportunity to travel to such beautiful places.'

'Titus and Freddie, why don't you take Eleanor to play outside?' suggested Hamish.

'Yes, Father,' Titus replied, in two octaves, his voice on the cusp of breaking. His eagerness suggested he was relieved not to have to sit through more adult conversation in the drawing room.

The boys took Eleanor into the garden and began a game of tag.

'What well brought-up sons,' Isabella said to Emily as they watched them play, noticing that they allowed Eleanor to get away from them, when they could easily have caught her.

'I think they would like a little sister, and a new female cousin is the next best thing,' Emily laughed.

'Tell me what happened in New Zealand,' Isabella said.

Emily shook her head sadly, and looked at her husband. 'I had been sure Hamish was dead, that I would never see him again. It was truly terrible. I felt alone and vulnerable being so far from family and with the responsibility of looking after our boys.'

'And I had no idea who I was,' Hamish added. 'Or what was going on. If it hadn't been for Ahurewa, the old Maori lady taking care of me, I don't know what would have happened. She hardly spoke, but used to sing to herself and mutter as she worked. When I came round, her big toothless grin was the first face I saw.'

'Where were you?' Isabella asked.

'At the time I didn't know. I was confused and in pain. I was attacked and robbed while on horseback, but it was so quick that I never saw my assailants. When I fell, after the horse reared, I hit my head and was knocked out instantly. My horse ran off. We never found her so we presume she was stolen. I don't know how long I was there before Ahurewa dragged me to her hut nearby. She cared for me and bit by bit my memory came back. She spoke some sort of pidgin English.

'After many days she told me her son had died at the hands of a white man, and I was the same age as him. I tried to find out more, and what I gathered was that she had been visited by someone – she called her a "Jesus lady" – one of her own people, though. This Maori Christian had told her about God.

'Ahurewa said her eyes were opened. She described this to me with sign language. She said she felt "belly joy" and her heart was comforted in spite of the loss of her son.

'When she prayed with this lady, she felt God speak to her heart that she needed to forgive the man who had killed her son. Ahurewa had been forgiven so she must forgive, and that would set her free from the pain she carried. She said she fought to forgive for a whole year, but eventually, broken and hurting, she prayed for help. She showed me a hard rock and then the porridge she had cooking over the fire. She told me God had softened her rock-hard heart until it was soft like the porridge, and this had helped her to forgive.' He paused, shaking his head.

'A week later she found me, a white man, unconscious on the road. If she had met me a week earlier, she would have left me to die, but her heart was open towards me and she took me into her home, caring for me as if I was her own son. Her face was radiant as she nursed me, and she cried when I eventually left, my amnesia fully lifted.

'Coming back to Emily and the boys was an emotional homecoming, I can tell you, but those weeks at Ahurewa's home were strangely very precious. I took Emily and the boys to meet her, and we have tried to support her.'

Emily, with her pale-blue eyes glistening, took Hamish's hand and smiled. 'She was a guardian angel; I am sure of it.'

Before Hamish and Emily left, Isabella told them about her time in Auckland, the tragedy of Elizabeth and Hubert's deaths and the steamer voyages. Then Emily asked about Hawaii.

'What were the Sandwich Islands like? I was surprised to hear that you were staying there for so long.'

'Oh, Emily, they were beautiful. I felt completely well and alive there for the first time in my life.'

'Well, I never – no back pain?'

Isabella shook her head.

'It must have been hard to leave.'

Isabella didn't say more. She was sure Catherine and Aunt Emily both knew there was something she wasn't telling them, but she was not ready to talk. If she spoke about Kainalu, and he became alive to her family, it would be too hard to shut him out of her mind.

Chapter Twenty-seven

Norfolk, winter 1881-82

Isabella wrote to Eleanor's grandfather, telling him that they were safely in Norfolk. She invited him to visit, informing him that she was hoping to make Eleanor's guardianship official. Sir Mark had also confirmed he would stand as a character reference if needed. Isabella posted the letter with a nervous heart, praying that it would be read by favourable eyes.

The Buckleys didn't hear from Eleanor's family straight away. Winter was now fully ensconced in Norfolk and showed off with blustery winds battling the bronzed leaves on the beech trees in the garden until they were all stark and naked. When Christmas came, it held a new excitement for the family through Eleanor's wonder.

As the New Year marched in, Kainalu and life in Hawaii seemed like a dream to Isabella, so different from the normal and mundane at home. The smell of polished wood, the ticking of the grandfather clock in the hallway, nothing had changed. Mrs West was preparing the same familiar meals, they had social calls most days, and dear Walter was still conscientiously cutting the lawn and pruning the hedges.

But the routine of daily life became Isabella's saviour. She painted, received callers with her mother, and accompanied her father as he visited the widows of the parish. Eleanor came with her in all she did. Isabella knew she would need a governess or a school to go to eventually, but for now they could spend their days together.

When Eleanor slept, Isabella began sorting out her paintings from Hawaii. She had more than fifty of the flora and a few landscapes, as well as sketches of the lepers. Isabella lay them out in the spare bedroom, on the twin beds, leaning them against the headboards, on the floor and dresser. She sat looking at them all, wishing she could somehow jump into the paintings and return to Hawaii.

'Well, I never!' her father said from the corridor. He came into the room and smiled at his daughter as he picked up one of the paintings. It was of an orange hibiscus and he took it to the window to inspect it more closely. 'My dear, this is quite impressive. You have come a long way. I'd say these are good enough for an exhibition.'

'Do you think so?'

'Botanical paintings are quite the thing nowadays. I may never see the flowers you have portrayed here in my lifetime, but I imagine you have drawn their exact representation.'

'I was so inspired by the beauty and colours in Hawaii, I painted nearly every day.'

'We must exhibit them.'

'I will need time to work on some of these, and then get them all framed...'

'Let us plan for May, when the weather is better. We can use the new parish hall... There is a framer you can use in Holt. I will help, my dear. How marvellous to have an exhibition!'

He left the room, and Isabella picked up a smaller painting of the view from Aolani's house, feeling excited to share the beauty of the islands.

In it all, despite the new distraction of planning an exhibition and the joy of Eleanor, Isabella was frustrated that Kainalu was still in her thoughts. She wondered if he was now married to the girl his mother had intended for him. The thought gave her a wave of nausea.

While she was walking away from love, even though unrequited, it seemed that her intuition about the change in relationship between William and Catherine was correct. Catherine had been spending more and more time helping in the surgery. She was being trained by the duty nurse to administer drugs and tend wounds. She and William would spend many hours talking about medical matters and how different ailments could be treated. Isabella realised Catherine was in her element.

At lunch, Isabella asked Catherine to come for a walk in the snow that had fallen a day earlier.

'Oh, I am sorry, I can't. William is coming in a few moments to take me to the surgery. I will be filling in for the nurse!'

'But how long will that take? Perhaps we could go when you return?'

Catherine looked sheepish. 'William mentioned something about a ride on Holkham beach. William said it is the perfect day for it as the snow has stopped and the sun is out... so I think I will not make other plans.'

Isabella found herself irritated by how often Catherine repeated William's name.

'Can *we* go riding on the beach too?' Eleanor asked, looking up at Isabella.

'Not this time, but we will soon.'

'That must be William now,' said Mrs Buckley, as the sound of a carriage crunching on the gravel could be heard from outside. 'Next time, do tell him to come a little later. You haven't even time to finish lunch.'

Catherine was already standing and she went over to the window to peer outside. 'Yes, it is him, I will be off,' she said with a lightness and joy that Isabella had not seen for a while.

Isabella could hear their happy chattering. She was pleased, of course, but there was also an inconvenient note of insecurity that she felt towards their new closeness.

'Wake up! There is a letter for you. Grandmama said it is from Hawaii!' Eleanor's face was almost touching Isabella's own. Isabella had slept late, which was unusual for her. She was glad for Hattie who now dressed Eleanor and took her downstairs in the mornings.

Despite her tiredness, Isabella was amused at Eleanor's eagerness as the child pulled the sheets and blanket from over her, and yanked her out of bed.

'Alright, I'm up!' she laughed, drawing a shawl around her shoulders and packing Eleanor out of the room so that she could get dressed.

A little while later Isabella walked downstairs. Not seeing the letters on the side table in the hall where they were usually left, she went into the dining room where breakfast was being served. Mrs Buckley and Eleanor were the only two at the table.

'Glad to see you, dear. I thought Eleanor was going to explode with excitement, but I told her she must wait for you to open the letters.'

'Thank you, quite right!' Isabella said, smiling at the twinkle in her mother's eye.

Eleanor had enthusiastically put the two letters on Isabella's place mat, one addressed to Isabella and one to Eleanor. Isabella picked them up. She didn't recognise the writing, so they weren't from Emma Fortnum, who had written a couple of times since their return. She realised her hand was shaking; could they be from Kainalu? Isabella let Eleanor open the first letter, which was addressed to her. A pressed orchid fell out as she unfolded it.

'Look!' gasped Eleanor, picking up the flower and smelling it. 'It still smells!' she said, putting it close to Isabella's nose for verification.

'Lovely,' Isabella agreed, the sweet fragrance immediately evocative of the islands. Her heart sank slightly when she realised the letter was from Leilani, with help from Aolani.

Isabella read the letter to Eleanor. Leilani wrote of how she missed her English sister, and told her of a recent fishing trip where her father had caught a turtle by mistake. She finished the letter with a drawing of a turtle and her name surrounded by flowers.

Eleanor asked Isabella to read it through twice, and then happily took the pages and pored over them at her seat. She couldn't read yet, but pretended to, and was completely content.

Isabella's letter had the same script as Eleanor's, so she guessed it was from Aolani. It would be the first time she had written to her.

Dearest Isabella,

I apologise in advance for my writing is not good. I wanted to write you, but it was too hard. I miss you with many tears. My Hawaii misses you. I want to tell you some news. Kainalu decided to sail the waters to find you. He said if you see him, you would return. He loves you and wants to marry you. Kapuna Wahine *has given up trying to provide him with a Hawaiian lady, and she gave her blessing. Kainalu did not get far, he landed in San Francisco, the weather was very cold and he was ill. He noticed a patch on his skin that was not normal. He had a thick, red skin with flaky, silver-white patches. It did not take long for him to realise he had leprosy. My brother did not go to the doctor, but returned on the next ship. Kainalu will have to sail for Moloka'i. My heart is broken, like a moon being parted from the stars. I cannot think of my brother, my good, kind, wise brother, having this fate. Please, sister, pray for him. I wanted to explain that he would have come, but for this dreaded disease.*

Aloha,

Aolani

Isabella's hand had involuntarily flown to her mouth as she read the first few lines. When she finished the letter, a teardrop fell into the empty plate in front of her. She blinked any more away, and got up quickly, before Eleanor asked questions.

'I am just fetching my shawl,' she said, as she hurried upstairs to her room where she reread the letter in privacy. *He did love me! He came for me!* It took Isabella a while to compose herself; she was overwhelmed with the news that he loved her, after telling herself for so long that she had imagined his affections. Kainalu had been coming for her; he had not given up on her. He had left his home to travel to England. But the joy of knowing her love was returned was marred inextricably by the pain of his illness. She remembered seeing the relatives saying goodbye to the lepers as they boarded the *Kilauea*. Their grief was now her own. He was not dead, but he might as well be. There was no life for him now.

She sat back and looked up at the ceiling; how could Kainalu get this disease now? It felt both painful and deeply unfair.

She could hear her mother with Eleanor downstairs, so she was not needed yet. Eventually, she went to find Catherine, who was in her room, writing a letter at her desk.

'Catherine, a letter has just come from Kainalu's sister. I need to explain something.'

Her sister immediately turned to her. Isabella passed the letter to Catherine. She read it quickly.

'Do you love him?' Catherine asked eventually, putting the letter down. Her eyes were wide.

'I do.'

'Why didn't you say?'

Isabella took a deep breath and told Catherine the whole story, how she didn't know what he felt for her, but had hoped; how his mother had disapproved and was arranging a marriage for him with a Hawaiian girl.

'I felt ridiculous having desire for Kainalu. When I realised his mother knew and was planning a marriage for him, I felt humiliated.'

'Is that why you came home when you did?'

'Yes,' Isabella admitted with shame.

'Your feelings were obviously reciprocated; you should not feel ashamed. I understand the strength of love,' she broke off, handing Isabella her handkerchief.

Later that morning Isabella wrote back to Aolani, thanking her for the letter and telling her that her prayers would be with Kainalu. She made sure that the tears she shed missed the paper, so as not to smudge the ink. She wanted to write to Kainalu, but it took her a long time to find the right words to say.

Eleanor's grandfather, Colonel Fennimore, replied to Isabella's letter. He explained that they had held a memorial service for Hubert and Elizabeth while Isabella and Eleanor were still in Hawaii.

> *The loss of my daughter has been hard, almost intolerable. I want to come and visit Eleanor, to see her, and to discuss the situation. I am grateful for the care you have shown her. When I said goodbye to her last year, I did not think I would see her face again, as I am old. Unfortunately, I have been too ill to travel, although I am gaining strength, and hope to visit when the weather is more clement.*

When, a week later, the country had a temporary thawing, Isabella received another letter informing her that the colonel would be coming to visit the following weekend with his son, Elizabeth's brother.

'Well, that is very short notice,' complained Mrs Buckley. 'But we will be ready, and show them that dear Eleanor is loved and happy with us.'

She went to talk to Hattie and Mrs West and the result was a flurry of cleaning and preparation. The brass shone, the wood had never been more polished, and there was not a cobweb in sight.

'Eleanor, can you guess who is coming to see you?' Isabella said as she dressed her the next morning.

'Who? Leilani?' Eleanor said, eyes wide with hope.

'No, but some very special people – your grandfather and your uncle.'

'Oh…' she said, sounding disappointed. 'Grandpa?'

'Yes, and your uncle, Anthony.'

'Oh,' she said, eyes lighting up as they came back to her memory.

The Fennimores would be arriving before lunch on the Saturday. William agreed to be present to help and give support.

'What if she is taken away from me?' Isabella asked Catherine in hushed tones as they sat together in the drawing room the day before the Fennimores were to arrive. She hardly wanted to voice her fear.

'She won't be, I am sure of it,' Catherine soothed. 'Once they meet you, and see how you love Eleanor, and she loves you, they will surely consent.'

Isabella was silent for a while. What Catherine said may be true, but Isabella could not ignore the nagging thought that perhaps it was actually best for Eleanor to be back with her family. She had to be prepared to let her go, however much the thought frightened and depressed her.

Colonel Fennimore's carriage pulled into the Buckleys' driveway at noon. The horse's breath was visible in the cold, misty air. The men were wrapped up like parcels in furs and hats. Isabella and her mother, who had been waiting in the hall, opened the front door and welcomed them inside. They were ushered into the warm drawing room, where there was a fire roaring in the grate.

Eleanor shyly watched them both, as Hattie took their hats and scarves.

'Hello Eleanor, do you remember me?' asked Anthony, hunching down to squat at her height. 'I'm your Uncle Anthony.'

Eleanor smiled shyly.

Isabella instantly warmed to Anthony, and felt some of her nerves dissipate. *He must be in his forties*, she thought, *with the same kind face as his sister.* His father, however, was not so warm and he did not smile as he entered the drawing room.

After lunch, Hattie was asked to take Eleanor down from the table to play. The adults were then able to talk more freely about what had happened. Elizabeth's father asked many questions, and Isabella answered as best she could.

'I am grateful to you for looking after my granddaughter, and although I would love her to live with me, I know I am too old to be bringing her up. Anthony travels so much it would be no life for a child. I received a letter from Elizabeth; it must have been written the day she died. She wrote about you.' The colonel coughed slightly. 'I wanted you to be able to settle back home, to give Eleanor time to recover; that is why we did not come immediately.' He paused, looking at his son, who gave a small nod. 'Now I am here, and have been able to assess the situation, there is one thing that concerns me.' He put both hands on the table, as if steadying himself. 'I have not come to this decision easily, but it has been troubling me. You are unmarried, Miss Buckley, and I do not think it best for Eleanor to be brought up by a single woman.'

Isabella opened her mouth in shock. She was about to protest, but he continued.

'She needs both a mother and a father. It is because of this that I am going to contest the guardianship, and see about arranging for Eleanor to be looked after by the cousins in Blanford Forum who have children too.'

Isabella felt a weight land on her chest, but stayed silent.

'I will not act rashly, and I need to contact them to see if they will be happy to have Eleanor, but I do think it is the right thing for her.'

Isabella could hardly utter a word, and Mrs Buckley took over the conversation.

'Of course, we appreciate that you have thought about this, but you must know we all love Eleanor very much. Isabella would not be alone in bringing her up; it would be a family affair.'

Isabella saw the colonel and his son exchange glances. Her parents were getting on in years, and she and her sister were spinsters. Isabella wished her father would speak up; she knew he would be very sad at the loss of Eleanor. He had been gentle with her and would patiently read Bible stories to her. He had taken on the role of grandfather wholeheartedly; indeed, Isabella had noticed that he was more affectionate with Eleanor than he had been with his own children.

'Sir, I want to remind you that Elizabeth asked me to *adopt* Eleanor. It was her dying wish, and one I feel privileged to accept.'

'She was desperate,' he said with a low voice. 'Far from home, and she needed reassurance. No doubt you have been a wonderful guardian, but I am sorry, Eleanor must return to her family.'

Isabella said no more, and the conversation moved on to trivial matters. She tried to listen and contribute, but she knew that Catherine was also holding back tears. If Isabella had looked at her, she would have lost her composure completely.

Thankfully the Fennimores were staying at a small hotel in Holt, and left soon after revealing their intended future for Eleanor. They promised to be back the next day when the details could be discussed.

'Can we go outside?' Eleanor asked Isabella after she had waved her grandfather and uncle off and the family had gone back indoors. Isabella raised a smile and reached out a hand to draw her in. She came close, and held Isabella's face in her little hands, looking into her eyes as if searching for something.

'Are you sad?' Eleanor asked.

'I'm not sad. How can I be, with you here?'

Eleanor accepted the answer. 'Let's play, then?'

'Why don't you ask Mrs West for some tea and cake first?'

'Oh, yes!'

When Eleanor had left the room, Mrs Buckley said, 'I wonder if we should engage a solicitor? I will write to Sir Mark.'

'I don't know how much one would help,' said Isabella.

'Well, it is worth a try,' Mrs Buckley retorted, and left the drawing room to go to her desk and put ink to paper straight away.

Even though it was cold outside, the sky was blue, and William and Catherine decided to take a walk before dusk fell.

'Come with us?' Catherine asked her sister.

'No, I think I might just stay with Eleanor, now that we don't know how long we'll have her.'

Catherine took Isabella's hand but said nothing.

'I'll just speak to your father before we go,' said William.

He was in the study for a while, and Isabella sat with Catherine in the hallway, waiting as she put on her bonnet and coat. Eleanor was happily eating cake by the fire in the drawing room. Eventually William came and they headed out, but not before Catherine checked one more time if Isabella would join them.

'No, you go. Have a lovely time.'

Isabella joined Eleanor and sat on the window seat looking out into the skeletal landscape, plants and trees stripped of foliage. She knew that when outside, having the vast sky as her ceiling, even the gloomiest days were full of beauty, but she was tired and had no stamina for a walk. She felt the old familiar pains in her joints and back, the ailments that had entirely left her in Hawaii. Her heart sank at their return as she remembered the discomfort she'd had to endure in the past. Everything seemed to be going wrong. She let out a desperate prayer: *'Why is life so difficult? Please help.'*

Despite the cold, Eleanor pursuaded Isabella to go out to the swing. Isabella obliged, wrapping her up in her woollen coat and scarf. As they opened the front door, Isabella tried to ignore the sense of heaviness that was ramming at her defences.

She followed Eleanor as she happily ran onto the frosty grass and skipped to the swing. Isabella stood behind her and pushed. 'Higher! Higher!' demanded Eleanor, her breath coming out of her mouth like little smoke clouds into the cold air. Her laughter was infectious, and soon Isabella found herself smiling too.

Even though he had been invited, William was absent at supper. Isabella learned he had gone to Holt to talk to the Fennimores. She did not have much appetite to eat the cold meat and potatoes. At nine o'clock, when her parents had gone to bed, she heard the familiar sound of the front door opening and closing. William had let himself in, and with a gentle tap on the door, walked into the drawing room. He looked grave and would not meet Isabella's gaze.

Chapter Twenty-eight

Norfolk, winter to spring 1882

'What did they say?' Isabella asked, getting up from her seat and walking towards William.

From his face, Isabella could only assume it was bad news.

'Tell us, Will,' Catherine said, sounding as anxious as her sister felt.

'I am sorry,' he said, looking at Isabella. 'I tried to talk them round, explain your bond with Eleanor… but they both think Eleanor should remain with close relatives. They don't want to hurt you, but have decided it is best for her.' He paused, and then added, 'They suggested you be made a godmother.'

Isabella let out the breath she had not realised she had been holding, and sank into the chair next to him. 'So, this is it,' she said, defeated.

'But her mother wanted *you* to look after Eleanor. She wanted *you* to be her mother. Why is he going against her wishes?' Catherine insisted angrily.

'Like he said, Elizabeth was dying. Maybe she just wanted assurance. In other circumstances she might not have done the same thing,' murmured Isabella.

William was silent, but Catherine paced the room. 'Of course she would have, she saw how you loved her daughter. That's what is important.'

'Family is important, Catherine. I know we all love Eleanor, but I can't hold on to her.'

The next day, when the Fennimores arrived, Isabella gave the colonel Elizabeth's jewellery, all contained in a small box.

He opened it and inspected the contents.

'Where is her engagement ring?' he questioned immediately, looking straight at Isabella.

'It is there, inside the pouch.'

He looked again, and found it. Pulling it out, he gave a satisfied nod.

They had sherry in the drawing room before lunch. Colonel Fennimore came straight to the point, addressing Isabella: 'We do not want to cause you undue pain or hardship, Miss Buckley, but we truly believe Eleanor having a mother and a father is best for her.'

Isabella wanted to let them know they *were* the cause of her undue pain and hardship, but knew the truth would not help forge amicable relationships at this time, so instead she said, with a polite smile, 'I understand, and agree, but Eleanor has been through such terrible loss. She is very attached to me, and I her. I fear taking her from our home will be detrimental for her at this stage.'

'You may be right, Miss Buckley; it will be a shock to her, but she is not going to an orphanage, or a home where she won't be loved. You may be forgetting I have lost my daughter and she is my only grandchild. I believe I know what is best for her.'

'We must make arrangements, so we won't rush to remove her from your care immediately,' Anthony said gently.

'I advise you not to fight us on this; it is very unlikely my daughter's deathbed letter will stand in court. For all we know, she was coerced into writing it!' Colonel Fennimore said. 'If you agree, we will collect her in the spring, once all the arrangements have been made. And, of course, we will reimburse you for all you have spent on her.'

Isabella tried to control her anger. 'Sir, I can assure you, there was no *coercion*.' Colonel Fennimore inclined his head. 'I do not want or need financial reimbursement. The love and care I have given her has been my privilege. However, I do request one thing – that I will be allowed to stay in contact with her. Please grant me that.'

'Of course,' Anthony replied. 'I am sure it will be a remarkable blessing to both of you.' He looked uncomfortable. 'I am sorry, Isabella. You have been a wonderful guardian for the child, but Eleanor must return to her own.'

Isabella's disappointment was overwhelming, but she also felt unwise to have believed she would have ever been able to keep Eleanor.

When the Fennimores left, Isabella took Eleanor for a walk on the beach. It was very cold, and her eyes involuntarily wept, watering down her face like tears. Eleanor ran on ahead of her, the wind blowing the long strands of light brown hair into her face and causing the fabric of her dress to flap around her legs. Once they got to the sea, the roar of the wind and waves meant Isabella had to shout to get Eleanor's attention.

They were elevated on the dunes, and could see the silty brown sea at high tide stretch out before them, the weak winter sun shyly dancing on the waves and reflecting off the wet pebbles on the shore.

'Come, let's sit,' Isabella called.

Eleanor, who had been picking up seaweed, obediently came to her side and plopped herself next to Isabella.

They were silent for a while, cheeks pinched red by the cold air. They looked out at the waves crashing on the pebbled beach. Eleanor was using the seaweed as a brush on the sand, stroking it up and down to make marks. They were both beginning to shiver, so Isabella knew she had to get to the point quickly.

'Eleanor, I have something to tell you, something very wonderful…'

'What?' Eleanor asked, looking up.

'You know that your uncle and grandpa have come to visit. They love you very much, and they want you to live with your cousins near them, so you will have another mama and papa to look after you, and brothers and sisters.'

'With Sybil?' Eleanor asked, hopefully.

'Perhaps. I am not sure,' Isabella answered.

Eleanor folded her arms and her brow furrowed. 'But *you* are my mama.'

'I will still be here. But with your cousins you will have a proper mother and father, and brothers and sisters of your own.'

'I want to stay with *you*.' Eleanor kicked her feet in the sand, and looked away from Isabella.

'Eleanor, I will always be here for you, but it is right that you go with your family.'

Eleanor was silent, and then said quietly, 'I want you to be my family.'

Isabella felt her heart was breaking. 'We are not blood related, but to me you will always be family. It won't be for a little while; you will stay with us for a few more months,' Isabella added, and Eleanor buried her head into Isabella's side. Isabella kissed the top of her head. 'I love you, you know.'

By now the wind had found its way through the woollen barricades of Isabella's clothing, and Eleanor's fingers were icy. They would have to start walking, as she could feel the chill meeting her bones.

'Home?'

Eleanor nodded. Isabella stood to her feet and held out her hand. Together they walked back to the house, more subdued than on their way out.

After Isabella put Eleanor to bed at seven, she excused herself from supper, complaining of a headache, and went to her room. She sat by the small bedroom fire staring into its flames, but not really seeing them. Kainalu's face came to her mind. She wished she could talk to him. She got up and readied herself for bed. Once she was lying in the warmth and comfort under heavy blankets, she attempted to engross herself in a novel to distract her thoughts. But *Jane Eyre* could not hold her attention, and the light of her lamp was too dim. In frustration she lay back on her pillows and shut her eyes, praying for sleep to come.

Winter had a tight hold on north Norfolk that year, but by March, it slowly loosened its grip. Eventually, warming winds blew through the Buckleys' home and the pink cherry blossoms in the orchard advertised that spring had come at last, and with that the reality that Eleanor would soon be leaving.

At church, Isabella's thoughts wandered as she stood with the congregation to sing *Love Divine, All Loves Excelling.* She was only mouthing the words, her mind imagining what the house would be like without Eleanor. The girl had brought such joy and purpose to everyone. She breathed in, trying to return to the present, and sang the next verse with gusto, focusing on the stained-glass window ahead, and not the tears that were stinging her eyes. She knew it was not just tears for Eleanor, but for every disappointment that seemed to amass into one huge feeling of loss.

After church, Eleanor was invited to play with a neighbour's daughter and Isabella walked Eleanor over to the house. She walked back alone along the high-hedged lanes to the rectory. In all the beauty of burgeoning spring, she felt bereft. She told herself she should be glad of Eleanor's confidence and growing independence; it would help her in her move.

The day came when Eleanor was to be collected. Anthony arrived alone to take her on the long journey back to Dorset. Eleanor, not fully understanding what it meant for her, was excited about packing her things. She had decided to keep her growing shell collection at the rectory.

'Please will you look after them, and when I come back, I will bring more shells,' she said to Isabella.

'Of course, my darling.'

When Anthony arrived, Eleanor was happy to see him. He hunched down to her height and gave her a kiss on the top of her head. 'How is my little niece? Ready to go on a journey?'

Eleanor smiled and nodded, and Isabella was relieved at her reaction.

'Can you stay for a meal, or a drink?' she enquired, desperate to eke out the minutes she had left with Eleanor.

'We have a long journey. I think it probably best if we make our way,' he said. Looking at the small trunk and canvas bag in the hallway, he asked, 'Is this Eleanor's?'

'Yes, we have some more things of hers that she would like to keep here, for when she comes to visit.'

'Yes, I see,' he said,

'Are we going now?' Eleanor asked, looking up at Isabella.

'Yes, dearest, you are going with your uncle.'

'But you are coming with us too?'

'No, remember, I can't come, you are going to your cousins now.'

Eleanor's face crumpled as she burst into tears. Isabella enveloped her into a hug. 'I will write to you, and you have Molly with you to look after.' She picked the ragdoll up and put her into Eleanor's arms. Eleanor held tightly to Isabella's skirts and tears streamed down her face. Everyone gathered to say goodbye. Isabella's mother's face was stony, and Isabella guessed it was because she desperately did not want to cry. But Isabella knew she had to be strong for Eleanor.

'You are going to have a wonderful time, I am looking forward to hearing all about it,' she said, as she lifted Eleanor into the carriage.

'There, there, Eleanor,' placated Anthony uncomfortably. He looked at Isabella apologetically. 'Isabella, I am sorry...'

'Yes, I know.'

Eleanor's tears had subsided, but she made huge sniffs as she clutched Molly. The carriage moved and slowly left the rectory. Catherine, Isabella and their mother waved wildly until it was gone from sight. Catherine gave Isabella a hug, and they held each other, looking out to where the carriage had just gone.

'It's for the best,' Isabella said eventually, and gave Catherine a squeeze, before going back into the house.

She would paint. That would help. As she walked into the garden room where she had been working, she stubbed her toe on the large wooden easel. The pain, though quick and excrutiating, was not long-lasting; however, Isabella opened her mouth in a silent scream. Then the tears came. She sank to the floor and, covering her face with her hands to muffle the sounds, she cried and cried – deep sobs that seemed to come in a tidal wave, and she couldn't stop them.

The next day, when Isabella returned from her early morning walk, she opened the front door to find the day's letters on the doormat still. She picked them up and looked through them. There was a letter for her with Honolulu as the postmark. She did not recognise the handwriting, but took it up to her room to read. She opened the thick manila envelope and looked at the signature. Her heart leapt: it was from Kainalu.

My dear Isabella,

Forgive me for taking so long to write. When I found out that you had left Hawaii bound for England, so many miles away, my first thoughts were to get on the next ship and follow you. My sister said she had told you about the arranged marriage. I should have spoken to you about it. I was going to Hilo to call it off, not to get married, but I was foolish and kept the truth from you.

And now the thing I feared most has come. If you do not know already, I have contracted leprosy. I was sailing to England, and recognised the skin lesions when I reached San Francisco. It would be easy to think my life is cursed, but I know that is not true.

I am sorry if I did not show you how very dear you are to me. I believe you were a gift and it was my fault entirely that I let you slip out of my hands. But maybe it was for the best, seeing my current condition. I never spoke to you about my intentions or my love for you. Isabella, I am sure you would not ever dream of a future with an islander like me, but if I was well, I would ask you to be my wife. The shame and despair of leprosy means I could never ask that of you now. You are a strong, wise and beautiful woman, your tender love for Eleanor and kindness towards Maima and the lepers touched me deeply. I wanted you to be my partner in life. Our trips to Kalihi will always be special to me.

This letter is to tell you that you captured my heart. I will overcome my sadness that in all likelihood we will never meet again, but if there is a chance you could write to tell me how you are, I would like that very much.

Aloha,

Kainalu

Isabella put down the letter and realised her hands were shaking. She put ink to paper straight away and told Kainalu she loved him, and that she would come to him if he wanted. She would wait for his response, and she told no one.

Breakfast at the rectory was a quieter affair without Eleanor's happy conversation. Isabella sat at her place in the dining room with her parents and sister in silence.

'Isabella, as it's your birthday next week, I thought we could host a little lunch party for you,' Mrs Buckley said, putting aside the letter she had been reading.

Isabella's heart lurched at the thought of her birthday. 'You don't have to.'

'Oh, come along, dear, it will be fun. Anyway, I have already invited Hamish and the family, and John will be coming from London…'

Isabella sighed, and took another sip of tea to mask her frustration. The decision had been made.

'Thank you, Mama.'

Isabella did not want to mark another year, especially this one that had seemed so hopeful and now was full of disappointment, but she didn't want to hurt her mother's feelings. Still, it would be good to see family, she thought.

It was a perfect May day for Isabella's birthday. She spent the morning working on the paintings for her exhibition, but her thoughts were on the letter, now on a boat bound for Kainalu. If he said yes to her coming, that would mean marriage. Could she marry a leper? Her thoughts went round and round in her head, thinking of possible scenarios. Then she thought of Eleanor; even though they were separated by many miles, they were in the same country. Could she leave Eleanor?

Her exhibition was in a week. Invitations had been sent out; it was called *An English Woman's View of the South Seas: Tropical Flora from the Sandwich Islands.*

She heard a knock at the door, and Catherine popped her head in.

'Birthday walk?' she asked.

'That is exactly what I need, yes!'

As it was warm Isabella felt no need to fetch her bonnet and coat. Together she and Catherine made their way down the driveway towards the sea, the air filled with the call of gulls as they circled over the fishermen's boats that were coming in with their bounty.

'What wonderful things will happen for you this coming year!' Catherine said, taking Isabella's arm in her own.

Isabella wondered about telling her she had offered to go to Kainalu, but decided against it, until she knew his reply.

'I do not dare hope. I have lost too much this past year.'

Catherine unhooked her arm and looked at her sister. 'You have sailed around the world, you brought Eleanor into our lives…'

'I have lost Eleanor, my voyage ended too soon, and the man I love…' Isabella felt a sting of vulnerability saying those words, '… is dying of leprosy.'

'You have not lost Eleanor! True, you will not be a mother to her, but she will always be connected to you, and you chose to come home when you did. As for Kainalu, I don't know what to say. That is indeed a deep tragedy, and I am very sorry.'

They walked on in silence, and Isabella felt guilty not sharing the growing sense that she would be taking a new voyage soon.

Despite Eleanor's absence, the birthday lunch was more enjoyable than Isabella had anticipated, and that evening she went to bed in a different mood. She was buoyed with love from her family. Aunt Emily, as always, made her feel as if she could succeed in whatever she attempted to do, and seeing her brother, John, reminded her of the security she had in him. She was where she belonged, that was what she told herself, and she tried to believe it. They were all encouraging and enthusiastic about her exhibition, having an early view of the paintings.

'You will make quite a sum if you sell these,' John said, admiring a sketch of Maima.

Chapter Twenty-nine

Norfolk, summer/early autumn 1882

The private viewing and exhibition of *An Englishwoman's View of the South Seas: Tropical Flora from the Sandwich Islands* was held in the newly built parish hall. Isabella had been immersing herself in the setup. It felt like she was being transported back to the Pacific as she arranged the hibiscus, frangipani and birds of paradise next to each other. She kept another section for the sketches and paintings of the lepers, with a short article about the colony and a request for support for Kalaupapa.

On the final day of the preparations, Isabella stood looking at her paintings. She had found enjoyment in it, and was appreciative of the praise of others, but she realised what she *did* could never be enough. It would not fulfil her to paint for the rest of her life, and nothing else. Creative gifting was a wonderful thing, and she was blessed and grateful for it, but she knew success in this area felt empty without the sense of belonging that gave her life purpose.

'People and relationships must always supersede what we make or craft,' she had said to Catherine as they discussed her work. 'This exhibition makes me even more sure of where I should be, and that is with Kainalu.'

Catherine said nothing, but looked at her sister with sad eyes.

Isabella's exhibition was very successful. She was praised by the press, and by a visiting fellow from the Royal Geographic Society who happened to be in north Norfolk. He wrote to Isabella to ask of the possibility of the exhibition being taken to London.

'This is wonderful news!' her father said, and even mentioned it in his sermon. The congregation fluttered to Isabella at the end of the service in congratulations.

'Success seems to breed friends,' Isabella laughed as she walked home with Catherine to the rectory, with abundant invitations.

A week after the private viewing, Isabella sat upright on the wooden pew between her mother and Catherine. Sunlight was pouring through the stained-glass windows, and she felt comforted by the familiar smell of incense and her embroidered hassock under her feet. The church service had been part of the weekly routine of her life since she was a child. It was once habit, or lip service, without any real reverence, but after her experiences in Hawaii, hearing Kainalu's story and seeing Eleanor get better, Isabella had taken to paying more attention. Was the God of the Pacific islands, the God of the Bible, present in this small country parish church? She did feel peace, and it was a peace that stayed with her, despite all the pain she had experienced in the past months.

The church was full, and Reverend Buckley was in the pulpit, giving a vigorous presentation in his sermon. As Isabella watched him speak, she noticed something change in his face. His words faltered, until he stopped talking altogether. He looked down at his notes, as if collecting his thoughts, steadying himself. The congregation seemed to hold a collective breath, watching in silence, willing him to go on. Instead of continuing, however, he clutched the wooden edge of the pulpit. He appeared to be trying to gain control over whatever was happening, but he could not, and collapsed into the small space provided by the pulpit. The congregation made a collective gasp. William immediately ran from his pew. Isabella, Catherine and their mother were close behind.

William held the reverend's head and loosened his dog collar. He kept talking to him, asking him to smile, to lift his arms up. He was still conscious, but weak.

'My first guess is apoplexy. We need to get him some fresh air,' William said to Isabella. 'We must keep talking to him so he doesn't go to sleep.'

With the help of Walter, William got the reverend into a carriage and he was driven to the cottage hospital in Cromer. The whole congregation exited the church with him, and solemnly watched as their parson was carried away. Mrs Buckley went with him in the carriage and Isabella and Catherine returned home to wait for news. Anxiety churned in Isabella's stomach, and she could not concentrate on any task.

Mrs Buckley returned with William late in the afternoon.

It was confirmed that the reverend had had apoplexy; the only comfort was that it was hoped he would make a good recovery. Isabella breathed a sigh of relief. She had been preparing for pain, bracing herself for the feeling of grief that she now knew well, so she was relieved when the promise of it was not fulfilled. She breathed a prayer of thanks that her father would live, but Isabella knew if there had been any possibility for her to pursue returning to the Sandwich Islands, it was abruptly halted now.

Reverend Buckley was in hospital for ten days before returning home, where he was bedbound. The turn had caused paralysis down the left side of his body and a nurse came daily to wash and dress him. His health cast a gloom on the house, and it was kept quiet so Reverend Buckley would not be disturbed.

Summer came with its long shadows and bright sunlight. William supplied a wicker wheelchair for the reverend, so he was able to sit and work in his study.

Isabella still had no reply from Kainalu, but she had received a letter from the Everards, Eleanor's new parents. They wrote that she was well and had settled in with her cousins.

She seems to be enjoying the older children, and mentions games taught her by a boy called Harry in Hawaii…

Even with the sting of missing Eleanor, Isabella smiled as she read it, and hoped Eleanor had as good a friendship with them as she'd had with Harry. She wrote to Eleanor weekly, and painted her little cartoon pictures. Painting was Isabella's only creative outlet, but now the exhibition was done, she needed something more immediate to look forward to. She knew she had to do something to stay occupied and busy.

She went to talk to her father, who was in his study. His left side had more feeling now, and he was getting stronger.

He would spend a few hours each morning working, studying the Scriptures, and then rest in the afternoon. He was planning a sermon series on the book of Revelation and the subject had brought new life to him. He was convinced of the imminent return of the Saviour.

'Come in,' he said, as she knocked on the door. Looking up from his desk, he smiled and removed his glasses.

'Papa, I was wondering about taking a painting course... or maybe teaching painting?'

'Well, my dear, you have a great talent. You don't need to work for money, thanks to your mother's trust fund, you know that. But if you'd like to, we can look into it.'

'Thank you.'

He sat back and stared at her. 'Is this really want you want?'

'Yes,' Isabella replied firmly. 'Thank you, Papa.' She had to do something to dull the sadness of no longer having Eleanor, and the growing need to be near to a man she had to accept she might never see again.

'Our time is short, Isabella; we have to live with purpose and surrender, not waste a day.'

'Yes, Papa,' she said and gently closed the door behind her.

As the summer nights were usurped by autumn's coolness, Isabella tried to embrace her position as a supporter and companion for her parents. She sat in the drawing room as her father read by the fire and her mother embroidered.

Isabella was pretending to read a book of poems, ones she loved and knew well, but her thoughts were on her parents. She watched her father, still in his wheelchair, not able to fully return to work in the parish yet. He had responded without bitterness or self-pity to the apoplexy, but embraced the humbling it gifted him and the need for others to care for him. He was even accepting of the loss of independenece. However, the weight of his care and worry fell on his wife. Isabella watched her mother; there was more grey in her hair: it had come suddenly in the past few months. She looked tired. Catherine too… Isabella could not leave her sister alone, even though she never seemed to be at home nowadays, always at the surgery. She knew it was her duty to stay with them. Or was it?

That night the dream of the island came again. This time she recognised the towering *pali*, the curve of the rocky beach and the flowering frangipani tree. She felt completely at peace. In the dream her arms were stretched out, and everything under her hands was growing and thriving. She somehow understood that her presence on the island was enabling things to flourish. Her life was bringing life.

Isabella awoke and then tried hard to go back to sleep, to return to the world that was so beautiful and inviting. She lay in bed in the darkness, trying to keep the pieces of what she could remember together, but the strength of the dream was losing its clarity and shape. The feeling of being in Hawaii, and the deep peace of it being home, was the overriding sensation that remained.

The next night, she had the same dream. Isabella awoke trying to understand what she was missing. Was Hawaii where she belonged? Kainalu had not responded to her letter; he had leprosy. It was impossible, she told herself. Frustrated, she turned over and shut her eyes tightly, willing herself to ignore the images of the island that had made her feel alive for the first time in her life.

I need guidance, she prayed desperately, lying in the dark in her bed. She decided to turn to her Bible. Surely if God would speak to her, it would be through His Word. She lit a candle and pushed back the sheet and blankets to get out of bed and find her Bible on the bookshelf. Bringing it back to the warmth of her bed, she flicked through the thin pages, not sure what she was looking for. She landed on the Gospel of John. John 15:13 seemed to jump out at her. 'Greater love hath no man than this, that a man lay down his life for his friends.'

Going to Kainalu would be laying down her life. Is this what it meant? Suddenly everything was very clear. She felt as if she could see what she had been blind to. The thought both terrified her and excited her. She must join Kainalu in Moloka'i as his *kōkua*.

Her mind raced as she blew out the candle and lay back in the darkness. 'If this is Your will, please give me courage, and make a way,' she prayed, before falling into a deep sleep.

The next morning, Isabella woke with a strong sense of peace in her decision. As she walked downstairs, she wanted to speak to Catherine straight away, but she could hear her talking to her mother, so she would have to wait.

After they had eaten breakfast, Catherine went outside to pick flowers for an arrangement in church. Isabella joined her and came to the point straight away.

'Catherine, I think I am going to go back to the Sandwich Islands.'

Catherine put down her flower basket and walked over to embrace her sister. She was silent, and then with a sigh she pulled away. 'I am not surprised. After you told me about Kainalu, I wondered if you would return one day.'

'But it's not for a short time. I am going there to be Kainalu's nurse.' She held her breath, searching for judgement on Catherine's face.

'You mean on the leper colony?'

'Yes.'

Catherine shook her head sadly. 'My dear sister, I don't know what to say. I want to dissuade you, but I fear nothing I say will stop you. You are so much braver than me.'

They moved to sit down on the garden bench.

'What do you know about leprosy? Surely we can get medicine for you to take with you?

'Yes, I plan to talk to William about it. He had so much experience of it in India.'

Isabella felt a slight shift in her sister at the mention of William. Perhaps old jealousy, or competition, even though there was no reason for either.

'Have you spoken to Mama and Papa?'

'No,' Isabella said. 'Not yet, and I feel guilty about them. Catherine, can I leave them? With Papa still not back to strength... they are both getting older.'

'I am here, and Papa is improving greatly. I don't want you to go, but I understand. I always believed you had a very different path from me.'

That evening, Isabella sat with her parents in the drawing room. Catherine was still at choir practice, so with trepidation, Isabella broached the subject of leaving.

'Isabella, you seem unsettled,' Mrs Buckley observed, before she had a chance to speak.

'I am thinking of going back to Hawaii,' Isabella blurted out in response.

Her father, in his wicker wheelchair, put down his glass of port.

'When?'

'I don't know, Papa, but I hope soon.'

Mrs Buckley looked at Isabella with a strange expression. 'I knew you would go back,' she said.

'I have a friend who has been ill, and I want to care for him.'

'How long would you go for?'

'I want to live there, Mama.'

'Isabella!'

'Who is this friend?' her father interjected.

Isabella explained about Kainalu.

'How can you consider living on such an island so far from home – with a native?' exclaimed Mrs Buckley. 'How –'

'Hush! Isabella, do you love this native man?' interjected her father.

'I do.'

'Does he even speak English?' Mrs Buckley asked, her face ashen.

'Yes, of course he does, Mama! He is well educated, and a cousin of the king of Hawaii.'

'To be related to royalty may mean something in England, but I am not sure how impressive it is in relation to an island in the middle of the Pacific. We...' her mother said, before glancing at her husband and changing to, 'I... no, Isabella, you must not go.'

Isabella's heart sank.

'And what about Eleanor?' Mrs Buckley added. 'You cannot leave her.'

'Eleanor has left us, and she is happy and settled with her cousins. I believe, I hope, she will understand,' she said hesitantly, lacking conviction. She turned helplessly to her father for support.

'Papa, you have often talked about having a purpose and serving others. I believe this is my purpose, to give my life to serve another. Surely that is an honourable choice? I have no vision for life here in England. I love you both, and parting from you all will be very hard.' She looked down at her hands and then, with a sigh of surrender, said, 'However, I won't go without your blessing.'

The grandfather clock in the hallway struck eight o'clock.

'We will think it over and give you our answer in the morning,' said her father.

Isabella's face was flushed with emotion. She returned to the book on her lap, but did not take in a word on its pages.

The next morning Reverend Buckley was stoical. He addressed his daughter at breakfast.

'You are old enough to know your own mind, and mature enough to make your own decisions. We will give you our blessing,' he said.

It felt as if they were blessing her to go to her death.

'We never want to hold you back, and so we must let you go. What you are doing is admirable. We would ask that you make sure you take furloughs, as we could not bear to say goodbye to you forever. We will support you with an allowance, just as we would if you stayed here, to help you live in some comfort,' her father told her.

'Thank you, Papa, and of course I will be home again.'

After breakfast, Isabella went up to her bedroom. She had slept in this room, with its chintz curtains and flower-patterned wallpaper, for so many years. It had been both her sanctuary and her prison. She had longed for a new home, but now she was grateful for the space and years she had had in the comfort of its walls.

She sat looking out to the cherry tree, the leaves beginning to turn bronze, gold and red.

I must see Eleanor.

Before she could think of leaving home for Hawaii, she would travel to Dorset to visit Eleanor and say goodbye in person.

Chapter Thirty

Norfolk, autumn 1882

Isabella wrote to the Everards. She hoped to spend a weekend with the family and did not know if her request would be accepted or welcomed. While she waited for a reply, there was another person she needed to speak to.

William was at home when she arrived at his cottage. She knew his housekeeper would be there, so they would not be alone. He looked surpised to see her.

'I wanted to tell you my news. May I come in?'

'Of course,' he said, ushering her into his small sitting room, overflowing with books on every shelf. He motioned for her to sit down.

'William, I am going to go back to Hawaii.'

'I see… what a loss for us.'

'I am going to help a man I met there. He is Hawaiian, and he recently found out he is suffering from leprosy.'

Isabella wondered if Catherine had told William about Kainalu, as he did not seem shocked.

'What sad news, Isabella. I am so sorry. Is this man…' he seemed to have trouble finding the words, '… important to you?'

'He is,' she replied, concentrating on the stone-tiled floor.

'Ah.' There was no way of knowing how he felt about that from his response. Isabella looked up, but his face was impassive.

'I wondered if you knew anything about treating the disease, or could advise me in any way?' Isabella asked.

'By strange coincidence,' he replied, 'I was reading a paper about medical advancements with leprosy recently. I have an interest after my time in India… would you like to see?'

'Yes, please,' Isabella said, grateful that he wasn't trying to dissuade her from going. They moved to the desk in William's adjacent study and he pulled out a large collection of papers from a drawer. He started flicking through the pages until he came to what he was searching for. He looked up. 'There is a chance that you won't contract the disease if you are living in a colony, but there is also a chance that you will.' He seemed embarrassed, but added, 'And if you marry this Hawaiian with the disease, and have full marital union, then I am sorry to say contracting leprosy seems to me to be inevitable. Have you accepted that?'

'I have,' Isabella replied firmly, blushing at his frankness.

'I will give you all the knowledge I have on how to treat patients with the disease, and I have an idea that we may be able to get sponsorship from a philanthropic society I have a connection with, so that you can take medication with you. I read a paper by a Professor Mouat about chaulmoogra oil bringing a significant improvement to patients, so we will see if we can get some supplies for you.'

'Thank you, William.'

'Upon my word, I wish I could do more.' William sighed. 'I must say, we will miss you terribly. It has been wonderful having you home.'

Isabella smiled. 'You have been so good to me, and to Eleanor, thank you. You are… like my brother.'

'And you…' He stooped to kiss her proffered hand, '… like my sister.'

Within a few days, Isabella had her reply from the Everards. It was suggested she travel with Catherine and they stay in a nearby guesthouse, as neither the Everards nor Anthony, who lived in the same town, had room to accommodate them. Isabella presented the offer to Catherine and she agreed immediately.

With approval from their parents, they left a few days later, to be in Blandford Forum in time for the weekend. Anthony had written that Eleanor was starting lessons with the cousins' governess and so the weekend would be more convenient.

'I wonder if she will have changed,' Catherine pondered as they sat in their train carriage compartment. The other passengers got off at Ipswich, leaving them alone en route to London.

'My only worry is that it will be unsettling for her to see us. Do you think it is the right thing we go?' Catherine said.

'We're on our way now, so I think that is probably a redundant question, dear sister,' Isabella said with a frustrated smile. 'I understand your worry, but we will be affirming to Eleanor that we are part of her life, and always will be, even though I will be further afield.'

Catherine nodded in agreement, and Isabella went back to staring out of the window at the passing green fields, her thoughts on Eleanor.

They arrived in Blandford Forum the following day, after staying with John and his family in Kensington and then taking another train west.

Anthony had made himself available to pick them up and take them to where Eleanor now lived.

'Welcome to Dorset,' he said, as they stepped off the steam train onto the station platform on a misty, damp morning. They shook hands and he took their canvas bags, carrying them both with ease. 'Follow me.'

In ten minutes, their horse-drawn carriage arrived outside a large Georgian house in the town.

'Here we are! I don't think Eleanor knows you are coming, so it will be a surprise.'

Isabella looked at Catherine, wondering why they hadn't told Eleanor of her visit. However, she had no time to be concerned, as Anthony had already jumped down from the carriage and knocked on the front door. It was opened by a boy of about fifteen. He had the awkwardness of a teenager, but when he saw Anthony he smiled brightly.

'Hello, young man, where is Mary? We are here to see your parents and little Eleanor,' Anthony said.

'Yes, sir. Mary has burnt something... she is putting out a fire. Father is in the study and Eleanor is in the garden with Sybil, but Mother is out visiting.' He looked at Isabella and Catherine who were now standing behind Anthony.

'Very good, let's see your father first, then.'

The boy showed them through the house to a small room with a desk in it, and a man sitting with his back to the open door in the room. He jumped up as he heard Anthony knock on the door.

'Cousin! We have arrived! Let me introduce you to ...'

'Very pleased to make your acquaintances!' the man said, enthusiastically, wiping down his jacket – Isabella noticed it had crumbs on it. His son had now slipped away. There was the sound of joyful shrieking from the garden, and two girls came running by the window.

'There, you will see Eleanor! She is a great friend of Sybil. Let's go and get them,' he said. There seemed to be an air of chaos about the house and a distinct smell of burning coming from somewhere. Isabella noticed the paint peeling from the walls, and curtains limping on their rails.

They stepped outside, and Isabella realised she was nervous. How would Eleanor feel, seeing her again? She needn't have worried, though, for as soon as they were in the large garden, Eleanor cried, 'Mama Isabella!' and came running to her, hurling herself into her arms. Eleanor had grown in the short time she had been with her cousins, and her cheeks had the rosy glow of fresh air.

'Am I going home with you?' she asked immediately.

'No, my darling, this is your home now. We came to see you.'

Eleanor went to hug Catherine, and Isabella smiled at the other little girl.

'You must be Sybil,' she said. The girl looked remarkably like Eleanor, a few years older, perhaps, but with the same expressive eyes. Her ribbon was falling out of her hair, and she had a leaf protruding from it, but she was smiling and nodded her head.

'I must say, Sybil in particular has enjoyed having a sister. She has two brothers who are not quite so amenable in playing the games she wants to play,' said her father.

When Mrs Everard returned, she seemed to revel in the disarray. Mary, the flustered housekeeper, was standing in for the cook who was sick. She appeared with a lopsided cake, but her employers just laughed good-naturedly and did not berate her for forgetting the milk and the teaspoons.

Once the tea was eventually served, the conversation remained polite. Isabella hoped she would have time alone with Eleanor, and Catherine, realising, orchestrated it.

'What a delightful garden you have. Why don't Isabella and Eleanor go for a walk in it?' she suggested.

'First-class idea,' said Anthony, and Isabella smiled gratefully. As she stood, Eleanor took her hand and they walked in the direction of the rose garden.

'Do you still have my shells?' Eleanor asked.

Isabella laughed. 'I have guarded them with my life.'

Isabella wanted to ask if Eleanor was happy, if her family were kind to her, if she was still having nightmares. But she felt in all the questions it would be hard to hear the answer if it was negative, because there would be little she could do to help.

'Do you miss Hawaii?' Eleanor asked, as she skipped along next to her.

'I do, do you?'

'Yes, I miss Leilei, and Uncle Kai. But I have to stay with my cousins. Sybil is nearly ten years old.'

'Is she?'

'Before we go back, I want to tell you something… let's sit here,' Isabella said, pointing to a nearby bench.

'What is it?' Eleanor asked, her face clear and open, looking up at Isabella.

'Uncle Kai has become sick, so I am going to go back to Hawaii to nurse him.'

Eleanor looked seriously at Isabella. 'Will he die?'

'No, he won't die, but he is ill... his skin hurts.'

'When will we go?'

'No, Eleanor, darling, I am afraid you can't come this time. I will have to look after Kainalu and we will live in another island away from our friends.'

'Why? Why won't you be with Harry and Leilei?'

'Because Uncle Kai's sickness could make them sick too, so we have to go far away to keep them safe. That is why you cannot come. I don't want you to get ill.'

Eleanor was quiet for a moment, taking it in, and then said quietly and forlornly, 'But I don't want you to go.'

'I understand, but Uncle Kai needs me. You are happy here, aren't you?'

Eleanor leaned on Isabella's arm. 'Yes.' She sighed. 'It is good for you to go and help him. When I am big, I will come too, with all the others. To help you.'

'You know this means you won't see me for a long time?' Isabella said gently.

Eleanor nodded.

They walked back to the house, and Eleanor sat close to Isabella.

'Can I show you my bedroom?' she asked.

Isabella looked up at Mrs Everard.

'Of course! Eleanor, you show Isabella and Catherine the way, and I'll follow behind,' Mrs Everard said.

'Can I go too?' asked Sybil.

'I don't see why not,' her mother laughed.

Eleanor proudly led Isabella and Catherine up the front stairs and into a pretty, south-facing room. It had two small beds in it, and Isabella immediately noticed the portrait of Elizabeth on the wall next to the bed Eleanor had sat on. Molly was lying on the pillow.

Mrs Everard joined them. 'She was lovely, wasn't she?' she said, referring to the painting. 'Elizabeth was my second cousin. As she was so much younger we were not close, but I always thought she was lovely.'

'She was,' Isabella agreed.

'Little Ellie is a blessing to us,' she said, giving Eleanor a large kiss on her forehead. 'I wanted lots of children, but I was getting on when I had Sybil. Mr Everard said another from my womb was out of the question,' she laughed heartily. 'But I always believed we would have one more somehow!'

The weekend ended well. Isabella was relieved to see that Eleanor was thriving. She was with her family. It gave Isabella peace of mind to know that even though she would miss out on being with Eleanor as she grew up, she would have a happy childhood.

When Isabella and Catherine returned to Norfolk, her paintings were being packed up and transported to London. She did not worry that Kainalu had not replied to her letter. She knew he would refuse her offer, so she must go without telling him. From that point her travel arragements moved quickly. She decided she would not stay for the Royal Geographic Society exhibition but would leave it to her parents and Catherine to represent her. She felt compelled to leave, and could not be detained any longer.

Isabella's father booked her passage. As she was now a seasoned traveller, Isabella was allowed to go without a chaperone. She would be sailing via New York again and by train across the States.

'You'll want to take presents for your friends,' Catherine said when the packing started.

'I hadn't thought that far... what can I take?'

'What about mustard? It would last the journey well. Or maybe lavender soap?'

Isabella knew Catherine was being brave, accepting her leaving for the other side of the world. The fact that she was becoming more involved in nursing, and her growing friendship with William, meant that Isabella felt she would be sustained. She knew Catherine loved home; she did not have the same desire to travel as Isabella did. It was a comfort to know she would be remaining with their parents.

A week before departure, Isabella made a final shopping trip to King's Lynn. When her carriage arrived home, Walter helped bring the packages inside. There were two large trunks in Isabella's room, filled with books, a few paintings as well as newly made muslin gowns in white and pale pink.

At night, as she drifted off to sleep, she wondered what it would be like to be with Kainalu, now that he was ill. Would the disease advance rapidly? She thought of the leper she had painted, with his disfigured nose. How would she feel if Kainalu's face had turned monstrous? She feared she would be repulsed.

Word soon got out in the close-knit north Norfolk community that Isabella was going back to the Sandwich Islands, and the gossip extended to her being about to marry a 'native'. That he was a leprous native was not yet known. At church, Isabella felt the full weight of the gossip. Mrs Sumner, Sir Mark's mother-in-law, leaned over her pew to stage whisper to Isabella, 'Do you not think you are too old for marriage now, my dear?'

'Not at all,' Isabella replied, coldly.

Mrs Sumner went on. 'My counsel would be to think again. You would have a good life with your parents. None of us believes you should go, and I am sure your family don't. Think of what you are doing. You are hurting so many.'

Isabella felt Catherine squeezing her hand, willing her not to respond in anger. She turned around to Mrs Sumner sitting behind them, 'Isabella has our blessing – she is doing something wonderful.'

With a superior glance at Isabella, as if to say 'mark my words', Mrs Sumner sat back to her seat. Isabella seethed through the rest of the service.

'She thinks she is helping you. She has a good heart,' soothed Catherine on their walk home.

'You are more gracious than I, sister. I fear her heart is clothed in dark prejudice. She is insufferable.'

On the final evening before Isabella's departure, Mrs Buckley hosted a party at the rectory. Speeches were made, and presents given. Isabella was grateful to her mother for organising it. If it had been up to her, she would have slipped away quietly, but she knew this was better. Her heart was already on the way to Hawaii; she would not feel at peace until she was on the ship.

The next morning, the carriage was made ready to take her to the station.

'My darling, I can't believe the day has come. I will miss you so, but we will be praying for you every day,' Mrs Buckley said as she embraced her daughter.

Mrs West popped her head round the door and handed Isabella a package. 'It's recipes, ma'am, your favourite, so you can make them where you are going.'

'Oh, Mrs West, thank you, what a wonderful present,' Isabella said.

'Go with God. You are never alone. We are proud of you,' Reverend Buckley said thickly, as he kissed Isabella's cheek.

Eleanor had written a letter for Leilani, and pressed a rose from the garden for her. The two little girls were going to have very different upbringings. Isabella fleetingly imagined Eleanor coming back to Hawaii when she was a young woman, or Leilani travelling to England. Perhaps it would happen one day.

When the goodbyes couldn't be stretched out any longer, Isabella got into the carriage.

'I have chosen this,' she reminded herself, as the carriage left the driveway for the open road. She didn't know when or if she would be back. It might be that she would never return. Isabella could not bear to think of that, so instead she tried to picture Kainalu's face. He was the reason she was going, and once she was with him, all would be well. Despite the sadness of leaving, she was urged on with a sense of promise.

The journey to New York was uneventful. She was sharing a cabin with a young Spanish lady called Angela-Maria Cortez, who spoke little English.

'You go where?' she enquired in broken English when they first met. She was a petite girl, with thick black hair, sparkling eyes and gold hoops in her ears.

'Hawaii,' Isabella said slowly, annunciating each syllable.

Angela-Maria opened her mouth, and then raised her shoulders in a shrug.

'Me go California. Me aunt, I live with her,' she explained with a grin.

'I have only been to San Francisco, but we did not see much,' Isabella replied, and realised this would be the extent of their conversation, but they travelled together well, miming their needs and smiling brightly at each other. Isabella was relieved she did not have to explain why she was going. She wanted to hold it all in her heart, and maintain the courage she had had from initially making the decision to go.

The first night, Isabella tucked herself into the narrow top bunk in her cabin and swiftly fell asleep to the now familiar chugging of the engines and rhythmic movement of the ship cutting through open seas.

In a dream, Isabella saw herself walking aimlessly through a deserted village. She knew it was the Kalaupapa leper colony. There was no one about, and she called for Kainalu. A sense of panic rose in her when she couldn't find him. She walked into a dark hut. Inside it was icy cold, even though the weather outside was hot. In the shadows, Isabella could make out a figure. She called Kainalu's name and there was no reply. She called once more and suddenly the figure came rushing towards her with a fearsome scream. At once she saw the face: it was a mutilated figure, with nose and ears eaten away and hideous growths. She cried out in her dream, and woke herself up. Angela-Maria was standing close to her, saying something soothing in Spanish.

It took a while for Isabella to realise where she was. She was covered in sweat, her heart still racing. A light from the side of the ship was coming into the cabin so she began to see the familiar fixings. She whispered an apology to Angela-Maria and turned over as if to go back to sleep, but every time she closed her eyes the image would come back. Blinking, she focused on the cabin wall in front of her, and hoped that sleep would take her gently.

Chapter Thirty-one

Voyage back to Hawaii, autumn 1882

After many nights of interrupted sleep, they at last arrived in New York. Isabella had hoped the nightmares would stop, but the same one had haunted her throughout her passage. She was starting to believe that what she had dreamt was what she was about to experience. She was staying again with Professor Ferrier and his wife at Yale before starting the train journey across the States. She hired a buggy to their home, and was greeted by Mrs Ferrier at the door.

'How lovely to have you back with us,' she said, beckoning her servants to take Isabella's trunk to the guest bedroom.

A little while later they were sitting in the Ferriers' comfortable drawing room. The walls were festooned with maps of different countries, Professor Ferrier being something of an amateur cartographer. He had arrived a few minutes after Isabella, and joined them. As it was a warm day, the windows were open and the sounds of the street below, horse hoofs clomping on the cobblestones and intermittent voices from pedestrians, drifted in.

'How is Eleanor?' Mrs Ferrier asked after they all had a cup of tea.

'She is flourishing with her cousins, but I never realised how much I would miss her, especially seeing the familiar sights of Yale without her by my side.'

'I can understand,' Mrs Ferrier sighed, with compassion.

'I hope you don't mind, but as you are going back to Hawaii, we invited the Hawaiian students to dine with us tonight,' said Professor Ferrier.

'I would be glad to see them again,' Isabella replied, genuinely pleased.

As Isabella changed for supper, she wondered if the students had heard Kainalu's news, or if she should tell them. Surely it would not be long before all the Hawaiians in Yale heard of his sad fate. She decided that if they didn't know she would not tell them; it was not her place. She couldn't bear Kainalu's bleak future to be the topic of their conversation during supper.

When she was dressed, she went downstairs and walked into the drawing room to meet James and Hani, their faces bright with the same jovial spirit she remembered from their last meeting. She smiled, feeling instantly at home with them both.

'I hear you are going to back to Hawaii. I am not surprised. Who would want to stay away for long?' laughed James.

Conversation flowed easily. The Hawaiians made even a formal situation light and full of laughter. Being with the students made Isabella think of Kainalu all the more, dispelling the horrible images of her nightmares. She longed to be with him.

After two days at Yale, Isabella began her journey west. She still felt some trepidation travelling alone, but the train journeys were straightforward, and soon she steamed through the rugged states of America until she hit the Pacific in San Francisco. She wrote home from every stop, describing to Eleanor the scenes that the little girl had witnessed herself. Passage to Honolulu was booked, the Fortnums were telegrammed, and this time no illness blighted the voyage. But as Isabella left the coast of the United States, her anxiety returned. What would it be like with Kainalu? Her feelings had only been expressed on paper, never in person. There was so much to navigate.

After twenty days at sea the islands came into sight and her heart leapt. When the vessel docked at Honolulu, the familiar scene of locals greeting the boat made Isabella smile. Everything was the same – the smell of flowers in the air, the vibrant turquoise of the sea and the luscious green of the palms. Isabella had dreamed of the tropical island long before she ever came to

Hawaii, and now she knew why. Her future was not in the respectable parlours of English society; it was on the warm, sandy beaches of the tropical paradise that she would call her home.

She spotted the Fortnums before they saw her and shouted a word of recognition, but the sound was stolen by other noises in the busy port. Harry eventually saw her and shouted hello, pulling his mother's arm and pointing up to where Isabella was waving.

'Hello!' she called back.

It wasn't long before the Fortnums were able to come on board.

'Where is Eleanor?' Harry asked straight away.

'Shh, Harry, we told you she was staying in England,' Emma chided.

'I am sorry she is not here with me, Harry. She is with her family in England, but she misses you and Hawaii very much.'

Harry looked very put out by this news.

They walked down to the waiting buggy, and driving to the Fortnums' house in the lush Manoa Valley felt like coming home.

'We were so excited to get your telegram!' Emma said when they were alone on the *lanai*. 'Tell me, is this a holiday, or have you decided to immigrate like we have?'

'Emma…' Isabella didn't know where to start. 'How is Kainalu?'

'Kainalu? We haven't seen him for an age; he moved to Kona, I heard. Aolani said he went to San Francisco on business quite a while ago and was sick when he returned. I think he went to Kona when he got back.'

'But isn't he in Moloka'i?' Isabella asked, confused.

'No, why would he be in Moloka'i?'

'Because he has leprosy.'

'Leprosy!' Mrs Fortnum exclaimed. 'You must be mistaken.'

'But Aolani wrote to me, she told me of his finding a patch on his skin in San Francisco. He was on his way to England to see me, but when he realised he was ill, he returned to Hawaii.'

'I think you are mistaken. Kainalu can't have contracted that terrible disease. I know he works with getting the sick to Moloka'i, but he is wise, and would not have put himself in danger, surely?'

'Aolani wrote a letter to tell me. I am sure it is true. Emma, he is the reason I have returned. To be his *kōkua.*'

'My dear Isabella, I don't know what to say… well, the only way to clear this up is to ride over to see Aolani. Would you like to go now? You can take the horse.'

That was exactly what Isabella was longing to do. 'I would be very grateful.'

The chestnut mare was saddled up and, changed into her Turkish riding trousers, Isabella rode astride again. She had butterflies in her stomach and her hands were sweaty as she rode. Aolani was unaware she was coming, and Isabella didn't know how she might react to the surprise. She cantered along the lanes, oblivious to the familiar beauty of her surroundings. Her face was set, and she could think of nothing but what she was going to say. Could it be true that Kainalu didn't have the disease after all?

Isabella arrived, hot and windswept, at Aolani's house and tied her mare to the pole outside their home.

'Hello!' she called, as she walked up to the house.

'Isabella? My sister! Is it a dream?' Aolani cried, running from the *lanai*, her arms wide open.

'It's not a dream!' Isabella said, laughing.

Suddenly Aolani stopped, held Isabella at arm's length and looked at her intently. 'You have come for Kainalu?'

'Yes, but Emma is insisting Kainalu is healthy and well.'

'You told her the truth?'

'I don't think she believed me.'

Aolani paused. 'Isabella, *hānai*, only our *ohana* know about Kainalu. If it got out that he is a leper, then we would all pay for this sickness. Kainalu didn't want us, especially Leilani and the children, living under the shame of being seen as unclean in some way. He went to Moloka'i in secret five months ago. He told us to say he had gone to America to start a new life. I have been unable to talk about him yet, for fear my tears would give away the truth. So I haven't told the Fortnums. We must tell them to keep this a secret.'

Isabella saw both grief and fear in Aolani's eyes.

'I had to say goodbye to my brother, I don't know for how long, but it is as if he is dead. I can't speak to him, or see his face. Isabella, leprosy is truly a curse.'

Aolani covered her face with her hands and wept.

Isabella sat close to Aolani, saying little. As she watched her broken friend, she was surprised to feel an internal strength. The peace she'd had in England when she first made the decision to go back to Kainalu had returned, and somehow it carried her.

'What happened to Kainalu?' she asked eventually. 'How did he know it was leprosy?'

'The symptoms showed themselves as just a circular patch of skin that was red and raised. It disappeared a few weeks after it first arrived, but any hopes were dashed when two similar spots returned on his legs a few weeks later.

'My brother could have stayed on Oah'u and received treatment in Kakaako, but because of his high profile, our connection with the royal family and his work with the lepers, he told us it would be better for him to leave immediately. He did not want us to suffer shame from his circumstances.

'He disguised himself when he got onto the steamer to Moloka'i, and none of us went to see him off. Our goodbyes were made the evening before. We prayed for him and anointed him with oil.

'Leilani did not understand what was happening, but when she overheard the word *leprosy*, she realised her uncle was now one of the unclean. Still, she has the faith of a child. She asked me, "But Jesus healed lepers in the Bible, why can't he heal

Uncle?" I told her that perhaps He can; it is something we can pray for. But for now, Uncle has to leave for Moloka'i.

'"Well, maybe he will get better and come back?" was Leilani's reply.'

Aolani sighed. 'I couldn't bear to explain that that would never happen. Kainalu has been furnished with provisions to keep him as comfortable as possible. Supplies to build his own home were shipped out, as well as a cow, chickens and seeds to enable him to start some sort of subsistence farming to add to the basic government-provided diet. My brother now has to put into practice what he preached – separating himself from everyone he loves.'

Aolani and Isabella continued talking as family members and servants came and went from Aolani's house. Each time Isabella heard a new footstep coming up to the *lanai*, her heart lurched, imagining it would be Kainalu. She knew that was impossible, but she was so used to his presence there that it seemed he was just in another room, about to come through the door with some story or joke.

The sense of loss that hung in the house was palpable. Isabella knew she couldn't stay.

'I am ready to go to Moloka'i, Aolani.'

'Are you sure?' Aolani paused and then said, 'You might get sick too. You don't need to go; it is too much.'

'It is what I came back to Hawaii for. I want to go to be his *kōkua*.'

'You cannot sacrifice your life for him.'

'I love him,' Isabella said, frankly. 'That makes any kind of sacrifice somewhat easier. I feel a call to do this. I cannot explain it, but I am compelled to go.'

'Then your obedience and sacrifice are beautiful,' said Aolani, hugging Isabella very tightly.

Fili returned home, and his eyes were large in shock at the sight of Isabella sitting with his wife.

'She is going to Kainalu,' Aolani said straight away.

Fili looked at Isabella, his eyes glistening. 'Isabella, that is too much to sacrifice.'

'I know it seems foolish, but I feel I have been prepared for this for many years.'

Fili's eyes seemed to convey both respect and compassion. 'Let me tell you about the colony; it is on six square miles of land, dry and nearly treeless, surrounded by a towering *pali* – like a vertical cliff. It extends for the entire length of north Moloka'i and blocks off the peninsular, meaning you will never see the sun rise or set. And quite apart from the conditions, you are in good health – you would not be allowed to go.'

Isabella knew this wasn't true.

'I know it will be possible for me to go as a *kōkua*, and I know you are being kind in trying to stop me, but I have made up my mind, and I would value your blessing.'

Fili looked at her sheepishly.

'Yes, sister, yes,' Aolani said, holding her hand and looking at her with tears in her eyes.

Fili just shook his head.

'I'm sorry, Isabella, if you are adamant, and we can say no more to dissuade you, then we will support you. You are a sign that there is a God. He has not forgotten Kainalu,' he said eventually. He left soon afterwards to speak to the superintendent in Kalihi who would approve Isabella's move to the colony.

'*Kapuna Wahine* is out North Shore side, but she is coming back today. She will want to see you, Isabella,' said Aolani.

'I'd like that, but I must return to the Fortnums' now. I will need to tell them the truth, but I can ask them to say nothing.'

'Make them promise, or this leprosy will ruin all our lives,' Aolani said with an intensity that Isabella had never seen before.

Isabella agreed and walked back to her tethered mare. She rode slowly back to Manoa Valley and the Fortnums' familiar and welcoming home.

Emma Fortnum was inside, telling Wilbur off for kicking his brother. She seemed relieved to see Isabella.

'How did it go? Please say you were wrong about Kainalu.'

'No, I wasn't. Kainalu is already in Moloka'i, but they haven't made the news public. Aolani asked that you wouldn't say anything; that you would promise. The disease has such a dreadful stigma attached to it.'

Emma just stared at her. 'He is already there? I am so sorry…'

'I am going to go to join him, to be his *kōkua*. Please don't tell me I shouldn't do it. I have made my decision.

Emma was silent, as if the news had winded her and it was taking her time to formulate any words. She placed her hand on the side table and she said quietly, 'I am devastated for you, Isabella. This is not the life I would have wished for an enemy, let alone you. It will be very hard.'

Supper was a quiet affair, the Fortnum boys having eaten separately, and Isabella excused herself early. She lay still under the thin cotton sheet, and was sure she saw Eleanor's gecko running across the wall. 'Hello, friend,' she whispered, wishing Eleanor was with her. It was a warm evening, and the gentle sound of the breeze in the palms outside her window was almost hypnotic. Despite the luxury of being with the Fortnums', Isabella felt eager to leave Oah'u.

The next morning, Fili came to the Fortnums' with news that Isabella could take the boat to Moloka'i in two days' time. He also invited her to a meal that evening so that she could see *Kapuna Wahine*.

'Are you sure she wants to see me?' Isabella asked.

'Yes, you will be surprised when you see her; she is much changed.'

When *Kapuna Wahine* came out to greet the buggy, Isabella thought she had shrunk in size somehow. Her firstborn was lost to Moloka'i, and it had obviously affected her deeply. As Isabella got down from the buggy, *Kapuna Wahine* embraced her with uncharacteristic warmth. Gone was her reserve, judgement and mistrust. Isabella was surprised, but hugged her back, and when *Kapuna Wahine* pulled away, she took Isabella's face gently in her hands and said, 'You are our *ohana*, God's gift to us. I will never be able to thank you enough for what you are doing for my son. Are you going to be his wife? Not just his *kōkua*?'

'If he will have me, yes.'

Kapuna Wahine nodded slowly, and with a look of humility in her eyes, she took Isabella's hand and they went inside. She handed her a package. 'Open it.'

Cautiously, Isabella sat down and unwrapped the box. Inside was a wooden bowl.

'This is for the Koa wood and *ti* leaf ring blessing for your wedding ceremony. I cannot be there, but I want you to tell Kainalu to make sure it happens. Koa represents strength, which you both have, and will need all the way through your marriage. The *ti* leaf is a sign of prosperity and the blessing of health for your mind, body and spirit. Kainalu knows what to do. The bowl is dipped into water first and then the leaf is immersed into the bowl and the water sprinkled three times over your rings.

'The priest will say, "*Ei-Ah Eha-No. Ka Malohia Oh-Na-Lani. Mea A-Ku A-Pau.*" It means, "May peace from above rest upon you and remain with you now and forever." The water represents a new beginning for you and Kainalu. Moloka'i is not the end; it is just the beginning.'

Isabella was deeply touched by *Kapuna Wahine*'s words. Her acceptance was the final blessing she needed.

Two days later, with an air of finality, Isabella closed her trunk one last time before she would open it again at her new home on Kalaupapa. On the top of her belongings were her Bible and *The Pilgrim's Progress*. She had read Bunyan's book through twice now, and found courage in its pages. She had felt spurred on with his description of the Celestial City. At least there was the hope of heaven for herself and for Kainalu.

Isabella arrived at the harbour just minutes before the steamer left. As she boarded the ferry, she looked around, hoping she would not recognise anyone. There were lepers on board, a group of about thirty, all of whom were kept away from the other passengers. Some had disfigurements on their faces, but on the whole they were not terrifying to look at.

The steamer stopped first in Maui to let passengers off and to take on more. When it neared Kalaupapa, Isabella rose from her seat in curiosity to see her new home. Fili was right about the cliff; the lush green *pali* soared into the sky. It was magnificent, and would have been a symbol of grandeur if it hadn't also acted as a wall to the lepers' prison. Isabella saw clusters of white, green and red buildings scattered across the stony peninsula.

There was no port, and the steamer had to cut its engines a few hundred yards out from the beach and ride the swells closer to shore. When they were near enough, the anchor was thrown and rowboats assembled to get the human freight onto dry land. Cattle were dumped into the churning surf and expected to swim ashore, herded by *paniolos*. The passengers were despatched into rowboats hanging off the side of the ferry. Isabella was given one of the first seats; she knew there was no other passage to shore, but the way to get there seemed both precarious and terrifying. The waves were high, and she clung to the side of the boat, her skirts getting wet from the seawater spilling over the sides.

With loud cries, the sailors pushed the boat away from the ferry. As the swell of the wave hit, the boat was carried forward, and the sailors rowed furiously to shore. When they got closer to the beach, they were met by a welcoming crowd, all seemingly eager to greet whoever the boat contained. Isabella wondered if Kainalu would be there, but she reasoned that he didn't know she was coming, so why would he be?

She clambered out of the rowboat and ran up the beach to escape an approaching wave. Her skirts were wet and felt heavy, dragging along the sand. Putting her hand above her eyes to shield them from the glare of the sun, she scanned the crowd. Kainalu was not among them. She would have sat down to catch her breath and gather herself, but there were too many people watching her. She felt unsure and self-conscious.

An official-looking man called her and told her to report to the *Kahuna* and register her arrival on Kalaupapa.

Isabella walked in the direction he had pointed, over to the nearest building. Through an open door, she saw a man sitting at a desk writing in a thick ledger.

'Name, and when did you first get leprous symptoms?' he asked, without looking up. She could smell the faint odour of stale alcohol emanating from him.

'I am not ill; I am here to be *kōkua* to James Kainalu Okalani,' she said, her cheeks flushing as she said his name.

The man looked up, interested. His weatherbeaten, stubbled face and unruly hair showed a distinct disregard for personal hygiene.

'Kainalu, hey? Lucky man. What is your name?'

Isabella Buckley.'

'Nice accent, lady. We don't have many foreigners here. I'll show you where to go. Kainalu lives a mile down the track.' The man heaved himself from his chair, revealing a rotund belly that had been hidden by the desk. He walked to the door and pointed Isabella in the direction she should take. 'His house ain't finished yet, but you can't miss it. It is away from the others and will be a beauty when it's built. Leave your belongings here, and he can come and get them in his buggy when you are ready.'

With that, the man went back to his desk and, head down, continued writing in the ledger, as if he had already forgotten Isabella. Her trunks had been left outside the office and, hesitantly, she started walking in the direction he had pointed. She smiled brightly at all she saw; hoping the confidence of her smile would mask her nervousness.

It took her twenty minutes in the hot sun, until she came to a wooden-framed house, with a man hammering on its roof. It was in an identical style to Aolani's. There was a half-finished *lanai* wrapped around it. Next to the house grew a small, blossoming frangipani tree. The fragrance was carried to

Isabella in the breeze like a welcoming embrace. She stopped and took it all in until, as if knowing he was being watched, the man on the roof turned around. He squinted in the sun, but after a moment, his eyes rested on her face.

Chapter Thirty-two

Moloka'i, January 1883

Kainalu just stared, as if not believing his eyes. Isabella felt joy rising in her and laughter pour out of her mouth, she was so relieved to see him. He looked just the same.

In a couple of seconds, when Kainalu realised it was not an apparition in front of him, but the woman he loved, he let out a whoop and descended the roof at lightning speed, jumping the final rungs of the ladder and throwing down his tools as he ran towards her.

'Isabella!' he said, with a mixture of disbelief and wonder.

When he got to the gate he slowed down, wiping the sweat off his brow and brushing his hands on his shirt in an attempt to clean them. Isabella was crying and laughing at the same time. Disregarding her reserve, she ran the final feet towards him. He came to meet her, but stopped suddenly, perhaps thinking she would not want to come too close. Isabella moved forward, and without hesitation fell into his embrace. It was the first time they had hugged; he had always been so formal in Honolulu. Now they were body to body, she could hear his heart beating and his breath against her cheek; he was so vital and alive. It was as if they fitted perfectly together and, in that moment, Isabella knew she had done the right thing in returning to him.

Eventually he pulled away. Holding her arms, he looked into her face. 'Is this a short visit?' he asked. She could see him bracing himself to hear when she would be leaving.

'Kainalu, this isn't a visit. I am here to be your *kōkua*.'

He shook his head as if in disbelief, but he didn't tell her she couldn't stay. He just looked at her, an unwavering stare that was so full of love she felt she was being filled up with goodness.

'I don't deserve you,' he said finally.

'It is not about deserving; there is no place I would rather be.'

'What about Eleanor?'

'She is with her cousins. She is happy and looked after...' Isabella said no more.

'I am sorry,' he said, realising her loss.

They walked onto the half-finished *lanai* and sat down on two wicker chairs looking out at the ocean beyond.

'Isabella, I think you received the letter I sent?'

'I did.'

'I wrote that I would have asked you to be my wife if I was well.'

Isabella nodded, heat coming to her cheeks.

'My desire to have you be my wife still stands, but I know that would be asking too much of you. But let me say this, you are a treasure to me, a rare find, rare gold. I have seen your character and your inward beauty. You stole my heart all those months ago, and you have my heart now. You are ravishing to me.'

'Kainalu, yes.'

Isabella felt a huge, almost supernatural, strength as she said yes. There would be no going back, but she knew she only wanted to go forward with Kainalu.

'No. You do not know what you are saying yes to. We could not be completely husband and wife, in all that means. I could not live with myself if you got sick.'

Isabella had thought about this. 'We can still be husband and wife within those confines. I am prepared.'

Kainalu looked out to the water. Tears escaped down his cheeks.

'How is your health?' she asked.

'It's strange, but I feel very well. I don't know how the disease is going to develop. It could be that I live a long time in relative health, or I may decline very quickly. Are you prepared for that?'

'I think so. I can't say in truth, but I am willing.'

'Isabella, when I was disease-free, I wanted to help these lepers. I felt I understood them because my wife had suffered from it. However, it was only when I became one of them that I fully understood what it is like to live with a death sentence and to be thought of as cursed and unclean. It is little wonder this place is known for licentious living: if you have no hope, what else is there to do but drown your sorrows in alcohol? I want to bring hope back to the people here, and your coming has given me strength to do it. I prayed for help, but never in my wildest dreams did I think God would answer by bringing *you* back.'

They stayed sitting, holding hands, until eventually they both needed food. Isabella's accommodation had to be arranged as well.

'You can stay with the other single ladies in the boarding house – there is a separate room for *kōkuas*. Father Damien built a church when he arrived here. We could marry there.'

The morning of Isabella's wedding, she woke early. The sun had not yet risen over the *pali*, but she could hear the sound of people already at work in the cook house preparing the *kālua* pig for the celebration. It was a cool morning, and Isabella put a shawl around her shoulders as she walked down to the rocky shoreline. She still had her daily constitutional, but now there was no pain in her back. Today she would become Kainalu's wife, in the coral stone church, to the sound of the ocean breakers a few feet away. She stood and breathed deeply, looking out to the horizon. She felt full of purpose. In laying down her life, she knew she was gaining so much, and even though she was aware it wouldn't be easy, and that there would be inevitable pain ahead, she had had overwhelming peace that she was in the right place. Even though it was very far from north Norfolk and all she knew, it felt like home.

Epilogue

1884 – a year later

My dear Catherine,
It is hard to believe a year has passed since I left you. I am sitting on the lanai. *It's early morning, but the air is warm, and the day is beginning to break over the cliffs that surround us. Dear sister, my only sadness, of course, is not being close to you and our family, especially Eleanor. I do hope she can travel here one day, that all of you can, before too long.*
Let me share more of what has happened with Kainalu. I wanted to write you a proper letter, telling you everything. I imagine I will write this over a few days as there is too much to say in one sitting!
In the early days of being his kōkua, and then his wife, I woke up each morning with a sense of dread, waiting for the sickness to worsen suddenly and for him to get ill. But the day did not come. We both worked together in the colony. I taught at the school – there are some small children here, and I longed to mother them, as most are without their families. So as not to spread the disease to those of us who don't have it, there are strict rules about touching. I found it so hard not to scoop the children up in my arms and hug them. There is one girl especially, her name is Maima, and Kainalu has a special bond with her. He was the one who discovered she had leprosy, so he had to enforce her leaving her parents to come to the colony. I think he feels responsible for her. We have become her second family in a way, and I am doing what I can to keep her healthy.

The people love Kainalu; they listen to him. Father Damien is sick with the disease, but there are still others here who work for the lepers.

Some months ago a strange thing began to happen. Kainalu's symptoms seemed to disappear, and his skin lesions cleared up. We wondered what was happening. Of course, I had prayed for healing, but never really had faith to believe it was actually possible. Kainalu had not received an official diagnosis. As he has worked with lepers for so many years, he thought he recognised the sickness in himself. He did question why he had not experienced the numbness that comes with the disease, and just assumed it would appear later. However, I began to hope and believe that maybe his self-diagnosis was wrong, and that he, in fact, did not have leprosy. We wrote to his sister, Aolani, and she was able to get a doctor to come to us in Moloka'i. And Catherine, we found that Kainalu did not have the leprosy bacteria in his blood! He is free from the disease.

Whether he was healed, or never had it in the beginning, I do not know, but I cannot express in words our reaction to the news. It was as if the dark cloud hovering over us was gone, and we could feel the strength of the sun for the first time. I think I had a smile on my face for a whole week. Kainalu reacted differently. He was very tearful, and he cried tears of joy at the faintest thing. He said he felt for all the others on the colony who will not get better.

I believe it is important we continue to live in Moloka'i. It is a place where we can make a difference, and I trust the Lord has opened up the way. I read a verse from the Song of Songs yesterday, and it encapsulates how I feel: 'My beloved spake, and said unto me, Rise up, my love, my fair one, and come away. For, lo, the winter is past, the rain is over and gone; The flowers appear on the earth; the time of the singing of birds is come ... [4]

---

[4] Song of Songs 2:10-12.

The season of singing has come. For you too, dear sister. So wonderful to hear of your engagement to William. Let us rejoice together!
Until we meet again,
Your sister,
Isabella Okalani

Author's Note

This story has been many years in the making. I stopped and started, and gave it up for a while, but it was in 2020 during COVID-19 when I left London and moved back to Norfolk that I was able to edit and rewrite until it was nearer a publishable story.

The inspiration for *Isabella's Voyage* was a woman called Isabella Bird (1831-1904) whom I came across when researching the historical connection between Hawaii and England. I had been interested in the heartbreaking story of King Kamehameha II and Queen Kamāmalu. They sailed to England in 1823 to meet King George IV, but they both died of measles when they arrived in London, not having immunity, and did not meet the king.

Isabella Bird was a British explorer and writer, and one of the first female members of the Royal Geographic Society. Isabella Buckley is not her, but I used some aspects of Isabella Bird's life for my protagonist. For instance, Miss Bird had one sister she was very close to, and she had a mysterious back ailment that used to disappear entirely when she went travelling. She travelled alone (when it was unusual for women to do so) to the Sandwich Islands, and wrote home of the flora and fauna she had seen there. She did not marry a Hawaiian surf-rider, but when her sister died of typhoid fever, Isabella Bird married the doctor who had taken care of her.

When I first started this story, I had no idea that Isabella Bird is in fact my third cousin, four times removed! My genius history-loving nephew, Henry, in the middle of A-levels, surprised me with his discovery!

Many of the characters set in Hawaii are real, but all events in the novel are fictionalised. King Kalākaua (1836-1891) was the monarch of the time and Archibald Cleghorn was a Scottish man who married Princess Miriam Likilike, fifteen years his junior, in 1870. Their daughter, Victoria Ka'iulani, was niece of King Kalākaua and the last heir apparent to the throne of the Hawaiian kingdom. When she was fifteen she travelled to England and was educated at Great Harrowdean Hall, a boarding school in Northamptonshire.

Isabella Bird travelled from New Zealand on a boat called the *Nevada*, so I was able to read her diaries to get a sense of what the journey was like. I was helped by two books in particular, Evelyn Kaye's *Amazing Traveller: Isabella Bird* (Bournemouth: Blue Panda, 1994), and *Isabella Bird's Letters to Henrietta*, edited by Kay Chubbuck (Lebanon, NH: Northeastern University Press, 2003).

Kainalu's family are entirely fictional, as are the Fortnums, but other characters mentioned, such as Henry Opukahaia (p.203) are real. As is the place of Kainalu's education - the Royal School which was founded by King Kamehameha III in 1839. Georges P Trousseau, born in Paris, was appointed to physician the Hawaii Board of Health in 1873. Father Damien was a Belgian priest who had a remarkable impact on the leper colony of Kalaupapa. While caring for the spiritual needs of the community, he built houses, schools, roads and a church. After fifteen years serving the lepers, he himself died of leprosy in 1889. Professer Mouat, whom William talks of, did write a paper on chaulmoogra oil as a treatment for leprosy in 1854. It can be found here.[5]

We know that leprosy, now called Hansen's disease, was once thought to be highly contagious, but in fact it does not spread easily. With the success of modern medicine, those who suffer from the disease no longer need to live their lives in quarantine. Kalaupapa closed as a leper colony when quarantine was lifted in 1969, although many of the lepers remained living there.

---

[5] archive.org/details/b22278217/page/8/mode/2up?view=theater (accessed 31st August 2022).

I first went to Hawaii as an eighteen-year-old, fresh out of school. Like Isabella Buckley, I grew up in Norfolk, and the furthest afield I had travelled was Spain... so to arrive in Hawaii, it really did feel like paradise. Added to the attractive climate, I was drawn to the Polynesian culture, and remember one night watching the *hula* danced by a group that was both beautiful and worshipful. The Hawaiian Islands had my heart at that point, and over the years I have been able to return for work – writing biographies of people based in Hawaii.

I have many people to thank for getting this book out. Madeleine Miller read my first draft and gave me hope that it had potential – she is a woman of faith! Before anyone knew of my idea to write a story about a woman travelling from England to Hawaii in the 1880s, my friend Alexandra Noel said while praying, she had 'a picture' of me writing a book, about Hawaii and England, about a woman from the nineteenth century travelling to Hawaii! It was extraordinary, and meant I didn't give up when I realised attempting historical fiction for my first novel was a potentially crazy idea. Another friend, Abigail Deacon, faithfully read through numerous drafts, giving feedback and editing my terrible punctuation. And there were many other kind, gracious friends who read through drafts and gave feedback when I was stuck. Amy Barreto was one such person. Also a novelist, her comments on the character of Isabella and my writing of her were so insightful, they enabled me to try to write from a more vulnerable place, instead of as a storyteller, from a distance.

I will also be eternally grateful to Nicki Copeland and Instant Apostle for believing in this book, and for Sheila Jacobs' extraordinary skill as editor, with a brilliant eye for detail, honing the story and editing masterfully!

My dad read an early draft and, as a romantic, he cried all the way through. He died in 2020, so was not able to see it in its finished form, but my love of sharing stories is from him.

When I started this book, I was writing the story I wanted to read. Like Isabella, I wanted hope that when life is hard, it can change suddenly and unexpectedly for the better. It happened for me, in 2021, when in six months I met and married my 'Kainalu'!

May my story, and Isabella's, show you that circumstances can change in a moment, and there is no hopeless situation.

Jemimah Wright
Summer 2022

*In Chapter Twenty-three, King Kalākaua's quote, 'Hula is the language of the heart, therefore the heartbeat of the Hawaiian people', can be found at
www2.hawaii.edu/~keahiahi/mmfhula.html (accessed 18th July 2022)

Glossary of Hawaiian Terms

Ali'i – nobility

Aloha – hello / love

E'kala mai – I'm sorry

Hale pili – traditional Hawaiian home

Hānai – adopted

Haole – foreigner / white person

He'e nalu – surfing

Heiau – place of worship

Holoku – A type of Hawaiian dress; *holo* means to go, and *ku* means to stop. Wearing the garment for the first time, the Hawaiian women are reported to have said, '*Holo! Ku!*' Roughly translated, this means, 'We can run in it – we can stand.'

Ho'onani – beautiful

Hula – dance performed by Hawaiian women

Kahili – standards handed down from ancient days made with human bones of enemy kings and decorated with feathers of birds of prey

Kahuna – priest, sorcerer, magician, wizard, minister, expert in any profession (male or female)

Kalo – cultivated taro plant

Kālua – traditional Hawaiian cooking method

Kanaka – a native or inhabitant of Hawaii

Kapa – barkcloth, traditionally made out of paper mulberry, hibiscus or breadfruit bark